A HEART DIVIDED

The flames in the fireplace suddenly shot higher. Someone had opened the door. Alethea looked around and found Jean-Claude standing in the doorway.

Closing the door softly behind him, he moved to her side and put an arm around her shoulders. "I had thought you must be asleep and dreaming by now."

A thrill went through her at his touch. Her voice was not quite steady and her heart was beating heavily. "You are home earlier than I anticipated."

"Yes." He moved away from her. "I am glad you are here, my dear."

His face was in shadow—but Alethea seemed somehow to be aware of the intensity of his stare . . .

Berkley books by Pamela Frazier

THE VIRTUOUS MISTRESS
A DELICATE DILEMMA

A Delicate Dilemma

PAMELA FRAZIER

BERKLEY BOOKS, NEW YORK

A DELICATE DILEMMA

A Berkley Book/published by arrangement with
the author

PRINTING HISTORY
Berkley edition/September 1988

ISBN: 0-425-11048-6

A BERKLEY BOOK ® TM 757,375
Berkley Books are published by The Berkley Publishing Group,
200 Madison Avenue, New York, NY 10016.
The name "BERKLEY" and the "B" logo
are trademarks belonging to Berkley Publishing Corporation.

PRINTED IN THE UNITED STATES OF AMERICA

10 9 8 7 6 5 4 3 2 1

PROLOGUE

THE SKY WAS vividly blue, but with an ubiquitous smattering of clouds, which not even winds that seemed to be leftover from March's arrival three weeks earlier could drive away. The poplar trees along the road to the Château de Mothancourt swayed in the breeze, and some of the new leaves fell to the ground as Jean-Claude de Bretigny rode toward the immense house. At this moment, everything seemed the same. He had grown up to cool spring days and colder winters. He had grown up in a château which had been old when Henry IV was fighting the battles that would eventually take him to the French throne.

Henry IV had said, Jean-Claude suddenly remembered, that Paris was worth a mass. He had straightaway abandoned his cohorts, the Huguenots, and cast his lots with the Catholics. What, he wondered, would Henry have thought had he been here in France at this time? Would he, with his protestant leanings, have yet been shocked to see monks and nuns turned from their convents and monasteries, some of them sent to the guillotine? Not only the clergy were in peril—all the powerful or, rather, once-powerful nobles of France were in similar straits. He shuddered as he reluctantly remembered his friends and some of his relations as well who had met that fate. Incredibly, Louis XVI and his beautiful, rapacious Austrian wife Marie Antoinette, whose folly might have helped bring down the French throne, had been executed.

The young man shuddered again, and then was reassured by the sight of the building before him. It remained untouched. There had been no invasion, not in his home nor in that of the De Mothancourts. Unlike many in this beleaguered land, they had never been absentee landlords, residing in Versailles rather than outside of Vire in Normandy. Ignoring the incentives proposed by Louis XIV and his descendants, they had remained close to the land, caring for their people—and now the people were returning the favor with protection. The estate of the De Bretigny family and that of the De Mothancourts might have ragged lawns, broken gates, and carefully shattered windows on sides where it did not matter, but that was all for show, all for protection. Inside, the tapestries, the paintings and the furnishings remained. Inside, the families survived, tended by servants who ignored the siren cries from Paris. He spurred his horse up the road and, arriving at the massive, iron-banded front door, let its knocker fall three times and waited.

To the accompaniment of rattling chains and squeaking hinges, the door was drawn back slowly, cautiously, to reveal an elderly, wary-eyed servant. The suspicion that leaped to his eyes in viewing one in the garb of a sansculotte was quickly allayed as he gazed into Jean-Claude's face. "Ah, it is you, Monsieur le Comte," he said on a sigh of relief.

"It is I, Rene," Jean-Claude acknowledged. Concern filled his tone as he added, "You appear unaccountably edgy."

"It is the times, Monsieur le Comte." Another windy sigh escaped the old man. He seemed on the point of becoming more expansive on that unfortunate subject. Then, he sighed again, shrugged and said, "Mademoiselle is expecting you. She will be in the music room."

She was a sight to remember in dreams, her adoring lover and soon-to-be-husband thought as he entered the lovely chamber with its pale blue walls and its high ceiling decorated with the nymphs and shepherdesses so popular in the days of Louis XIV, when the room had been done over. However, Jean-Claude's eyes were not on the painted ceiling. They lingered on the face of his fiancée, committing every detail about her enchanting person to mind on this, his last visit for a month. Her hair, golden brown and newly washed, curled back from a lovely, piquant little face lighted by immense blue eyes under winged brows. Her figure, slight but well-proportioned, had always reminded him of one of the nymphs in the ceiling—no, not always, he amended mentally. There had been a period when she was shorter and much more compact. There had been a period when she had groaned over her plumpness. It was only in this last year, her seventeenth, that she had become so slender, so ethereal, so incredibly beautiful!

He held out his hands. "Denise," he said huskily.

She ran to him and melded into his embrace, standing on tiptoes, gazing adoringly up at him, saying as always, "Jean-Claude, have you grown another inch? I vow you are becoming a giant."

He laughed down at her. "No, my lovely, I am still no more than six feet in height."

"Six feet . . . but that is gigantic! Papa is but six inches over five feet. It is that you are English, my love. You will feel very much at home there, I am thinking." Sadness vanquished the gleam in her eyes.

An expression of regret banished his own smile and dulled his gray eyes. "I will never feel at home anyplace where you are not, my Denise."

"Oh, Jean-Claude," she said yearningly. "I wish I might go with you. I would clothe myself in the garments of a peasant woman or . . . or a drummer boy, perhaps?"

"My dearest, I wish you might, but we both know it would not be safe. The eyes of those vultures who guard the gates of every city are keen. You must remain here in this charmed corner of France . . . Only here is it still safe."

Anxiety leaped into her eyes and colored her voice as she replied, "There are times when I do not feel safe even here. I will feel much less safe when you are gone."

"But nothing will happen to you here, my love. That has been proven time and again," he said staunchly over that ever-present fear which he, in common with Denise, had never quite succeeded in obliterating. Still, rumor had it that the terror in Paris would soon be abating, and with it, the marauders who roamed the countryside seeking out stray pockets of the nobility would also be discouraged from their endeavors. Furthermore, they had been in this district twice and had been turned back twice. He was reasonably positive that they would not make a third visit. Yet, he could wish that his dear friend and teacher, the renowned chemist, Antoine Lavoisier, had not insisted that he bear the papers of his latest experiment to the Royal Society in London.

The chemist's words came back to him. "You, my dear Jean-Claude, are fortunate. You are as tall as any Englishman. You resemble your mother's side of the family and you speak the language as well as a native. Furthermore, if you travel in company with Lord Jerard, they will not question your passport or your right to leave the country."

Jean-Claude sighed, thinking of Lavoisier's own danger. Marat, that unmitigated scoundrel who had not been slain soon enough by Charlotte Corday, had denounced the chemist to the Assembly, calling him a tool of the late king and citing all the offices he had held under the crown.

Quite as if she had read his thoughts, Denise said, "You have not been here often, my dearest. I become very jealous of Monsieur Lavoisier."

He was not surprised by her perspicacity. Save for his three years at school in England, he and the girl beside him had known and loved each other all their lives and, on occasion, it seemed to him that their thoughts flowed from head to head—without the need of speech. In truth, they had hardly to listen to the priest who would marry them. Already it seemed to him that they were one person, and though he knew he had no need to offer the comfort hovering on his tongue since she was all too well aware of her foolishness, he said, "My love, once I have returned, we will have all the days of our lives. This misery will end soon, I am sure of it."

"It must . . . oh, it must." She clasped her hands. "It is so terrible. So many dear, dear friends . . . Jeanne de Champfleury, my best friend at the convent, and all the poor nuns—"

He put his hand over her mouth. "Shhh, you must not think of them, my Denise. You are safe here. Thank God, our people have remained faithful."

"But unfaithfulness is spreading like a plague, Papa says, and—"

"It has not come here." There was the slightest trace of impatience in his tone. "I hope you will not dwell on this, Denise, my dearest. It is our last day."

"Our last day, yes." She shuddered.

He was immediately regretful for an implication he had not meant. "Our last day until I return, my dearest," he emphasized. "Then, we will spend all the days of our years together, Denise. You are my life, you know."

She took a step back and stared up at him, her expression doubtful. "Am I?" She held up a hand against his burgeoning reassurances. "Of late, I have thought that chemistry is your life, and now it is upon the account of Monsieur Lavoisier that you are leaving me."

A tendril of impatience glimmered fitfully in his mind and was summarily banished as he said, "It is important that I go, my love. He has no one else to send. Surely, you can understand that, Denise. I can easily pass for an Englishman, and I will be in the company of an English diplomat—Lord Jerard. But I have told you that. My dear, these papers must be brought before the Society."

"Why cannot this Jerard bring them?"

"Because they must be explained, and I am the one who is most familiar with the matter contained in them. It will be only a fortnight, and then I will return. You must believe that I will not tarry in London or anyplace where you are not, my Denise."

She forced a smile. "I do know that, Jean-Claude, and I have something for you." She started to unfasten a thin gold chain around her neck and then stopped with a little

sigh. "My fingers are all thumbs this afternoon. Will you
take the chain off, please?"

He obliged, his own fingers trembling slightly as he
touched the smooth, satiny flesh of her neck. The catch
was difficult to manipulate, but at last it was open and he
found that there was a small gold and enamel locket
hanging from the chain. He handed the necklace to
Denise, who opened the locket with a flick of her
thumbnail, showing it to him.

"Ah, your likeness," he breathed.
. "I had it painted last week," she told him. "Is it not
well-done?"

He scrutinized the miniature closely. "It is well-done,"
he said finally, "but it does not do justice to you, my
Denise. No artist ever could."

"You grow extravagant, Jean-Claude," she chided softly. "Maman thinks it flatters me."

"She is wrong," he said strongly. "One day, I will have
the greatest artist in France paint you."

She pretended to pout. "Then, this is so paltry a thing,
perhaps you will not wish to take it with you?"

"Ah, my love, my dearest, dearest love," he said
warmly. "Of course I will take it with me and cherish it
all the days of my life." He drew her to him, embracing
her fervently.

"Oh, Jean-Claude." She sighed as they finally drew
apart. "I wish . . . But no, I will not voice it. I know that
you must do what you must do."

"I must, my dearest." He sighed. "The master is in
danger, and I go not only to present his papers but to
summon help. My uncle Lord Lenster is the earl of Brace
and he has powerful connections. If anyone can prevail,
it is he."

"It is terrible that poor Monsieur Lavoisier, who has
done so much for France, is now in trouble." Denise
sighed.

"God willing, there will be those who can save him.
But enough . . . " He embraced her again and again. "I
must go now, Denise, my dearest, but I promise you that
I will be back, and all will take place just as we have

planned. I will not leave you again, and we will live—"

"Happily ever after," she murmured and was silent as he caught her in yet another embrace.

It was not safe—but Jean-Claude could not resist the impulse that drove him to seek out his teacher in his small laboratory in Paris, where he stubbornly remained despite the protests of his friends.

As Jean-Claude had suspected, he found cauldrons bubbling and beakers filled with fluids in various stages of preparation. On a chair near one of several worktables lay a large bag, fashioned from varnished silk. Since nothing in this room was without purpose, he wondered why it was there and was about to ask Seguin, the chemist's assistant, when Lavoisier himself hurried into the chamber. He had been frowning, and the frown did not vanish at the sight of the young man he, who was always frugal in his praise, did not hesitate to call his most promising pupil.

Raising thin, dark eyebrows, he said, "My lad, I thought you must be on the channel by now."

"I will be leaving very soon, sir." Jean-Claude frowned. "And I beg you will change your mind and join us."

"No," the chemist said firmly. "My work is here and there is an experiment which I must do." He pointed to the silken bag. "This has only now been completed."

"But what is it?" Jean-Claude asked with pardonable confusion.

"It is to be my shroud," Seguin said before the chemist could reply. His crooked smile belied his ominous explanation.

"But no, my friend." Lavoisier laughed. "You must not listen to Seguin. It has, you see, two openings only. The first will allow our friend Seguin to get inside, and then it will be sealed. The second, which we dare not seal, is for breathing. Everything—everything emitted by his body will be retained in the bag, save for the air escaping from his lungs. We will take the respired air and put it into these bottles and flasks and we will analyze it . . . I wonder if I need tell you why?"

Jean-Claude was silent for a moment. Then, he said slowly, "Would it be because you wish to try and understand breathing?"

"Ah, yes, I knew I would receive so sensible an answer. You are right. It is to learn the process of respiration and perspiration and . . . But enough. If I begin to explain all that I hope to achieve from this experiment, I will keep you here far too long. You already have my papers, and now I beg that you go. One never knows what strange visitors one might entertain during the course of a day."

Jean-Claude felt his heart beating in the location of his throat, a sensation he had no desire to discuss with his teacher. He said, "I will go, but also I will find the means for you to follow . . . before I return to France."

"You will return?" The chemist frowned. "I would strongly suggest—"

"Sir," Jean-Claude interrupted, "I am to be married by the month's end, and you know how matters are in my corner of the world."

Lavoisier was silent a moment. Then he said with a tiny trace of regret, "I do know, my lad, you have been singularly fortunate and, of course, I wish you and your Denise well. But we waste time. You must leave and you will take with you my best wishes to your uncle for whom I have always had the very greatest respect."

They exchanged a few more words, and then Lavoisier kissed Jean-Claude on both cheeks and bade him a serene farewell. Indeed, the young man had a strong impression that the chemist had mentally dismissed him at the same time as he said his farewells and was already concentrating on his forthcoming experiment. He was sure of it as, opening the door, he heard him call, "What—you are not undressed yet, Seguin? I beg you hurry, please. You know our time is limited."

The journey from Paris to Calais was accomplished with dispatch by Jean-Claude and Lord Jerard. However, it was not without a few tense moments, these at the gates of the city where the scrutiny by the armed soldiers of the Revolution was close, suspicious, and ever-hopeful as they ferreted through covered vans and produce carts in search of fugitive aristocrats or, as they said roughly, "Fodder for Madame la Guillotine." Oddly enough, as they surrounded the coach holding Jean-Claude, their attention was focused on Lord Jerard, who bore their scrutiny calmly enough and answered their questions in his cool, precise but heavily accented French.

To the wary soldiers, the undaunted lad of eighteen, looking much younger than his years, his eyes alight with interest but not fear, seemed to confirm the French opinion that all English were mad.

If they had been able to see Jean-Claude or, rather, hear his low-voiced anger expressed to his lordship as their coach rolled beyond the gates, they would have been at him like a swarm of infuriated wasps—but they did not. At this point in time, they were not concerned with the English.

There were, of course, similar questions at all city gates and often on the road, but finally the two men arrived at Calais and some days later, Jean-Claude was hurrying up the steps of his uncle's house on Jermyn Street in London.

Shown into the library, he was embraced by a tall, dignified man, who had much the look of Jean-Claude's late mother. "Lad, lad." His uncle, usually so cool and dignified, kissed him on both cheeks, French style, and sighed. "I have not drawn a single easy breath since you began this journey! Oh, how you do resemble your dear mother . . . I have grieved long for the accident that took the lives of your parents . . . but I do not grieve now."

"We are safe in our château—" Jean-Claude began.

"Safe?" his uncle interrupted. "That is a word that must not be used in France. But enough, my boy. You will stay with me. I have much to tell you, and yes, of course, I will take you to the Royal Society, where you may read Lavoisier's papers . . . But enough! You will want to rest after your journey." Then, as he seemed about to open the library door, he paused and turned an intense and slightly frowning gaze on his nephew's face. "You know, Jean-Claude, on one of my estates in the country there is a tower, part of the old castle. I am sure you remember it. You were wont to play there as a lad, and it would be admirable for a laboratory, were you to decide that you wish to remain in London. Oh, yes, I know you plan to be wed . . . but that girl would not cavil at such a change, I am sure."

"Uncle," Jean-Claude said gently, "I am grateful for the suggestion and certainly, I will put it to Denise, but . . . I fear that she, in common with myself, is deeply rooted in Normandy."

"Yes, I understand," Lord Lenster said. "Still, a great many Englishmen have made the journey from Normandy to Britain, their viking blood having made them wanderers. William the Conqueror was not the least of them, but we will not concentrate on that at this time, lad. I will see you at supper."

London's streets were clamorous and crowded. Hawkers shrilled their wares, pedestrians were rudely jostled by running footmen and by pickpockets, too. Drays clattered past, and often coaches, curricles and hackneys crashed against each other to the angry denunciations of their various drivers. But none of these travelers coalesced into a mass, into a screaming mob, demanding death.

Jean-Claude, waking each morning in his large, comfortable chamber, could contemplate the rising sun without the tendrils of fear he had never been quite able to suppress in France. He was not wholly at ease in his mind. Despite the situation in his section of Normandy, he was still worried, and some part of his mind wished himself there. But he could not deny that he was enjoying himself. He had met many members of the Royal Society, and it was a heady experience to have them hanging on his every syllable as he described the most recent experiments of his great teacher. Furthermore, on being asked about his own work, he found his experiments received with undeniable interest and considerable praise, something it was Lavoisier's habit to withhold.

Too, there were men in the Society whose celebrity ranked with that of Lavoisier, and whose theories he was writing down to discuss with his teacher. Indeed, he was in the midst of inscribing them in his notebook on the morning before his departure for Dover. It would take a fortnight to reach the port, and he had tarried too long already. He was so deep in his work that he did not hear the knock on his door until it was repeated thunderously, bringing him to his feet in alarm.

"Come in, please," he called, but as he started toward that abused portal, his uncle entered swiftly and reaching him, put his hands on his shoulders. His face, Jean-Claude noted, was pale and his eyes bloodshot. The fear that was never entirely absent from Jean-Claude's mind grew from a small tendril to a great plant. "What is it?" he mouthed.

"Jean-Claude, I have grave news," Lord Lenster began. "And I beg you—"

"What news, Uncle?" Jean-Claude demanded through stiff lips. "Lavoisier?"

Afterwards, he remembered that it was his teacher's name that had sprung to his lips, not that of Denise. He had bitterly castigated himself for that, praying that wherever her soul had flown, she had remained in ignorance of that cry.

His uncle had shaken his head, saying brokenly, "Lavoisier, we have learned, met his death on the guillotine a fortnight ago. And in Normandy . . ." He had paused.

Jean-Claude had felt numb, he remembered that later, numbed by the fate of his teacher. Otherwise, he could never have said in tones that remained cold and calm, "What of Normandy?" He had stared at his uncle and received the silent answer. "Denise . . ."

Lord Lenster nodded. "In the night . . . soldiers . . ."

"You are not telling me that Denise . . ." Jean-Claude began and found his uncle nodding as he began to speak again. He did not hear that second explanation— because, for the first time in his life, he had fainted.

Jean-Claude cried out in his sleep so loudly that he woke himself with that same cry. He stared confusedly about him at the shifting square of moonlight on his chamber floor. The cry that had escaped him still echoed in his ears, but the sleep-fragmented visions accompanying it had, fortunately, disappeared. No longer did he need to witness what, in actuality, he had never witnessed but only envisioned. Those tumbrels carrying his teacher and Denise toward the guillotine, thrust beneath its knife by the minions of Robespierre, a scant fortnight before Robespierre himself met that same fate.

Having roused himself, he wondered why he had been visited by those horrid images. They came only when he was disturbed and, of late, his experiments were successful and his life serene. Yet, something had disturbed him—disturbed him enough to bring that bloody spectacle back to his sleeping mind.

He stared at the moon-thrown shadows on the walls of the chamber his good friend, Mrs. Drusilla Truslow, had compared to a prison cell, chiding him roundly for remaining there as sequestered as a hermit.

"If I were so sequestered, I would not come to take tea with you and little Alethea," he had replied reasonably and a trifle defensively.

"Alethea!" he exclaimed.

Had her plight occasioned his nightmare? Alethea Unwin. She had Denise's coloring, save that her hair was a shade more blond. She was delicate and gave promise of great beauty. She was also despised as a bastard, a fact her mother, poor wretch, had made abundantly clear before dying.

He frowned, wondering as always upon whom the woman had wished to be revenged? The lover who had deserted her or the child that, contrary to her sister Drusilla's wishes, she had caused to be christened "Unwin"?

"Unwin for unknown," the woman had told a shocked and disapproving clergyman.

"Unwin . . ." Jean-Claude whispered now, glad to concentrate on the child rather than on the forces responsible for her arrival in the world, this imperfect world which was like unto one of his dear master's failed experiments.

Lavoisier, too early dead. He should have had a

lifetime ahead of him, or at least thirty more years. But the guillotine . . . He would not concentrate on the dead, would not go through that litany of names again. He shook an impotent fist and lay back on his bed, watching the moonlight-illumined wall of his room. Outside a shriek filled his ears—some night bird had caught its prey . . . for was the world outside not divided between predator and prey?

Yet, he thought as sleep dispersed his memories, he would have to do something for that lovely child. Something must ease the strain in Drusilla's face and cheat the dying bitch, who had inadvertently given Alethea life. Alethea must not be thrown to the predators, too. He had been unable to save those he loved, but he would do his best to save Alethea from the fate that undoubtedly awaited her unless someone prevented it. He would be that someone.

PART ONE

CHAPTER ONE

ALETHEA UNWIN, WALKING in the direction of the tower that stood at the edge of Lord Lenster, earl of Brace's property, looked at the immense square structure with affection. It was tall as became a tower, and there were battlements and what she could now recognize as circular bartizans on each of the four corners of the roof. The door she was now approaching was deep-set in a pointed archway. Made of stout oak, it was iron-barred and could be blocked from the outside as well as the inside. When it was open, one could see into an immense, square room with thick stone walls. A circular flight of stairs led to another large room, and above that was the smaller chamber where Jean-Claude slept. There had been a time when the tower had been flanked by outer walls and by a house, built later, and even later destroyed by the Puritans.

The tower had suffered under the siege, but had proved happily impregnable. In revenge, Cromwell's army had stabled their horses on the ground floor, using the upper rooms to store weapons which they took with them into battle and also used to ruthlessly subdue those local residents whom they believed loyal to King Charles I. Some of these men were shot on the village green as an example to anyone else who might be cherishing similar loyalties. They also hanged several women, elderly and judged to be witches. The Puritans were hot after witches, but they were gone, were dust and ashes in graves and crypts throughout the country. However, Alethea reflected with some satisfaction, the tower remained largely intact and was, she guessed, even more permeated by odors, many of them vile, because no sooner was one compound finished and stored in a glass container than another was boiling up in its place.

Affection had long ago replaced the awe with which she, hearkening to the tales of the fearful and ignorant villagers dwelling on the outskirts of the town called Helmsley, had bruited about concerning Jean-Claude. Fortunately, everyone must now be used to his eccentricities. Furthermore, in this enlightened age, she could not imagine that anyone would dub him an alchemist and suggest that in his search for the Philospher's Stone that would turn base metal into gold, he was consorting with the devil.

Yet, once he had definitely given that impression. That had been on a never-to-be-forgotten day when she was but seven and her Aunt Drusilla was away from the house on an errand. Alethea had been bidden to remain at home, but the sun had been bright and she had been minded to go to the fields where there was a brook. In the brook were silvery minnows and small tadpoles, some with legs and arms, suggesting that full froghood was not far away. Above its gushing waters, there were bright blue and orange dragonflies with iridescent wings. She loved to sit by that stream, and sometimes she made people out of sticks using the green moss that floated on top of the waters for hair. She would talk to them and pretend that they answered her. In those days, only the sticks had answered her, for the village children either chased or avoided her. Their elders had also looked on her with disdain and, on occasion, loathing. Invariably, they muttered, whispered, and pointed whenever they saw her in company with her Aunt Drusilla.

In order to reach the brook, she had needed to pass the tower, and in those days she had been terribly afraid of Jean-Claude or, rather, of the idea of him because he lived in the haunted tower. Her aunt, who had some acquaintance with him, had chided her about her fears. However, it had been impossible to disassociate him from them—for she had heard him called "wizard" and "sorcerer." He had, the name-callers insisted, chosen to live in the tower because it was haunted, peopled with various apparitions—ghostly veterans of the many wars that had taken place since the tower had been erected, soldiers who had died there, impaled on spears or struck by stones from a catapult or burned alive. There, too, dwelt doomed wives and ravished maidens and, of late, strange odors and, on occasion, mysterious explosions.

"'Tis the devil comes to visit him that makes the noise," Sally Price said, with the authority of one whose older brother Matthew was apprenticed to that same sorcerer. Sally, age eight to Matthew's twelve, had been chastised by her brother for her tales—but he had not succeeded in silencing her.

Consequently, it had taken considerable courage on the part of Alethea to go to the brook but, she decided, she would whisper a little prayer as she passed the tower. She was steeling herself to do just that as she came in sight of the edifice—but at that moment, Sally Price had happened upon her and, with a pack of village girls, chased her to the tower, screaming words that yet echoed in her ears.

"Bastard, bastard, ugly little bastard, yer mother were a whore 'n yer father's the devil!"

Coming within a few feet of the tower, they had formed a circle around her, their shrill voices loud in her ears, their hands thrusting her back as she tried vainly to escape. There had been stones, too, showers of them flung at her, and there had been great chunks of mud, for the ground was wet from a recent rain.

Then, as she had lain there, vainly trying to protect her face from the missiles, her tormentors' screams had changed to cries of fright as a tall, thin figure emerged from the door to the tower. He had been clad in a long black gown, and his hair, also black, had been wildly tousled about his thin, dark face. His eyes, large and also black, had been bright with anger. With raised hands

clenched into fists, he had reproached the girls, ordering
them away in loud, threatening tones.

They had not needed a second order. They had fled,
still screaming and she, mud-covered and bleeding from
a dozen places on her face and body, had been unable to
move. She had not moved even when he had lifted her in
his arms and carried her inside the haunted tower!

She remembered Matthew coming forward and click-
ing his tongue as he said sharply, "That Sally . . . She be
a little demon, she be, even if she is my sister." He had
helped his master wipe off the grime and the blood.

Then, the man whom everybody—save Matthew and
her aunt—appeared to fear had taken her upon his lap
and had spoken to her so gently, so soothingly, that she
could no longer be afraid. She could not remember all he
had said, but his tone had been so gentle. She remembered, too, that once she was soothed and the mud
washed from her dress, he had carried her back to her
aunt's cottage.

Aunt Drusilla had wept, frightening her, who had
never seen her aunt cry before and later, there had been a
discussion which she, washed and put to bed, had not
been permitted to hear. The result of that colloquy was
Mrs. Metcalfe's School for Young Ladies, located in
Bath, to which she had been sent the following winter,
remaining there until her eighteenth birthday, last year,
at which time, she, having served as a student teacher—
working with the younger pupils and, in the summer,
receiving practical lessons in the skills and teaching at
homes in the district—was pronounced ready to undertake the position of governess.

Mrs. Metcalfe had arranged such positions for her with
various families, and she had earned high recommendations from pupils and parents alike. Indeed, she had
done so well at one establishment that the lady of the
house had suggested that immediately upon graduation,
little Miss Unwin must take a permanent position in the
household.

Alethea, excited by what had appeared to be a fortuitous beginning to her career as a teacher, had arrived at

the household and had been rapturously welcomed by the children. The first part of the summer had been an unqualified success but, unfortunately, in the latter part of that summer, the lady's eldest son had come home from Oxford and favored the governess with his many and unwanted attentions.

His mother had discovered him trying to persuade Alethea to open her chamber door to him one evening, with the result that the girl, severely reprimanded for having intentionally invited his advances, was sent back to the school within hours of the episode. Her employer had further stated that Alethea need not expect to be hired by any of her wide acquaintance in that district, for she fully intended to write letters alerting her friends to the dangers of so "disruptive" an influence in their households!

The schoolmistress, much to her weeping pupil's amazement, had assured her that she believed none of the slander. "However, my poor child, this scotches plans I had made to eventually take you on as my assistant. I will need to send you home, and I can only hope that you will have a better chance in the country. I do not think that the gossip here will titillate the ears of those dwelling in Yorkshire."

Once more, Jean-Claude and his uncle, too, had come to her rescue. He had prevailed upon the earl to find her a position, and the latter had managed to place her with a family some three miles distant. After nine months in that position, she felt happily secure. Her pupils, Lady Alison and Lord Robert, called Robin, were fond of her. In fact, they were never weary assuring her how much better they liked her than the governess dismissed the previous year for a health disorder.

Alethea flushed. The health disorder which, according to Alison, had caused the lady to grow fat of a sudden, was not unknown to her. It was impossible to remain in a girl's school and not hear the scandal that the teachers tried so hard to keep from young ears. Indeed, she was quite aware that had she committed the folly of opening her door to the earnest solicitations of the young man from Oxford, she might have been in similar straits!

It was well that gossip had not reached as far as Yorkshire, for even with the earnest recommendations of Jean-Claude and his uncle, she was positive that her employer, Lady Dysart, would have been reluctant to employ her, given her heritage and an appearance which, at school, had driven several pupils to develop a transitory passion for her. She sighed. She did not wish to be conceited and was not, she assured herself. Still, she could not help knowing that she was good-looking. Looks, as had already been proven during that fateful summer, were not an asset to a governess.

They invited, if not intimacies from the gentlemen of the house, certain familiarities, and her employer's son had been prepared to be more than merely familiar. Fortunately, in the household where she was currently employed, she had only to deal with the languishing glances of the footmen and butler. Lord Dysart, earl of Hawtrey, was often away from home, and when he was there, he gladly spent his time with his wife. He seemed deeply fond of his children, too. He had come to the schoolroom on several occasions, but he had never cast a look in her direction.

Unfortunately, when Lady Alison became ten and her brother twelve, they would both be sent to school, and she must needs seek another position. In two years, she would be twenty-one. That was old, but it was not old enough to rob one of an appearance sufficiently striking enough to warrant her second and even third looks from passing gentlemen whenever she accompanied her charges to Helmsley.

Alethea grimaced and then smiled, castigating herself for being a ninny of ninnies! Her employers had chosen this particular March to visit relatives in Scotland. They would not be back until Tuesday week! She was relieved from her duties until that time—a boon she had not actually appreciated until this moment. She would be able to visit the tower more than once, and perhaps she would be allowed to participate in some of Jean-Claude's experiments, as she had when she was little.

The future was . . . the future, and need not concern her at this moment. She hastened toward the tower, and a few minutes later had lifted the knocker on that formidable door and let it drop against its plate. It was only then that she wondered if he were there—but, she reasoned, he was always there. Yet, the door remained closed. Disappointment filled her. She had assumed that Jean-Claude was in the midst of one of his eternal experiments, but evidently she had been wrong. She knocked a second time, slamming the knocker against its plate with all her strength. Then, she waited. Still, no one came to answer her summons—not Jean-Claude, not Matthew.

With a little sigh of disappointment, she turned away and was starting down the path to the gates when an impatient voice behind her demanded, "You there, what do you want?"

Alethea recognized the voice. She turned quickly and there he was, in his leather apron which, he had always said, made him look more like a blacksmith than a scientist. His hair was cut more fashionably than usual, and the occasional one-to-two day old beard that coated his jaws when he was in the middle of a particularly demanding experiment was also absent. His one white lock caused, her aunt had once told her, by a terrible shock was hanging over his forehead and, as usual, there were burns on his slender hands and one angry welt on his arm. She was once more amazed at how strikingly handsome he was—even given the fact that his appearance seemed to mean nothing to him.

All this flashed through her mind with the speed of thought which, Jean-Claude had always averred, traveled faster than the wind.

Consequently, it was little more than half a minute before she replied, "I do hope that I have not disturbed you, Jean-Claude. I did expect that Matt would open the door. Aunt Drusilla—"

"Alethea!" he exclaimed, striding out of his tower. On reaching her, he held out both hands, which she grasped shyly. "But I did not expect to see you here so soon!"

"They sent me home in the gig," Alethea spoke breathlessly, feeling the warmth of his grasp all the way up her arms and wondering at the flutter it was occasioning in her throat.

He continued to hold her hands while he regarded her searchingly. "But how is it possible that in a mere six months, you have changed so entirely?" he demanded.

Surprise threaded her answer. "I have not changed . . . at least my mirror has not revealed it, Jean-Claude. I have only grown a little taller, I think."

He was silent, staring at her again. "Have you?" he asked finally. "Yes, I believe you are right. But still, that is not all."

"How have I changed? Is it that I am six months older, Jean-Claude?" she demanded.

Laughter gleamed in his silvery eyes, "No, I do not see that the ravages of time are now written large upon your countenance, my dear. You are yet a child."

"No, I am not, Jean-Claude," she retorted. "I am turned nineteen!"

"Are you telling me the truth?" he demanded incredulously.

"I am." She smiled. "I became nineteen on the fifteenth of April."

He bowed. "My belated congratulations, and also my regrets."

"Your regrets, Jean-Claude?" she questioned with pardonable surprise.

"Your grand accumulation of years have pointed up how very long I have know you . . . I must be an ancient, indeed." His smile belied his words.

"You are not ancient!" she said indignantly. "You are but thirty-five."

"I must correct you, my dear. I became thirty-six in August. I was born under the dangerous sign of Leo."

"But that is splendid for a chemist!" she said lightly. "Leo is a sign of fire, as is Aries."

"Are you Aries? But of course, you are. April born and with an April face."

"What, pray, is an April face?" Alethea asked, liking

his teasing mood and yet surprised by it. She had never known him to be quite so jocular.

"An April face . . ." he murmured. "I think it must belong to Persephone or one of her nymphs . . . before they were summoned to Pluto's dark and noisome lair." A curious shade passed over his countenance, and he added brusquely, "But why do we stand here talking nonsense? Come in, at once. Matthew will brew you some—"

"Alchemical potion?" she finished with a laugh.

"Shhh!" He put a slender finger to her lips. "I beg you will not mention alchemy out here. I shall be thrust from my tower."

Alethea's smile fled. "They are not whispering of witchcraft again, are they? Those plaguey boys—those, I mean, that sneak about the tower."

"No, they have not pointed accusing fingers at me lately, but every so often there will be another outbreak, and then my poor Matthew must either knock their heads together or appeal to the minister to bless this edifice." He cocked an amused eye at her. "I beg you will not look so alarmed, my dear little Alethea. I am talking pure nonsense." He put an arm lightly about her waist. "Come, my child, come to my dark tower or, to my dark tower come, as the ancient balladeers would say."

He led her to the door and she would have followed him inside but he bowed, insisting that she have precedence. He had, she thought, bowed very gracefully, and as she came into the vast chamber, she knew a moment of deep regret. He had confided the tale of his lost Denise to her aunt and, on occasions similar to this one, the tragedy arose in her mind. Despite his rough attire, he was a very elegant figure and it was a pity that he was not in his proper environment which, of course, would be in a château or at court. The French court as his family had known it was gone, but he with his British ancestry would have been quite at home in its English equivalent.

As Alethea came into the vast chamber which Jean-Claude called his laboratory and, on rare occasions, his atelier, she defensively prepared herself for the amalgam of odors that invaded her nostrils and on occasion clung to hair and clothing longer than was either comfortable or desirable. Yet, despite the momentary discomfort of these, she had, as always, the same sense of coming home that she experienced when she returned to her aunt's cottage.

The crucibles, the vials, the receptacles, the retorts, the ovens, the peculiar apparatus for the decomposition of water which had been invented by Lavoisier, his esteemed and mourned teacher, the apparatus for analyzing oils, a copy of that which also had been in the laboratory of Lavoisier, and many other items which were replicas of those found among the late chemist's effects evoked a stream of memories. In her mind's eye, she could see her younger self perched on a high stool, her teeth clenched against the questions that begged for answers, but which had not been asked because Jean-Claude was in the midst of an important experiment or an equally important preparation for an experiment. She also remembered Matthew looking at her anxiously, fearful lest she interrupt his master's flow of thought. Occasionally, Jean-Claude did exchange a word with the lad, but his language was largely incomprehensible to the child she had been.

Eventually, however, she had been allowed to assist Matthew as he prepared some mixture for Jean-Claude. She was never quite sure what she was doing, but she followed instructions very well and in so doing, she had won Jean-Claude's praise—words she had committed to memory and mulled over with pleasure once she was back in her aunt's cottage.

She had always loved him. As a child, she had worshiped him, and now that she was grown up and knew that love had many facets, she still worshiped him—but at this particular moment, she was conscious of an entirely new feeling and also of a latent surprise. In other years, Jean-Claude had seemed so old but today, he appeared younger to her—as if, indeed, he had imbibed one of those magic potions with ingredients which reason told her no chemist, however brilliant, could duplicate. She wondered what had occasioned the change in him. Was it the trimming of hair and beard? No, she had often seen these minor transformations.

"Alethea!"

She started and turned toward him. "Yes, Jean-Claude."

"Did you hear me?" he demanded. "I think not."

"Hear you?" she repeated, looking at him blankly. "Were you speaking to me?"

He laughed indulgently. "I was, and you were wool-gathering, indeed. Where were you, my child? With your lover—wandering through some enchanted glade?"

"My lover?" Alethea looked at him even more blankly.

"Surely, you have a lover." He smiled.

"No, never!" she exclaimed. "Why would you imagine I had?"

"It is far easier to think you have than that you have not," he said teasingly.

She said stiffly, "I have not a lover, Jean-Claude."

"Then, I will have to imagine that you dwell among the blind or the demented," he commented lightly, his eyes on her face.

Once more she was struck by the change in him. He, who had been so deadly serious on all the other occasions she had been with him, was now teasing her. She felt warmth in her cheeks and was pleased that at least the interior of the laboratory had not suffered a change. It was still dark with only an occasional light—a burning candle or an oil lamp—neither giving enough brightness for him to see that she was blushing. She said reproachfully, "I dwell in a respectable house, Jean-Claude, as you know perfectly well. And if I were to have a lover, I would not have a position." She was surprised to find that she could speak so coolly to Jean-Claude, surprised, too, at the anger and the hurt his comment had engendered. She felt, indeed, as if he had attacked her character—and in that same moment, she saw his face change.

"But, child," he assured her hastily, "I was only having my little joke with you. Of course, I know that you are everything that is good and virtuous." Moving to her, he slid his arm around her waist and gave her a little squeeze. "Will you forgive me?"

His arm was warm on her waist and, oddly, his touch seemed to have deprived her of breath. She said, "Of course. I . . . I should not have chided you, Jean-Claude."

His eyes were grave. "You must always chide me when you believe I deserve it. Your honesty is a trait I have always admired."

"You are . . . kind," Alethea murmured. Before he could respond, she added, "Aunt Drusilla tells me that you have been showing her great wonders . . . magic, she calls it. Might it be possible for me to see these wonders, too? I mean, if it will not be too much trouble. Indeed, I expect I should not have asked." She fell silent with a sigh, afraid suddenly of having stepped too far out of her place. If she had waited, he might have suggested showing her what her aunt had called marvelous chemical effects.

"But, of course, you should have asked," he assured her. "And tomorrow afternoon, I will consider it a great privilege to show them to you, my dear Alethea. There is also something you could do for me tomorrow, if you do not mind?"

"I will do anything you want me to do," she said eagerly.

His eyes gleamed with laughter. "You must not be so extravagant with your promises, my child. Suppose I wanted to send you up to the stars in the basket of a balloon?"

"I would go," she said with a giggle. "Is that what you want me to do when I reach home?"

"No, alas, it is much more mundane. I wish only that tomorrow when you come, you will bring with you a red cabbage. Your aunt tells me that she has some fine ones growing in her vegetable garden."

"She has," Alethea affirmed. "But—a red cabbage? That is all you want?"

"That is all," he said. "And now, I thank you for

visiting me, but I have work I must do."

"Oh, dear, and I have interrupted it!" she cried.

"No, you have not interrupted it," he contradicted. "I had not yet begun it. You will be here tomorrow, then? At two?"

"I will," she promised. "And I must bring you only a red cabbage?"

"No, only a red cabbage in the morning, yourself and your aunt in the afternoon." He smiled.

She nodded. "Very well, Jean-Claude." She hurried out of the tower.

"A red cabbage?" Mrs. Drusilla Truslow's gray eyes lighted. "Ah, that Jean-Paul . . . what transformation does he hope to effect upon a red cabbage." She pushed a strand of gray hair out of her eyes and looked up at her niece, now half a head taller than her small compact self. She had a sigh for the passing years—they had come and gone so swiftly. It seemed a very short time since her sister Dorinda had come home to bear her child and die no more than a week after the babe's christening. It seemed to Drusilla that Dorrie had willed her death and, left to her own devices, might have destroyed the child she had done her best to leave nameless. Yet Unwin was not Unknown, and had she not babbled out her frustration to anyone who would listen, she might not have succeeded at all. As it was, she had succeeded only in part; Unwin was Unwin, and only a few people in the vicinity knew otherwise. If there were any virtue in gossip, it was that there always existed a tale to match a tale, and the first would be forgotten in the titillation of the second. There were few who remembered Alethea's birth, and those few were in no haste to recount the circumstances surrounding it—if, indeed, they now remembered them.

The tale had surfaced once or twice—the first time having been that unfortunate moment when Sally Price and her cronies had stoned the child. The second time had been when Lady Dysart had inquired about her new governess's parents and had mentioned that someone had told her the girl was illegitimate. Drusilla had been quick to deny that. She had explained that her sister's husband, an apprentice tailor, had been run over by a London dray, and his grieving widow had come home to have her child alone. Lady Dysart, living beyond the village of Helmsley in her sequestered manor house, had accepted the story without question.

"I do not know what he might want with cabbage, but he did specify red . . . we have a large head in the garden. Are you listening to me, Aunt Drusilla?" Alethea spoke a trifle severely as if, she suddenly realized, she were speaking to one of her pupils rather than to her beloved aunt, who was both mother and father to her.

"Yes, I am listening, and you are very pert, Miss Alethea, to tax me with this." Drusilla's tender smile took the sting out of her words. She put an arm around her niece's waist. "It is good to have you back again, even for so short a time. Did not Jean-Claude think you had changed?"

"I thought that *he* had changed, Aunt," Alethea said slowly.

"Did you?" Her aunt regarded her in some surprise. "I am not aware of it."

"Do people ever grow younger . . . is it possible?" Alethea questioned and, without giving her aunt an opportunity to reply, she rushed ahead. "Jean-Claude seemed younger to me today."

"Well," Drusilla said thoughtfully, "he is not very old, no more than thirty-six. He was thirty-six in August, I believe. Still," she bestowed a warm smile on the girl, "I expect that at nineteen, thirty-six must seem ancient."

"No," Alethea said. She added, "I grew up believing that he was very old."

"That is the way of children. Poor man. Many of the émigrés have had experiences that have served to render them old before their times. Jean-Claude is not exempt, I am sure."

Alethea gave her a narrow look. "I have the feeling that you know a great deal more about him than you have ever told me, Aunt."

"If I do," Drusilla responded, "it is nothing I can share . . . for it was told to me in confidence."

Alethea said, "I know that he was a pupil of Antoine Lavoisier, who was beheaded so cruelly, so unjustly." She shuddered.

"Yes," Drusilla agreed. "It was a great tragedy, not only because it cut short his life far too early, but because it was a great loss to the study of chemistry, so Jean-Claude has said."

"It was a very great loss," Alethea agreed. "I have read about his experiments. He also changed the entire nomenclature of chemistry. Jean-Claude was fortunate to have known him, more fortunate to have been his pupil, since he has been able to preserve so many of Lavoisier's papers and also duplicate his experiments."

"Indeed." Drusilla nodded. "But my love, tell me more about your pupils."

"Do you know that we are both signs of fire?" Alethea asked.

"You and your pupils, both of them? That is certainly an odd coincidence, my love," Drusilla commented dryly.

"Jean-Claude and I, Aunt. He was born under Leo in August, and I—as you know—am an Aries."

"And I put no stock in signs," Drusilla said. "As a young girl, I had my so-called horoscope cast. It promised much and delivered nothing."

Alethea shrugged. "Nor do I, actually, but I did think it interesting." Hopefully and, at the same time, hopelessly, she continued, "Can you not tell me more about him? Were you to impart some of his confidences, I swear to you that none would ever pass my lips."

Meeting her niece's eyes, Drusilla found a certain evasiveness in them. She said, "Confidences, my love, are told in confidence. I think," she continued with a finality to her tone that Alethea had learned to recognize, "that we have discussed Jean-Claude long enough. I would prefer it were you to tell me about your duties with Lord and Lady Dysart."

Alethea sighed and tossed her head like a fractious horse. "They are not interesting, Aunt."

"But where you are is interesting. Tell me about the house. I do have a fondness for ancient piles." There was a wistful note in her voice that did not escape her niece. Drusilla had spent the greater part of her life caring first for her family, then for her sister, and finally for Alethea. She had had scant opportunity to view any house that was not in the immediate neighborhood and, apart from the tower, none of these were particularly interesting—being built mostly of gray stone.

Alethea said contritely, "Well, the main part of the manor house was built in 1585, after the son came back from an expedition to . . ."

Finally, she was able to escape and go to her own small room. From her window, she could see the mass of trees hiding Jean-Claude's tower—all but the very top. She found herself thinking about him again—or had his image ever left her mind? She wished it might have still been winter. Then, the leaves would have fallen and she would see the tower clear. She laughed at her fancies. To see it could not bring him any closer. Yet, in a sense, it did.

"Fancies," she murmured, chiding herself for a flight of the imagination that had nothing to do with reality.

Jean-Claude was no closer here than he was when she was in her little chamber at Dysart Manor. What did that matter? It was a question for which she was reluctant to provide answers, because those stirring in her mind were perilously close to madness. Yet, the feelings that had risen in her when he had hurried her into the tower were unlike any she had ever entertained before. The difference was indefinable, rather, it *was* definable, but that definition was something she did not wish to consider—even in the fastness of her chamber. She might as well, she thought bitterly, reach for the moon.

CHAPTER TWO

THE RED CABBAGE, a large, compact head, was heavy in the blue cotton sack that her aunt had given Alethea, with instructions to bring it back once it had served its purpose. As to the purpose that the red cabbage was to serve, she had waxed mysterious, saying only, "You must remember that Jean-Claude is a chemist, my love. I have also found that he loves to surprise and, on occasion, shock with his chemical resources."

"And will I be shocked and surprised, Aunt?"

"It depends," Drusilla had said with a smile and a wink.

Alethea had another moment of wishing that she shared her aunt's rapport with Jean-Claude, and then it fled as she saw a face she knew. It belonged to Katie Kirk who, as far as she knew had hired out to be an abigail last year. "Katie!" She hurried forward. "But I thought you were in London."

The girl came to a stop and turned a sober face toward Alethea. "I thought you was bein' a governess," she said. Without giving her a chance to reply, she continued, "Belike you'll be a-goin' wi' me, too."

"Going where, Katie?" Alethea responded in some surprise.

"To the hirin' fair wot's comin' up in a fortnight's time . . . or don't governesses go to such?"

"You are going to the hiring fair?" Alethea gasped.

"Aye," the girl said glumly. "I 'ad it 'ard in Lunnon . . . Nothin' I could do 'd please the fine lady wot 'ired me. Said 'as 'ow my fingers were all thumbs but that were mainly because o' 'im."

"Whom?" Alethea demanded, guessing what Katie was going to say almost before she said it, her fair hair and pretty face providing strong enough clues to her problem.

"'Im wot was 'is lordship. 'E was always meetin' me in the 'all or 'appen I were on the upper stairs, there 'e'd be, grinnin' at me, 'n later comin' closer 'n . . . " Tears rolled down Katie's face. "She caught 'im wi' 'is 'ands on me 'n said as 'ow I'd led 'im on, *me*, wot was always tryin' to avoid 'im."

Alethea shook her head. "I am sure you were . . . but she would not have wanted to think you were. Still, do you want to go to a hiring fair, Katie?"

"'Aven't any choice." The girl sighed. "Goin' fer a dairy maid. There won't be many gentlemen comin' to see the cows."

"But you will have to agree to work for fifty-two weeks, and if you do not like your position—"

"'Aven't any choice," Katie groaned. "My mom won't keep me 'ere. I 'ave an older sister in service 'n she told 'er that if'n I 'ad this trouble, 'twere my fault. 'Sides, there be Meg 'n Bonny, my younger sisters wot Ma 'as to keep, they be no more 'n seven 'n nine. Can't 'ire out until they be ten an' meanwhile there's another on the way. You was lucky, you was, bein' sent off to school."

"Yes, I expect I was, very lucky." Alethea nodded, repressing a little shudder as she thought how easily she might have been in Katie's shoes. The poor girl would have to don a white apron or put a bit of straw behind her ear to signify that she was willing to work in a dairy or a farmyard—but perhaps that was better than being a housemaid or an abigail. A thought struck her and she said, "Perhaps you could find work in a shop?"

"I t—tried, but 'twasn't nobody wanted me. I got all mixed up, the one place that gave me a chance. Sally, now, she done good for 'erself . . . 'prenticed to a milliner, she be. Seen 'er last night 'n she told me the work weren't 'ard, an' she quite liked it . . . seein' all them fashionable ladies 'n the men wot keeps 'em.''

"I am sure she must," Alethea responded, hoping that she did not sound as regretful as she felt at this unexpected information. "She's home, then?"

"Come 'ome yesterday night, off the Lunnon stage. Be 'ere a week, she will.''

"I see." Alethea repressed a sigh. "Is it not unusual that Sally was allowed to come home at this time?"

"It be 'ighly unusual," Katie acknowledged. "Mrs. Ellis wot is the milliner 'ad a death in the family 'n closed the shop for a week.''

"Sally must be pleased," Alethea commented, feeling an unwelcome tension in her throat. Years had passed since her bête noire had tormented her, and it was ridiculous to be experiencing a sudden feeling of unease. She could do nothing now, and undoubtedly, they no longer had anything in common. She was a well-situated governess and Sally was a shop assistant, and never need they meet unless Matthew took it in his mind to bring her to the tower. She frowned, but her brow swiftly cleared. There was no reason to imagine that they would be in the tower at the same time. Matthew worked there all day. Sally, however, would not be allowed to remain there all day.

"Guess I'll be off, then," Katie said.

Alethea regarded her with some chagrin. Lost in her thoughts, she had completely forgotten that Katie was with her. She said hastily, "I hope that I will see you again.''

Katie shrugged. "May'ap you will, may'ap you won't.'' She walked away swiftly, giving Alethea the uncomfortable impression that her feelings were hurt. She started to go after her but came to a stop. There was nothing she could say that could make matters better, and an apology might render them even worse.

A sigh escaped her. She had an unfortunate habit of falling into deep thought at times when it would have been better to remain alert. An idea would occur to her,

and she would follow it with the tenacity of a bird dog to
its final solution. She had been teased about this habit by
her pupils. She smiled at the thought of them and of their
father, who had never looked at her with anything more
than the most impersonal of glances. She was, she
thought for the hundredth time, very, very lucky, and she
owed all that luck to Jean-Claude . . . and to want more
than she had been vouchsafed was not only greedy, it was
totally unrealistic. Despite the gulf that stretched between herself and Katie, she must needs remind herself
that while education could soften and correct speech and
could provide a position which, while not lofty, was also
not menial, they were, in essence, sisters. Without the
interference of Jean-Claude, she herself might have been
off to a hiring fair.

She arrived at the tower a few minutes later and was
admitted immediately by Matthew. It was on the tip of
her tongue to inquire after Sally when she heard the
laughter. Then, staring about her, she encountered a
vision or, more specifically, she found herself looking at
a young lady of fashion, tricked out in a bright blue tunic
covered by a pelisse split up the front and heavily
embroidered in blue and red thread, a fanciful design of
improbable daisies. The vision was wearing little kid
shoes of a similar bright blue, and her bonnet was
adorned with a red ostrich feather. Around her neck, she
wore a bright gold chain.

"La," said the vision, "seems as if ye don't know me.
But I know you. You're little 'Lethea . . ." She paused
significantly before adding, "Unwin."

"You see," said a voice behind her, "that Miss Price
has deigned to pay us a visit." Jean-Claude moved
forward. He was, Alethea noticed, better dressed than he
had been yesterday, and she wondered jealously whether
he had chosen his wardrobe with Matthew's sister in
mind. However, before she could dwell very long on that
subject, he said, "I am twice-honored, for here you are,
too, Alethea." Stopping in front of her, he surprised her
by taking her hand and bringing it to his lips.

Alethea felt a warmth on her cheeks. With something

less than her usual poise, she said, "G—good morning, Jean-Claude." She reluctantly turned toward Sally, adding, "Good morning, Sally. I heard you were home."

"Did you now?" Sally's blue eyes were glacial. "My, news travels to all corners, does it not?"

Though there was nothing offensive in her words, there was a certain edge to Sally's speech that went with the look in her eyes and suggested to Alethea that she was experiencing a resentment very similar to her own. She could only hope that her feelings were not as obvious. Certainly, she was no more pleased to see Sally than the latter to see her. She remembered her earlier fears and concealed a grimace. They had, indeed, come to pass. She and Sally were in the tower at precisely the same time!

Sally had arrived only the night before and, evidently, she could not wait to present herself to Jean-Claude in all her overblown and tasteless glory. Yet, to be accurate, Alethea herself had come to visit as soon as she might and with, possibly, even less excuse than Sally, whose brother was employed here. No, she decided quickly, she had a very valid reason for coming here. All she was, she owed to Jean-Claude, and furthermore, he had seemed pleased to see her. Was he as pleased at the sight of Sally?

She slid a side-glance at him and was much discomfited to meet his eyes. However, she received no answers to that silent query. Jean-Claude appeared at peace with his world and manifestly unconscious of any sword-wielding on the part of either of his female guests—if she could employ so large a description. Actually, she could not. She was not a guest. Even though she had been asked to come, the invitation had been by word of mouth and casual. If Jean-Claude were to entertain one or another member of the fair sex as guests, they would be of the ilk she had glimpsed from between the rails of the staircase at her current place of employment.

At the earnest solicitations of her little charges, she had, on occasion, reluctantly stood with them in the upper hall to watch guests arrive for a dinner or a ball. Since her employers were both young or, at least, reasonably young, their guests had been much the same age. The men were elegantly clad in the black coats and white stocks deemed de rigueur for evening wear by Beau Brummel. The women, slender, beautiful, and patrician of feature, were garbed in the latest fashions—not garish ensembles like the one so proudly displayed by Sally Price, but fine silks or brocades, simple in cut, but bearing the stamp of the expert mantua-makers. Indeed, had Alethea not been sent to a good school, she might have deemed Sally's attire the last word in female elegance! Yet, in a sense, she was different from Sally. Her features were more delicate and her hands were slender, as slender as those of her ladyship's guests. She might owe the delicacy of features and hands to the father she had never seen, but to think of him was to become lost in impossible fantasies, and now was not the time.

"Did you bring the cabbage?" Jean-Claude asked.

"Yes, I did." Alethea held up the bag.

He took it from her. "Ah, a nice round one," he remarked on scooping it out. He folded the bag carefully and handed it back to her. "Your aunt will not want to lose this," he said.

"Thank you, Jean-Claude," she said gratefully, and forebore to ask him why he wanted it.

"Oh, Lor," Sally said. "If you needed a cabbage 'ead, we 'ave them growin' all over our garden. Should've asked Matt, 'ere, to bring you one." Her eyes, resting briefly on Alethea's face, were filled with an anger which, however, passed so swiftly that Alethea wondered if she had really glimpsed it. And, indeed, what did Sally have to be angry about?

Jean-Claude dispelled her thoughts as he said, "The cabbages that grow in Mrs. Truslow's garden are of a red that Matthew tells me he does not cultivate."

"Oh, I see," Sally said. "'Tis the color and not the quality that you want."

"It is the color or, rather, the strain of cabbage that I need," Jean-Claude affirmed.

"Well." The incipient crisis dissipated, Sally fixed a

slightly derisive glance on Alethea's face. "Matt, 'ere, tells me yer a governess?"

"Yes." Alethea nodded. "And I understand that you are apprenticed to a milliner."

"Aye, but 'tisn't just any milliner," Sally said importantly. "The shop's in Mayfair where all the ton goes. Dressed to the nines, they be. Beau Brummel 'imself comes there to advise—"

"To advise the milliner?" Alethea interrupted in some surprise.

"Bless you, no," Sally said, her grin and tone making mock of Alethea's ignorance. "'E comes to advise the ladies wot dote on 'im . . . 'e bein' a friend o' Prinny's. An' in case you don't know 'oo Prinny be, 'e be the regent 'n 'as been since February, 'n 'igh time since 'is pa be madder than an 'atter. Talks to 'imself, 'e do."

"Poor man," Alethea commented.

"You needn't be sorry for 'im. 'E be rich as Creases, that's wot they say in the shop. Mrs. Fitz'erbert, she come in once. She be pretty but gettin old 'n I don't care much for blonds," Sally directed a telling glance at Alethea's fair hair. "An' they say . . ."

For the moment, Alethea ceased listening to Sally's chatter. A glance at Jean-Claude, however, told her he was both amused and possibly even interested in her gossip. She experienced a sharp pang of disappointment. Jean-Claude, of all people, ought to be above such frivolity! In that same moment, she discovered within herself a deep desire to be out of the tower and away from Sally's obtrusive presence, but even as she framed the excuse she wished to deliver to Jean-Claude, he said as Sally paused for breath, "My dear, it has been delightful to see you again, and I hope you will return this afternoon for my little experiment with the cabbage."

"Wi' the cabbage?" Sally echoed.

"Yes, it is something that might amuse you . . . but at this particular moment, I must ask you to leave. There is work I must needs complete."

"Oh." Sally reddened and looked miffed. "I did not mean to out-stay my welcome," she said grandly.

"You did not," he assured her hastily. "And I do want you to return this afternoon, as I said. The experiment I mean to perform might amuse you, and there will be others, as well."

"Well," Sally said, "I suppose I will, then."

"Good," Jean-Claude said cordially.

Sally fixed her eyes on Alethea. "I expect you'll be comin', too?"

"Yes." Alethea nodded, wishing she need not leave with Sally. Undoubtedly, she would be treated to more of the girl's far from subtle innuendos. She did not want to quarrel with Sally, but at the same time, she would not accept her barbed speech passively. Consequently, were they to leave together, which they must, there was bound to be some manner of confrontation.

"Alethea," Jean-Claude said. "I will need you to help me, my dear."

Sally appeared to stiffen. She said sharply, "Wot about me, Jean-Claude. I can 'elp you."

"No, my dear Sally, you could not." Jean-Claude spoke gently but firmly. "This requires the dictation of some rather complicated formulae. But I do thank you for offering."

A deep flush stained Sally's cheeks, and the look she visited upon Alethea was hot with resentment. She said pointedly, "If'n anyone'd sent me to school, I'd've been able to read, also."

Jean-Claude looked embarrassed. "But, Sally, my dear—" he began.

"Sally," Matt snapped. "Go along 'ome, now. Ye've been 'ere long enough 'n as for readin', I'd've taught ye myself, if you'd ever 'ad the slightest bit o' interest in learnin', which you didn't."

His sister visited an even angrier look on him and, holding her head high, she stalked out of the room and slammed the ponderous door behind her.

"She'll get over it." Matt shrugged, breaking the small silence that had ensued after his sister's noisy departure. He looked apologetically at Jean-Claude. "You know 'er . . . always does."

"Yes." Jean-Claude nodded. "Her angers are usually short-lived."

Alethea was not so sanguine. Sally might make peace with her brother and Jean-Claude, but her resentment toward Alethea had been refueled. Still, what could the girl do? They were no longer children. The time had passed since Sally could persuade her friends to join her in harassing a defenseless child. She could only simmer futilely until the time came for her to return to London and Alethea to her pupils. Certainly, it was most unfortunate that their visits home must needs have coincided.

"My dear, a penny for your thoughts." Jean-Claude smiled at her.

She gave him a startled glance and produced a self-conscious little laugh. "They are not worth half that sum," she assured him lightly. "Now, what is it you wish me to read?"

He moved across the room to his bookcase and returned with a formidable leather-bound volume. He set it down on a lectern and opened it to a marked page. "You can begin halfway down the page . . . starting where the red line is," he explained.

As Alethea took her place at the lectern, she felt a sharp jab of disappointment. She had believed—or had she merely wanted to believe—that the reading he required had been merely an excuse to rid himself of Sally's obtrusive presence. She had even allowed herself to hope that he wanted her to stay because . . . but as she glanced at the close-written pages, some of them in Latin, she felt earth meeting her feet with a bump. Stifling a sigh she had no right to be emitting, she began to read while Jean-Claude, settling down in a chair, took notes in his small, fine handwriting.

Returning with her aunt, late that same afternoon, Alethea had not expected that Sally would put in an appearance. However, she was present, seemingly recovered from her anger and chatting gaily with her brother and Jean-Claude. She nodded briefly as Alethea and her aunt entered. Then, she greeted Drusilla with an enthusiasm which, to Alethea's ears, was patently spurious.

From her aunt's dry responses, she was sure that the older woman shared her opinion. However, Drusilla tactfully complimented the girl on her appearance and admired the blue ensemble. Alethea's thoughts fled as Jean-Claude came forward.

"You will please take your seats, my ladies," he said, pointing to three chairs set side by side. Sally was the first to sit down, putting herself in the middle so that she was flanked by Alethea and Drusilla. Having assured herself of what she appeared to believe was the most important position, she proceeded to look at neither woman. Instead, she fixed her eyes on Jean-Claude. Her face was slightly flushed and, to Alethea's mind, she did look quite amazingly pretty. The blue of her gown matched the blue of her eyes, and Alethea, who was wearing one of the three round gowns she possessed, a gray kerseymere she had had for two years, felt like a sad dowd beside her, even though, she assured herself, nothing, nothing in the world, would have induced her to don anything as blatantly showy and vulgar as Sally's so-called fashionable attire! A side-glance informed her that Sally had further gilded the lily by adding a necklace of patently spurious pearls. And . . . Her thoughts ended abruptly as Matt brought out a small table, setting it down a few paces to the front of the chairs. He moved back into the depths of the lab and returned a second time with three wineglasses, which he also set down on the table.

"Oh, are we to 'ave a feast, then?" Sally demanded.

Her brother visited a frowning glance on her. "No," he said shortly. "An' I charge you, Miss, you be'ave yerself."

Sally flushed and glared at him. "Just 'oo are you to teach me manners?" she demanded hotly.

"Stow yer gab," Matt snapped. "You be makin' a cake o' yerself." Without giving her a chance to respond, he moved away again.

"Well, I like that!" Sally said to no one in particular. Her cheeks were flushed, Alethea noticed, and there was a fiery gleam in her eyes—one she knew only too well. Sally looked as if she were spoiling for a fight, and in that same moment, she met Alethea's gaze.

"Just 'oo are you starin' at?" Sally demanded belliger-
ently.

"Gracious, Sally, dear, whatever is the matter?"
Drusilla asked.

She also received a glare, but her calm, gray gaze
remained untroubled. "It is a warm day for this time of
the year," Drusilla observed. "I imagine that all of us
would be better for a cooling breeze."

"I 'spect so," Sally growled.

A response had been trembling on Alethea's lips, but it
was just as well that her aunt had, inadvertently, prevented her from giving it. Had she answered Sally's angry
question with a corresponding anger of her own, she
would have been descending to her level and, furthermore, she might have created a scene, for obviously Sally
was extremely miffed by her brother's reproof and, she
was sure, even more miffed by her own presence in the
room.

She concealed a derisive smile. Actually, Sally seemed
to be treating her as a rival for the affections of a man
who had earlier proved that he had no interest in either
of them, only poor Sally would never guess the reasons
for that! Unless told the bitter truth, she would not
understand that the Prince-Regent, excepting, Jean-
Claude was more aristocratic than any of the so-called
gentlemen of fashion who graced the milliner's shop.
They might cast a favorable eye on one or another of the
pretty girls employed there. Indeed, Sally must already
have had her share of admiring glances, but Jean-Claude,
Alethea knew instinctively, was far too fastidious to give
carte blanche to a mere shop assistant.

Indeed, it was a pity that Sally had never enjoyed that
second, secret education that she and the other girls at
her school received through the medium of forbidden
midnight meetings in the rooms of one or another
well-informed pupil. Most of those nubile young ladies
came from wealthy and aristocratic homes. They were
wise in the ways of dalliance, having been the recipients
of confidences—if not from their parents, from elder
sisters or brothers and even from knowing abigails!

It was from them that she herself had learned about Harriette Wilson, the famous courtesan who, in 1809, when that information had been imparted to her, had been on the London scene for some seven years, her clientele including earls and even dukes! She had also heard about Mrs. Fitzherbert, the Prince's wife, who was not really his wife—even though they had gone through a real marriage ceremony. The royals, due to a recently passed bill, were not allowed to marry commoners. However, the girls had dwelt with even more salacious detail upon Perdita Robinson, the prince regent's beautiful ex-mistress, loved and discarded by his Highness, mainly through her own folly. That had been a long time ago, twenty years to be exact. And Alethea's mother must have been living with her father at that same time!

Had he been a member of the regent's set? The regent, who had not been a regent then, but merely the Prince of Wales, and George III still in command of his senses. What had her father been like? But now was not the time to mull over that question, for Jean-Claude had appeared, carrying a glass pitcher filled with a dark red fluid that looked like wine, his presence scattering her thoughts and causing her to wonder why she had been thinking about such things in the first place.

Jean-Claude was the answer to that. He had brought them out. He was looking at her. No, she realized with a flash of disappointment, he was looking directly at Sally!

He said, "Now, my dear Sally, you will soon be witnessing a minor miracle." He turned toward Drusilla. "This is the cabbage you so kindly gave me."

"Don't look like no cabbage to me," Sally commented pertly.

"It's an infusion of cabbage, stupid," her brother told her. "If you was to 'ave a whiff o' it, you'd know it were cabbage."

Sally appeared unconvinced but, evidently, she had taken her brother's swift admonition to heart, for she lapsed into a rather sullen silence and fixed her eyes on Jean-Claude.

Jean-Claude turned to Drusilla. "And do you have

similar doubts?" he inquired.

"No," she responded equably. "I have witnessed many of your miracles, Jean-Claude. Consequently, I stand prepared for anything."

He smiled at her. "You never disappoint me, my dear Drusilla."

"I am glad of that." Drusilla winked at him.

Listening to them, Alethea wished that he had addressed his questions to her. Not for the first time, she also longed for the rapport that appeared to exist between her aunt and Jean-Claude. She had a third wish, but she refused to let that one remain in her mind. She might as well wish to fly to the moon in one of Jean-Claude's small, experimental silk balloons.

"And now," Jean-Claude said, "Matt will fetch the three solutions."

Matt nodded and moved toward a table pushed against the far wall. In a second, he had returned with three small bottles filled with a clear liquid which appeared to be water. Setting them down, he grinned and moved back as Jean-Claude, picking up the pitcher, filled the three glasses with the cabbage mixture. He then picked up one of the bottles and let a few drops fall into the first glass. "Voila!" he said in the voice of a magician and, smiling, stood aside as the mixture suddenly became a bright purple.

"Lawks!" Sally exclaimed. In a voice that trembled slightly, she added, "'Ow'd ye do that?"

"Well, Jean-Claude, that is a miracle," Drusilla commented.

"And here is another, my friends." Jean-Claude poured liquid from another bottle into the second glass which straightaway became filled with a bright green fluid. Without waiting for the audience's amazed exclamations to subside, he poured the contents of the third bottle into the third glass and smiled as that mixture became a vivid crimson.

Sally fastened wide eyes on Jean-Claude. "Ye . . . ye must be a wizard," she gasped.

"Oh, no," Jean-Claude assured her smilingly. "It is

only a demonstration of one liquid acting on another. That sort of wizardry is often to be found in chemical laboratories."

"I've 'eard as 'ow the old wizards used to consort wi' the devil 'oo taught 'em to turn base metal into gold," Sally said. "Can you do that, Jean-Claude?"

Matt guffawed. "Those be fairy tales, Sally, right enough."

As she reddened and shot an angry look at her brother, Jean-Claude said pacifically. "It is true that chemistry can bring about many changes but, although in years gone by many learned scientists believed it was possible to turn base metal into gold—even without instruction from the devil—that belief has been proven to be a fallacy."

"Wot's a fallacy?" Sally asked.

"It's a mistaken notion—" Alethea began.

Sally glared at her. "I did not ask you!" she snapped.

"Sally," her brother protested. "Mind yer manners. Alethea was only tryin'—"

"I know what she were tryin' to do," Sally snapped. "She were tryin' to queen it over me on account I never went to any fine school like 'er. Nobody wanted to send me, it seems."

"Sally, I never meant to—" Alethea began.

"Hush, both of you," Jean-Claude interposed. "My experiments are not at an end." He smiled at Sally. "Should you not like to see more?" he asked coaxingly.

"'Appen I would." She appeared somewhat mollified.

"Matt." Jean-Claude looked in her brother's direction. The latter nodded and brought out a metal container, which he set on the table. Then, he laid out a richly carved tobacco pipe and lastly, he set down a small glass jar in which there was a colorless liquid.

"Wot do ye need a pipe for?" Sally demanded in some surprise.

"Wait 'n see," Matt admonished her.

"Now . . ." Jean-Claude picked up the container and passed it before his three-member audience. "You will see that there is nothing inside this receptacle save a little white powder . . . indeed, it might be powder for the face, might it not?"

"Aye." Sally was looking interested again. "'Tis, ain't it?"

"It might be." Jean-Claude smiled.

"I distrust you." Drusilla gave him a narrow look. "I am beginning to distrust every liquid and substance I see in this laboratory!"

"Aunt Drusilla!" Alethea looked at her in pained surprise.

"Hush." Drusilla smiled. "Jean-Claude knows I am teasing him."

"Indeed, he does." Jean-Claude gave her a fond look. "Now, Matt . . . you may continue."

Matt picked up the pipe and thrust the narrow end of it into the glass jar.

"Be careful, Matt," Jean-Claude cautioned hastily. "No more than one drop, if you please."

"One drop it is." Matt carefully held the pipe over the container. Then, taking it away and setting it down hastily, he backed off as in that same moment there was a bright burst of flame accompanied by a rather unpleasant odor.

"Ahhh!" A long scream issued from Sally as, leaping to her feet, she shrank away in utter terror. "'Tis 'ellfire . . . the devil's work," she wailed, turning a face drained of color in their direction.

Alethea laughed. "Nothing of the sort," she said condescendingly. "'Tis only a bit of sulphur. Am I right, Jean-Claude?"

"Yes, my dear." He smiled at her. "You are quite right."

"You!" Sally whirled on her. "Damn 'n blast you to 'ell! I'll teach you to laugh at me, you misbegotten little bastard!" Launching herself at Alethea, she thrust her from her chair to the floor and before anyone could stop her, she had struck her hard across the face.

"Sally!" Drusilla cried.

"Sally!" Jean-Claude echoed that cry and, thrusting Sally roughly aside, he lifted the shaken Alethea to her feet. Turning back to Sally, he said angrily, "Get out of here . . . get out, get out immediately!"

Sally glared up at him. "She—"

"Get out!" Jean-Claude repeated angrily.

"She will that," Matt growled. Seizing his trembling, furious sister by her shoulders, he half-pushed her, half-carried her to the door and thrust her out, slamming it behind her. "I am sorry," he growled as her strode back. "Always was an 'andful."

"Are you hurt?" Jean-Claude kept his arm around Alethea.

"No—no," she said in a shaken tone of voice. "I . . . ought not to have laughed at her."

"No." Drusilla nodded. "You certainly should not have laughed."

"Why not?" Matt demanded. "Sally be three-fourths of a ninny, always was. I'll 'ave somethin' to say to 'er when I get 'ome, I will."

"No," Drusilla said quickly. "I would think that there's been too much said already. Sally was truly shocked and frightened. And my niece should have refrained from laughter."

"I expect I should have," Alethea said in a small voice.

Jean-Claude's eyes were on Drusilla's face. "You are right," he continued ruefully. "I am afraid I depended too much on the element of surprise. No, I must be truthful, I wanted to astound and shock . . . but I had no intention of frightening poor Sally. Still, if I had thought about it—"

"She'll get over it," her brother said unsympathetically. "See if she don't."

Alethea said a trifle reluctantly, "I expect I had better go and find her so that I can apologize to her."

"No," her aunt said hastily. "You will only make matters worse, dear. Sally is in no mood to see you . . . much less listen to you."

"I agree, my dear," Jean-Claude said. "And, after all, it is of no great matter."

"I'll 'ave a word wi' 'er," Matt growled. "'Adn't no cause to act that way."

"Please," Jean-Claude said edgily. "I think it were better if we all forgot the incident."

"Yes," Drusilla nodded. "And the sooner, the better." She turned to Alethea. "It is time we were going home, my dear."

Alethea nodded and stifled a sigh. She was sure her aunt would have more to say about the incident, and any reproach regarding her ill-timed laughter was well deserved!

Sally, walking home, found herself both angry and hurt. But the farther she walked, the angrier she grew— at Alethea and Matt and Jean-Claude. Though Jean-Claude had certainly been harsh with her, he bore the least of the blame. The main force of her anger fell on Alethea—Alethea, who had dared to laugh at *her,* Alethea, that misbegotten little brat, daring to laugh at her betters, daring to laugh at one who was born in wedlock, not dropped from the loins of a whore. And who could say who or what her father had been—he might have been the devil himself, for all anybody knew. Indeed, he could very well have been the devil, the way she always had people taking her part, sending her to school so she could queen it over her betters.

"Ought to 'ave been scrubbin' the floor o' the poor 'cuse," Sally muttered resentfully. "There's somethin' strange about 'er . . . the way she gets folks to do for 'er . . . Jean-Claude an' Matt, too, turnin' 'im against 'is own sister. 'Tisn't natural!"

By the time, she had reached home, she was thinking about Jean-Claude again. "'E were nice to me 'n 'twas 'er set 'im against me," she muttered. "Well, two can play at that game," she continued darkly. "'An we'll see 'oo'll be the winner, we will. Damn 'er to 'ell."

CHAPTER THREE

ON REACHING HOME, Sally told her mother that she had eaten something that disagreed with her and, obtaining her permission to try and sleep off her discomfort, she climbed to the part of the loft she shared with her younger sisters. Crawling into bed, she pulled the covers above her ears and resentfully glanced at the afternoon sun. It would not be setting in any great hurry, and it would be a chore to lie here on her hard straw mattress, pretending illness for the next three hours or more. Still, it was warm in the loft, and she did manage to sleep, despite the noise made by her family at dinner in the common room, directly below.

Meg, her ten-year-old sister, came up and tried to get her to join them, but Sally, pulling the blankets about her ears, growled, "Lemme 'lone, I'm sick."

A half-hour later, she said the same thing to a belligerent Matt, who gave it as his opinion that she was only miffed and well she should be, given her shocking display in the tower.

Hot words formed on her tongue, but she swallowed them. Nothing would have been gained by quarreling with Matt, especially since her parents might join in the fray. Her father was not above giving her a good hiding if he felt she deserved it—even at this late age! Furthermore, if she got mad enough, she might say something she would regret later. She lay passively staring out of the small window, watching while the light faded. The sky was nearly dark when she quietly arose and, moving past the beds where her sisters lay sleeping, she made her way down the narrow stairs. She paused below, cocking an ear to hear if her parents were still up, but they usually went to bed with the sunset, and Matt would be sleeping, too, she guessed.

She moved quietly through the common room and, in a few moments, she was out in the chill darkness. She shivered, half with anticipation and half because there was a cool wind blowing. London was warmer in the autumn, and she would give a monkey to be back in the cozy bedroom over the shop which she shared with Mattie and Jenny, two of the five girls employed by the milliner. If she were with them now, they would be discussing the gentlemen who came to help their mistresses and, very occasionally, their wives, choose hats for which they paid three times what they were worth!

They would also be comparing notes, deciding which gallant they preferred and like as not one or another would be giggling and saying that she had gotten the eye when a certain top-lofty female's back was turned. There was one young gentleman who had given her the eye—but he wasn't a patch on Jean-Claude! He was not stylishly clad, but even with his hair too long, he was more handsome than anyone she knew. And though Matt had told her the girl he loved had died—had had her head chopped off, in fact, like so many of those Frenchies—he could not spend his life grieving over that.

A man needed a woman, not necessarily to marry, but she would not mind being without a wedding ring and with Jean-Claude. She flushed. She had to have Jean-Claude because she had told the girls at the shop that he was her lover. That was partly because she had wanted an excuse for discouraging Harry Gordon, a young clerk who wanted her to walk out with him. She had turned him down, and Mattie had scolded her for being unkind and had also accused her of being too top-lofty. That was when she had told Mattie about Jean-Claude, and now the whole shop knew.

She had vowed she would bring back a gift from him.

"Maybe a ring," she had murmured.

"An' 'e he did look as if 'e liked me," she muttered. "If 'twasn't for 'er . . . makin' mock o' me because I was scared. Oh, if I could get my 'ands on 'er . . ." The possibilities attendant on that brought a smile to her lips, but it soon vanished.

"Sent 'er to school, 'e did," she muttered resentfully. "An' . . ." She came to a stop because looming directly in front of her was the tower. It looked extremely tall in the intermittent moonlight. She shivered, remembering stories she had heard about it when she was younger. There was only one light in the window and, for a moment, it appeared blue to Sally's fevered imagination, but it was not. It was white enough, casting a glow which enabled her to see the door. She hurried up to it and, seizing the knocker, she shivered because it was chill against her flesh. But still she slammed it against the plate twice and then stood back, nervously waiting for the door to be opened.

In a second it was, and Jean-Claude stood in the aperture, looking surprised. "Yes . . . ?"

"Jean-Claude, it be me." Sally had intended to speak boldly, but much to her chagrin, her words emerged in a whispery, weak sort of way.

"Sally!" he exclaimed. "What are you doing here at this time of night?"

"It can't be very late . . . it's beginnin' to get dark earlier. It do, this time o' year. I 'ad to see you 'n tell you 'ow sorry I was to . . . to be so rude an' unmannerly. Matt's that angry, 'n 'e should be."

"My poor child, come in," Jean-Claude said quickly, emerging from the doorway and putting an arm around her shoulders. *"Sacre-bleu!* But you are shivering and 'tis no wonder!"

She had been cold, but a sudden rush of warmth came with his nearness. "It be cold out there for September," she acknowledged shyly as she let him lead her inside.

"It's far too cold for you to be wandering about," he said almost sternly. "Come," he added, indicating a fire roaring on the grate. "You must stand there until you are warm. Else you could catch a quinsy."

He had dropped his arm, and Sally wished that he had not. She also wished that she might tell him she needed no other warmth than his arm around her, but a sudden shyness had descended upon her. She slowly walked to the vast old fireplace, so high and so deep, it could accommodate huge logs—half-trees in fact! The flames were warm and warming. She said with some surprise, "Oh, it do feel good."

"Yes." He nodded. "As I told you, you should not have left your house in this weather. It has been uncommonly cool all day."

"I expect it has," she murmured. Then, remembering that she had been out that day, she added, "I did not much notice."

"I imagine that it is warmer in London," he said.

"Oh, yes . . . it be much warmer," she agreed. "It be nice in London. Whyn't you ever come to London, Jean-Claude?"

"I have no need," he explained.

"'Aven't you never been there? If you 'aven't, you'd like it, you would."

"I have been there." He nodded. "I prefer the country. I have little liking for cities. Besides, my work is here."

"Yer work, yes. I . . . I wanted to . . . to tell you 'twas ever so interestin', all wot you showed us." Sally felt more than the warmth of the fire on her cheeks as she continued haltingly, "An' I didn't mean to 'urt Alethea. I'm ever so sorry. I 'ope you'll forgive me."

Jean-Claude said gently, "There's nothing to forgive, child . . . and I beg you'll not think on it now. I expect you were startled by the experiments. I should have given you more warning."

Sally moved away from the fire. "I wasn't exactly frightened. Matt's told me you do some strange things 'ere. It was 'er laughin' at me." Anger rose in her throat again as she envisioned the scene. "She shouldn't 'ave laughed. 'Oo's she to laugh at me, I'd like to know?"

"Come, child, we have all agreed to put the episode out of our minds. Alethea has admitted that she should not have laughed. She did not mean it unkindly, I assure you."

"She meant it!" Sally exclaimed angrily. "But I don't want to talk about 'er. She don't mean nothin' to me . . . less 'n nothin'!" She faced him. "It's you I care about," she cried passionately. "I've told them all about you."

He regarded her confusedly. "I do not believe I understand," he said finally. "You've told whom?"

"All the girls wot work at the shop," Sally cried. "I—I told 'em I love you . . ." Her hand flew to her mouth as she looked up into his astonished face. She made an effort to stem the words that seemed to be forcing themselves out of her throat, but she had not the art to hide her feelings. "I love you, Jean-Claude. Seems to me like I've loved you all my life."

He looked at her, caught between embarrassment and pity. "My dear child . . ." he began.

Sally moved a step closer, crying. "No, no, no, you must stop callin' me a child. I be nineteen, an' soon I'll be twenty. I be a woman!" She brought her hands up to her bodice, unbuttoning it with trembling fingers. "Look 'ere," she cried, releasing her full breasts and pushing them forward. "Look, look, look! Do these belong to a child? I be a woman 'n can do anything you want me to do—anythin'! Take me . . . take me to yer bed 'n you'll see."

Retreating a step, his eyes fixed on a point above her head Jean-Claude said gently, commiseratingly, "Sally, my dear, you do not know what you are saying."

"I do . . . I do . . . I do . . ." She flung herself at him.

He caught her by the shoulders, thrusting her back. "No, child," he said firmly. "That part of my life is over . . . has been at an end for many years. My work is all."

"I could make you forget yer work, I'd do anythin' . . . I love you," Sally wailed.

"My dear girl," he began and came to a startled stop as, flinging her arms around him, Sally kissed him passionately.

He pushed her back, gently but firmly. "It is no use, Sally," he said with finality. "As I have told you, that part of my life is at an end . . . it has been over for close on eighteen years."

"I don't believe ye," she shrilled. "Yer not old . . . there be someone else."

Jean-Claude bit down a strong desire to order her out of his presence, to order her out and, indeed, thrust her out. His patience was fast leaving him. He said, however, "There is no one, my child. I had one love in my life, and she is dead."

"'Ad 'er 'ead chopped off, I suppose," she cried. "Ye can't be in love wi' no corpse."

His fists clenched. "I must ask you to go, Sally. I thank you for . . . your suggestion. It is a very great compliment, but—"

"Damn you," she shrilled, her face distorted by fury now. "May'ap, it's that scrawny little wench Alethea you'd bed . . . an' wot does she know about pleasurin' a man?"

"That is enough," he said coldly. Striding to the door, he pulled it open. "It is growing late, and you should be at home. I want you to go, Sally."

"I'm goin'." She glared at him. "An' . . . an' you'll be sorry, ye will . . . see if yer not. I 'ave friends in these parts, I 'ave." Head held high, she went past him and out.

He was already sorry, as he closed the door. He had not handled the situation well. He had never liked Sally. If it had not been for Matt, whom he thoroughly liked and respected, and upon whom he depended, he would have had nothing to do with her. He ran his hand through his hair, grimacing. Her protestations of love had made him want to laugh in her face. At least, he had not committed that particular folly. Then, when she had made reference to Denise's terrible death, he had wanted to shake her until her head swam. However, he had controlled himself, and for that, he was grateful.

He sighed. "How can she love me?" he muttered. "I have never so much as . . ." Another sigh shook him, one of pure exasperation. "I should never have invited her to

the tower today. I would not have done so were it not for
Matt . . . and I do not believe he wanted her there,
himself. And to bring her together with Alethea was pure
folly! She has always hated the child."

A vivid image of the moment when he had found poor
little Alethea being tormented by Sally and her compan-
ions rose in his mind's eye. He had disliked the girl since
that day. True, she had been a child, but her actions had
proved her a bully. Elements, heated in a crucible, might
change—characters did not, and Sally had not changed.
That was only too obvious and, judging from what she
had said regarding his intentions toward Alethea, perhaps it were better to warn her.

"Tomorrow," he murmured. "Tomorrow, I will speak
to Drusilla." He sighed and, returning to his library from
whence he had come at Sally's knock, he picked up a
book just sent him from London dealing with the experiments of one Dalton. Settling down in a chair, he began
to read and, in reading, forgot all about Sally and
Alethea, too.

Seething from hurt and embarrassment, Sally walked
in the direction of her home. Her hands were clenched
into fists and, in her present mood, she would have not
hesitated to shove both of them into Jean-Claude's gray
eyes. In fact, if she could, she would like to wreck his
laboratory. Maybe if she were to tell Matt that he had
tried to have his way with her . . . but as well speak to a
lump of clay for all the attention Matt would pay. He was
that fond of Jean-Claude and thought it a feather in his
cap that he could work for him, damn them both to hell.

"An' 'oo be this out so late?"

Sally came to an abrupt stop. There was a pounding in
her throat as she saw a tall man, his face in shadow,
staring down at her. She had an impulse to run, but he
was blocking the path and, besides, she was not one to
turn tail in the face of danger, if danger there was. She
lifted her chin and said pertly, "An' 'oo is it wants to
know?"

"Well, well, well." A thread of laughter ran through the
voice. "Ye've got a tongue in yer 'ead, an' yer not afraid
to wag it, seems."

"Why should I be afraid?" she demanded. "You want to do me a mischief?"

"May'ap yer new to these 'ere parts."

"May'ap I'm not. You suggestin' I ought to be scared?"

"If'n yer not new to these parts, maybe ye've 'eard o' Charlie Denwick."

Sally loosed a crack of laughter. "Charlie Denwick, 'tis . . . an' maybe Mr. Charlie Denwick's 'eard o' Miss Sally Price."

"Sally Price . . ." Interest sharpened his voice. "Ye'd not be Matt Price's little sister."

"Far's I know, I am. One o' 'em."

"Thought you was in Londontown."

"I am."

"Yer mighty solid for a ghost." He reached out a hand and grabbed her shoulder.

"'Ere where do you come off bein' so familiar," she chided.

"An' where do you come off bein' out 'ere in the dark?"

"May'ap it were stuffy up in the loft where me 'n my sisters sleep, 'n I took myself a walk."

"Cool night for a walk. May'ap ye 'ad other fish to fry?"

"May'ap I did. May'ap they're fried now," Sally said with a touch of bitterness, while she sent her mind back several years into the past, trying to form an image of Charlie Denwick. He was the leader of a gang of rowdy lads. Out for a lark, they were, and not above stealing or burning a man's field if they took a mind to it. Most of the people in the village tried to keep on Charlie's good side, giving him odd jobs. And . . . Her thoughts came to an abrupt end as she was suddenly swept into his arms.

"'Ere," she cried. "Wot're you about, Charlie? I—" But anything else she might have said was turned into gibberish as his mouth fastened on hers in a hard and invading kiss. She tried to cry out, tried futilely to struggle as memories of Charlie's ways flooded back into her mind. However, no matter how hard she struggled, she could not break free of him and, after a futile few minutes, she gave up. Charlie's kisses were not unpleasant, and later on when he became even more familiar, she found herself responding in kind. He was not Jean-Claude, but he wanted her and that was something.

"Sorry, I'm late," Matt said to Jean-Claude the following morning.

Jean-Claude, looking up from a mixture he was stirring, asked, "Are you late? I did not notice."

"It's close on ten. There was a real dust-up at 'ome. Sally, o' course."

Jean-Claude tensed as the events of the previous evening came rushing back into his mind. "What happened?" he asked edgily.

"She were gone all night. Come back this morning 'n now she's gone again, bag 'n baggage."

With a calm he was far from feeling, Jean-Claude said, "And why would that be?"

"Took up wi' Charlie Denwick, that's why." Matt rolled his eyes. "An' you know wot I say? I say 'good riddance!' "

"Charlie Denwick?"

"Aye, she come in bold as you please, 'angin' onto 'is arm. Ma was that put out. She was for takin' the strap to 'er . . . but when she went lookin' for Pa, Sally 'n Charlie didn't wait. She grabbed 'er clothes 'n took off wi' 'im. She'll 'ave her 'ands full wi' 'im, an' 'im, too. Sally's got a mean temper, she 'as. Never did care two straws for 'er."

"She's your sister." Jean-Claude felt it incumbent upon him to protest—over the great relief that had filled him as he had listened to this sorry tale.

"May be my sister, but I didn't choose 'er." Matt shrugged.

Jean-Claude abandoned his remonstrances. In the face of Matt's casual acceptance of his sister's downfall, there was no use for them or for commiseration. He merely said, "Who is Charlie Denwick? What does he do?"

"Anythin' 'e can. Odd jobs 'n maybe a spot o' skulduggery 'ere 'n there. 'E 'n 'is pals'll do anythin' that don't mean 'ard work. Last year one o' 'em were transported to New South Wales for 'ighway robbery. Could 'appen to Charlie. I 'ope he don't leave Sally wi' a full oven. God 'elp the brat . . . she won't be welcome 'round 'ome, I can tell you. May'ap it'll be the poor 'ouse for 'er. Now wot do ye want me to do?"

Jean-Claude told him, and they set to work.

Lying with Charlie in his hovel of a house and on a rickety bed that shook and groaned under their combined weights, and with sheets that from the smell and feel of them had not been washed in a month, Sally had tried to pretend that her lover was Jean-Claude, but it was a futile pretence that sent the flame of her rage even higher. It would have been different lying with Jean-Claude, she was sure of that. Charlie was rough in his lovemaking. Everything about him was rough, from his wild, unruly yellow hair to clothing that served only as a covering for his big body. He and style were strangers, and she did not want to be his doxy. She could do a sight better in London.

"Wot're ye savin' it for?" one of her friends at the millinery shop had asked her.

Well, she was not saving it anymore, and she felt three kinds of a fool for having held out so long, longer than anyone she knew! Even though she did not feel anything like love for Charlie, having him make love to her was exciting, but it might be just as exciting with that young man who had been so hot after her—and him with money and a title! He could have her now, and welcome, now that her foolish dreams were at an end. But Jean-Claude was going to regret his rejection of her—and before he was much older. She only had to drop a word or two in Charlie's ear. Hell-raising came naturally to him. One might say it was his meat and potatoes, and she meant to see he had a good meal of them. And Matt, too, damn him for the unnatural brother he was and always had been! Once these scores were settled, she would be on a stagecoach back to London, and Charlie none the wiser.

"Now that is pure nonsense . . . old wives tales, as they say." Drusilla was speaking and sharply to Mrs. King, a neighbor, who had just stopped in, wide-eyed with fear and big with news.

"I dunno as 'tis, Mrs. Truslow. Used to be strange things 'appened 'ere abouts. My grandma, she talked about 'ow there was witches 'n sorcerers puttin' curses on cattle 'n such."

"Have any cattle died recently?" Drusilla demanded edgily.

"Not that I know of, but . . . 'twasn't so many years back that they swum a witch in the millpond."

"Not so many years?" Drusilla echoed. "'Twas close on ninety."

"All the same," Mrs. King said stubbornly. "They be sayin' as 'ow that Frenchie be doin' some very peculiar things in 'is tower. An' look at 'im. 'E be peculiar, too, that long 'air 'n all."

"There is nothing peculiar about him," Drusilla retorted indignantly. "He's a scientist and cares nothing about his looks."

"Be that as it may, I'd think twice afore I'd be seen there," Mrs. King said darkly. "I suppose ye've 'eard o' alchemy?"

"Of course, I have heard of it," Drusilla snapped.

"Them alchemists . . . My Martin says as 'ow they used to brew potions 'n were in league wi' the devil."

"The devil?" Alethea came down the stairs. "Who is in league with the devil?"

Mrs. King gave her a narrow look. "You oughta know seein' as yer so friendly wi' 'im."

Alethea's eyes widened in indignation. She said coldly, "I expect you must be talking about Jean-Claude."

Mrs. King nodded. She said solemnly, "If the shoe fits—"

"The shoe does not fit!" Alethea retorted sharply.

"Tha's not wot folks're sayin'," Mrs. King told her. "That Sally Price said as 'ow 'e were turnin' water into wine."

"Nonsense," Drusilla snapped.

"Tha's wot they be sayin', an' everybody knows only the Good Lord can do that, less'n a person be in league wi' Satan."

"Sally Price knows full well that Jean-Claude was

merely performing a chemical experiment," Alethea said coldly.

"That is true," Drusilla corroborated.

"Tha's not wot she says. Said as 'ow she'd seen it wi' 'er own eyes 'n tasted it, too. Says as 'ow it tasted like wine when it'd been nothin' but plain water, afore."

"She's lying through her teeth!" Alethea cried hotly. "Does Jean-Claude know about these evil rumors she's been spreading, damn her?"

"May'ap. I expect Matt wot works wi' 'im would've told him. 'E been keepin' to 'isself, 'e 'as."

"It's disgusting." Alethea stamped her foot. "There's not a word of truth in it."

"No, there certainly is not," Drusilla agreed hotly.

"I 'ope not. Wouldn't want no trouble. Lots o' people'd get 'urt." Mrs. King rolled her eyes. She added, "Well, I expect I oughta be gettin' along."

"Mrs. King," Alethea said. "Do tell people that this is nothing but silly gossip. Indeed, I do not know what has gotten into Sally."

Mrs. King looked grim. "Well, whatever 'tis, she's turned out to be no better 'n she should be, takin' up wi' the likes o' Charlie, 'oo'll turn 'is 'and to any mischief. It's for 'er poor mother I feel sorry . . . brought shame on 'er 'n on 'erself as well. Thass wot comes o' lettin' 'er go to Lunnon. I said at the time t'wouldn't no good come o' it. An' I were right." Having delivered herself of that melancholy pronouncement, Mrs. King left.

Alethea turned a worried face toward her aunt. "I feel I ought to go to him."

"No, child," Drusilla said quickly. "What could you do? If there is trouble, you could get caught in the middle of it and, besides, there'll be little likelihood anything could happen, and if it did, Jean-Claude can take care of himself."

"But people have been gathering around the tower in the last two days," Alethea said worriedly. "And maybe a lot of them share Mrs. King's opinions. Do not tell me she doesn't concur with the gossip . . . I could see that she does."

"Mrs. King is not very bright," Drusilla said soothingly. "Jean-Claude has been performing experiments in his tower for many years now. It will take more than a Sally Price to get him out. Besides, it would not be seemly, you going there alone—and my ankle will not let me walk more than a few steps."

"Oh, your ankle," Alethea said quickly. "I had forgotten you turned it this morning." She looked down and said concernedly, "It is swollen. Maybe I should fetch the doctor."

"No, child, I have done the doctoring. Perhaps you will read to me. Some of that poetry by Coleridge in the book you brought with you. *The Rhyme of The Ancient Mariner* is one of my favorites. And you bring such drama to it."

Stifling a sigh, Alethea did as she was bidden. Then there was the midday meal to be prepared, which she also insisted on doing, needing to keep her hands busy and her mind as well, so that she could avoid worrying about Jean-Claude, whom she had not seen since the experiment.

She had not ceased to think about him. At odd moments, the mellifluous sound of his voice would be in her ears and his face before her mind's eye. There was no doubt but that her feelings for him had undergone a change. She had always loved him, but at first it had been the love of a child for one who could have been either father or uncle. It had been a long time, she realized, since she had thought of him as either. More and more, she was thinking of him as a man one could love in another way, a way which set her heart to beating faster and made her wish to touch him or, more pertinently, she wished to feel his arms around her. She had been experiencing these feelings ever since the day of the experiment and, now that he might be in trouble, she longed to be with him—to protect him. Yet, was it not the man who protected the woman? It was both, she thought. There was a hint of the mother in the wife, even when there were no children, she knew. Yet, of what use were these speculations when the man she loved was so far above her—as unreachable as a star? It were wiser if she could put him out of her mind.

At length, the chores were done and again Alethea had an urge to go and see Jean-Claude, but she had no reason—none! She was home, he knew it, had asked for her that one day—the same day he had invited Sally to the tower . . . What about Sally? How had she happened to leave home, and why was she spreading these ridiculous rumors regarding the experiment she had witnessed? True, she had been frightened and had turned ugly and was thrust out, but it was her brother who had done the thrusting! And later, Matt must have explained what chemical changes had taken place to cause the liquids to alter their hues. Something else must have happened. But unless Alethea were to ask Matt, there was no one else who could tell her . . . unless Katie knew. She was Sally's friend and, furthermore, her house was no more than a half mile away and not in the direction of the tower!

She hurried up to her aunt's chamber and knocked on the door. "Come, my dear," Drusilla said in a drowsy voice.

"Aunt." Alethea, standing on the threshold, said, "I am going out for a bit."

"Are you, dear? Where?"

"I am going to see Katie. I'll be back shortly."

If she had been more wakeful, her aunt might have questioned her, knowing that she was not fond of Katie, but she was weary and so Alethea, flinging on her cloak, hurried down the street and was soon at the cottage— little more than a hovel—where Katie lived. Praying that the girl was at home, she knocked. The door was opened so hastily that she had the impression Katie had been directly behind it, waiting for someone else. That was very evident. Disappointment was in her voice and manner. "Oh, 'tis you," she said in a dragging tone. She seemed paler than the last time they had met, and her eyes were swollen and red.

"Katie," Alethea said concernedly. "What is the matter? Have you been ill?"

"No, 'aven't been ill." Katie shook her head. "Wot was it you wanted?"

"I thought you might be able to tell me about Sally and—"

"Sally!" Katie snapped, a deep frown creasing her brow. "'Er . . . wish she were in 'ell, I do." She moved back into the house and it was obvious that she intended to slam the door in her visitor's face.

"No, please, Katie, I beg of you," Alethea said hastily. "You and Sally are no longer friends, then?"

"Friends!" Katie shrilled. "If I 'ad 'er 'ere, I'd skin 'er alive, I would, for wot she done to my Charlie, 'oo I been walkin' out with 'til she come 'ome."

"I am sorry, Katie."

"You can be sorrier for 'im wot's in the tower. She's got Charlie 'n 'is pals all stirred up, she 'as . . . sayin' as 'ow Jean-Claude's in league wi' the devil 'n practicin' black magic. Says as 'ow she seen the devil rise right outa 'is cauldrons. Tonight they're goin' to march on the tower an' get the demons out."

"Oh, God," Alethea said. "Why would Sally do a thing like that?"

"You didn't know she were sweet on Jean-Claude?" Katie asked.

"I thought she might be," Alethea admitted.

"Well, she were, right enough. Matt told me that. 'Appen 'e wouldn't look at 'er, 'n why should 'e? 'Im bein' a gentleman for all 'e's 'alf a Frenchie."

"When are they going to march on the tower?" Alethea demanded.

"Come sundown when Matt's gone 'ome. None o' 'em wants to tangle wi' 'im. 'E'll 'ave 'is 'andsful, 'e will. Jean-Claude, I mean."

Alethea glanced at the sky. It was darkening. The idea of going to the constable entered and left her mind. She must first warn Jean-Claude and then go for him.

"I thank you for telling me, Katie," she said.

"You take care," Katie warned. "They be a angry lot, they be."

"I'm not afraid," Alethea said staunchly.

The distance between the tower and Katie's house was longer than she had imagined, and as she reached her destination, she saw some rough-looking youths milling about. She did not like their lowering expressions. She quickened her steps but as she reached the door to the tower, one of them yelled loudly, "Keep away from there, you—if you don't want the devil after you."

"There are no devils here!" she dared to retort and then, turning her back on them, Alethea knocked purposefully on the door.

"'Oo be she?" someone called.

"May'ap she be 'is doxy."

"A cozy armful, 'n too good for the likes o' 'im." A tall young man came forward purposefully.

Alethea pounded on the door. "Jean-Claude," she called. "Jean-Claude, let me in."

The young man caught her arm. "Come away, love . . . by God." He stared down her. "Yer a beauty, ye are." Grinning, he tightened his hold on her arm.

Fear chilled her as she stared up into his grimy face and saw the look in his eyes. "Jean-Claude," she cried hopelessly as she vainly tried to wrench her arm from her captor's hard grasp.

In that same moment, the door was pulled back and Jean-Claude, a pistol in hand, his face grim, stood in the aperture. "Alethea!" he said and thrust the pistol at the head of the man holding her. "Let her go," he commanded. "Release her at once, damn you."

"An' be damned quick about it, or ye'll get the contents o' this pitcher in yer face 'n ye'll wish ye'd never been born." Matt appeared behind Jean-Claude, holding a smoking metal pitcher.

Startled, the young man dropped Alethea's arm, but at the same time, a hail of rocks fell about them as more of the men came forward, their faces menacing. Jean-Claude hastily thrust Alethea inside and, turning to Matt, he muttered, "Get back." Then, slamming the massive door, he looked at Alethea concernedly. "Did he hurt you, my dear?"

"No." She looked up at him with equal concern.

"I . . . I had thought to warn you. I did not know they were already gathering."

"'Ave been for the last hour," Matt said grimly. "Ye can blame my damned sister for that . . . 'er 'n 'er wild tales."

"I should have gone to fetch the constable immediately," Alethea said regretfully.

"I hope he will come later," Jean-Claude said. "But meanwhile, we are safe enough in here. It is my hope that they will grow weary of this prank."

"It be more 'n a prank, thanks to my damned sister 'n that long tongue o' 'ers . . . 'er 'n that Charlie wot's always spoilin' for trouble."

"You'd best sit down, Alethea," Jean-Claude said concernedly. "I wish I might send you home, but it would not be safe for you to leave at this time. Later in the evening, perhaps. Meanwhile, you can rest in my room."

"I do not want to rest," she said determinedly. "I will stay here. It might be that you will need my help."

He did not answer at once. He stared at her in silence. Then, in a curiously constricted tone of voice, he said, "You are very brave, my dear Alethea. I hope you will not have cause to regret that bravery."

"I will never regret it, no matter what happens, Jean-Claude," she said steadily.

He regarded her in silence for a long moment and seemed about to say something more when shouts, yells, and pounding on the door interrupted him.

"Wot 'n 'ell's gotten into them?" Matt growled.

"Bloodlust," Jean-Claude said bitterly.

"But they know you," Alethea cried. "And they know Sally. Their reason should tell them . . ."

Jean-Claude whirled on her. "Their reason?" he demanded. "Their reason has fled . . . as it fled in France not very long ago. The mob does not reason, it does as it is directed, mindlessly and obediently. And the guillotine falls, and the heads roll."

"Oh, Jean-Claude." Alethea rose from her chair and flung her arms around him. "Do not think of that . . . Do not remember, I beg you will not remember."

He looked down at her bemusedly. It was a moment before he said huskily, "I should not have used such a comparison. It is not the same. They will calm down eventually." He put a finger under her chin and tilted her face up. "Do I see tears, my dear? You must not be afraid, my Alethea."

"I . . . I am not afraid for myself," she half-sobbed. "Only for you. Oh, why, why, why did this have to happen?"

"We have not to wonder why . . . and the siege will be over before the night is through, I am sure of it. Meanwhile, the tower is impregnable. Out there, they will only wear themselves out and go home. There will be no tribunals." He led her to a chair and, gently but insistently, pushed her down. "You will see that I am right, my dear," he said as he turned away.

Watching him, Alethea wished he might have let her remain at his side. Her thoughts fled. The yelling and screaming had grown louder and, to her fury and horror, she heard the words, "Sorcerer . . . devil . . . come out and show yourself."

Others, she knew, had heard those same words here in this very tower, but centuries ago. It seemed incredible that they should be hearing them again—that concentrated outpouring of rage and hate, mindless and terrible! No matter what comfort he had been able to offer her, he must be suffering dreadfully as the mindless fury outside brought back a replica of the agony he must have endured before he left France. And all because of Sally Price's wounded pride. It was possible that many witchhunts had arisen out of similar causes . . . And meanwhile, how long would this madness continue? There was no guessing; they would have to wait and see.

The battering against the door grew louder. There was cursing, and there were cries for the "wizard" to show himself. There were also threats concerning what would happen if he did not. An hour passed and then another and still the raucous cries and ugly threats smote the ears of the beleaguered trio. Matt occasionally tried to refute the hoarse accusations that were being screamed through the door. More often, he paced back and forth across the room like a caged lion while Jean-Claude tried to soothe him—a difficult task, given his own frustration and anger.

"Will they never go away?" Alethea cried finally.

"Not until—" Jean-Claude began and then paused, adding thoughtfully, "Not until they are distracted. Matt!"

"Yes, sir." Matt frowned. "I could shoot over their 'eads," he spoke pleadingly, and Alethea guessed he must have made that suggestion more than once.

"No," Jean-Claude told him firmly. "I have thought of something I should have remembered much earlier. Then, I think, the crowd would have dispersed. It may very well go now—even though they are warmed to their task and out for blood."

"Oh, no!" Alethea could not quell the exclamation that burst from her.

He was at her side in a minute, kneeling by her chair and taking her hands in his warm grasp. "They will not achieve their purpose, my dear, never imagine that they will!" He moved away from her and turned back to Matt, saying, "We must prepare a mixture." He went on to mention ingredients that meant little to Alethea. She heard the words "potash and phosphorous."

Matt, who seemed to understand very well what was needed, fetched them, putting them into a mortar. She saw that he was suddenly grinning.

"My dear." Jean-Claude stood before her again. "You must put your hands over your ears and stay as far away as possible from this . . . mixture." He pointed to the mortar. "It might even be better were you to go upstairs."

"No," she protested. "I wish to stay here."

"Very well, but you must stand on the other side of the room. Come." As she rose, he added, "You are very brave, child." He put an arm around her shoulders and gave her an affectionate little squeeze. "But now—go quickly, there, by those scales."

She nodded and hurriedly crossed to them, wondering

what Jean-Claude had in mind. Then, as Matt applied a pestle to the mortar, bringing it down hard on whatever mixture was inside, there was a series of very loud explosions that startled her—bringing a cry of fright to her lips, which she determinedly swallowed. Outside there were other cries and screams, the while a hoarse voice yelled, "They be shootin' at us, damn 'em!"

Matt put more of the mixture in the mortar and, as he stirred and pounded, the explosions continued, while outside there was the faint sound of running feet and that hoarse voice angrily exhorting them to remain.

Finally, there was quiet.

"May'ap we can go now," Matt said.

"It is possible," Jean-Claude spoke dubiously. "You may try opening the door."

Matt nodded and, loosening the chain, he pushed the door open to a chorus of angry threats—not as many as there had been before, but enough to prove that safety lay only within.

"Damn ye all for a pack o' village idiots," Matt yelled and slammed the door again, hastily fastening the heavy chain as those outside evidently tried to force it back.

Matt turned angry eyes on Jean-Claude. "Shall we gi' 'em another round?"

"No." Jean-Claude sighed. "We will have to wait until they go home. It is a cold evening. There is frost in the air. They will eventually grow tired of this futile siege." He crossed the room to stand beside Alethea, saying ruefully, "I think you must try and sleep, my dear. It is possible that you will not be able to return to your home until morning."

She regarded him anxiously. "My aunt," she began timorously. "She does not know where I am."

His eyes mirrored her concern. "It is a pity that she must be uselessly distressed, my child, but there's no help for it. It would be exceedingly dangerous for you to leave at this time. There's no telling what would happen. Let me take you up to my room . . . You can remain there for the night."

"But where will you sleep?" she demanded anxiously.

"I do not expect to sleep," came the grim reply.

"Then, I shall not, either," she cried.

"Child, you cannot help us by remaining down here. Come with me now, my dear. I insist."

"No, Jean-Claude," she said mulishly. "I will stay here . . . I insist."

He smiled regretfully. "I will not continue this argument, my child, but it will be a long night."

"I am prepared for that," she said, lifting her chin.

"Here is bravery." He put his arm around her shoulders, giving her a little affectionate squeeze—before turning away.

She looked after him yearningly, loving him with all her being. Despite her very real concern for her aunt should she wake and find her gone, she was glad that she would be with him through this long night—no matter what happened. There might be danger, to be sure, but at least she would not be in ignorance as to the outcome.

The sun, shining through the open window, awakened Alethea. She opened her eyes and then hastily shut them against its brightness. A moment later, she opened them again and sat up, looking confusedly about her. She was in a small room, furnished only with a bed, a chair, and a tall clothespress. She sighed, realizing ruefully that, after all, she must have fallen asleep and Jean-Claude had brought her to his room. She remembered nothing of that. Then her cheeks flamed as she realized she was wearing only her shift. Her gown, neatly folded, lay on the chair. Had he also undressed her? He must have, she knew. He would never have delegated that task to Matt! And how, how, how had she happened to fall asleep? She had intended to remain below the whole night through. Yet, the last thing she recalled was the tumult outside, the angry voices, the continued demands for the "sorcerer" to show himself . . . and how could she have fallen asleep through that racket?

The drink?

Vaguely, she remembered Jean-Claude pouring wine for them all. Had he drugged her wine? It was not outside the realms of possibility. He had been concerned over her losing sleep and had said as much more than once. He had also continued to stress the fact that she was not needed below. Perhaps, she thought guiltily, he believed her presence more a hindrance than a help and had been too polite to say so. And what had ultimately happened? Had the crowd finally dispersed? The tower had windows all around; she would be able to see if any of them remained below.

She slipped out of bed and, going to one of the front windows, she leaned out. Then, she hurriedly shrank back. There were a few people still milling about. She hoped none of them had seen her, for she would have been caught in a most compromising position since she was wearing only her shift! And when would she be able to leave? Her aunt would be frantic! Looking about her, she saw an ewer and basin. There was water in the ewer. Hastily performing her ablutions, she pulled on her gown, buttoning it with equal haste, and then she hurried down the stairs.

"Jean-Claude," she called as she reached the laboratory. She received no answer and, looking through the vast room, she realized that neither he nor Matt were present. Nor were they in the small inner room. Where were they? What had happened to them? Had the mob broken through? No, her common sense told her—even before a glance at the door saw it well-chained and intact. If the tower had been invaded, she would not have been lying in Jean-Claude's bed. She flushed, wishing . . . but she dared not follow that thought to its inevitable conclusion. It was her Aunt Drusilla she must needs concentrate on. How could she leave the tower without being seen? But that would not be difficult—there was a way out through the back, through the trees and over a surrounding wall! Jean-Claude might be concerned on returning and not finding her, but it was of her aunt, she must needs think. He would realize where she had gone, she told herself.

She had no difficulty in leaving the tower, and though she had not climbed the wall since she was a child, she found the old footholds and in a few minutes was on her way back to her aunt's cottage.

As she had anticipated, she found Drusilla well-nigh distracted as she limped up and down the floor of her small living room under the sympathetic eye of an elderly neighbor, Mrs. Griswold. The latter had given a small shriek as she came in, and Drusilla flew at her, clutching her by both arms.

"Where have you been?" she cried, caught between anger and relief.

"I went to see Katie . . . while you were asleep, aunt," Alethea began, wishing that Mrs. Griswold was not present. She was a known gossip, and often her word-of-mouth was far from accurate, but there was no help for it. She continued reluctantly, "And, she told me—"

"You've been with Katie all this time?" Drusilla interrupted. "Why?"

"No," Alethea said. "She told me what Sally was planning and I thought to warn Jean-Claude. But when I reached the tower . . ." As she told her story, both ladies listened closely, Mrs. Griswold avidly and Drusilla, to Alethea's surprise, angrily, once her worries had been alleviated. As Alethea reached the end of her account, Drusilla said sharply, "You should not have gone! It was madness."

"I expect it was," Alethea said contritely, "but I thought he must be warned."

"There were others who could have warned him," Mrs. Griswold commented with a sharp look at her.

Alethea's own anger rose at what she could tell was their combined disapproval. "I thought I would tell him and come home, but the temper of the crowds was such—"

"That you were required to remain there," Drusilla finished with something of a snap. She fixed her eyes on Mrs. Griswold. "Jane, now that you have heard the explanation, I hope that you will be kind enough to counter any gossip that should arise."

"Oh, I will that, Drusilla," Mrs. Griswold said hastily. "And I am sure it happened just as Alethea has described."

Alethea looked at her with no little surprise. "Are you suggesting that I . . . I am not telling the truth?"

"Alethea—" Drusilla said on a note of caution.

"Of course, my dear, it is obvious that you are telling the truth. I, for one, would never doubt you," Mrs. Griswold said in an ameliorating tone of voice. "It's just that that Frenchman bein' a bachelor, 'n Matt, too . . . an' you bein' there all night . . . if folks was to 'ear of it—"

"They will not hear about it," Alethea said quickly. "No one knew I was there except . . ." She paused, frowning as she realized that a whole crowd had watched her go in—but, she assured herself, they would hardly have remembered that, given the subsequent commotion.

"No one knew you were there except . . .?" Drusilla said edgily.

"Exceptin' whom?" Mrs. Griswold demanded.

"There were people there, but they were all in such a state of fury." Alethea shook her head as her own anger rose again. "It was Sally Price set them off!"

"I can imagine anything of Sally Price," Drusilla said sharply. "That girl's a fool and a busybody to boot."

"An' no better 'n she should be," Mrs. Griswold said. "She's like to drive 'er poor mother into an early grave, she is . . . a-throwin' in her lot wi' the likes o' Charlie Denwick. 'E were born to be 'anged, 'e were. Sally'll regret the day she ever met 'im, an' that's a fact."

"Sally deserves whatever comes her way," Drusilla said. Her eyes rested on Alethea's face. "I only hope . . ." She shook her head and sighed. Then, she added, "I don't expect you had much sleep last night, my dear. You'd best go to your room and rest."

It was on the tip of Alethea's tongue to assure her aunt that she had slept very well, but fortunately, she was preserved from that folly by a vivid memory of where she had slept. "I will do that, Aunt," she said, and thankfully left the room.

"Jane Griswold." Drusilla fixed a stern eye on her friend. "You have heard what my niece has told you, and

you may believe that it is the truth. Alethea always tells
the truth, you have known her long enough to be aware of
that, yourself."

"Oh, I am, I am, Drusilla," Mrs. Griswold assured her.
"Nobody will get a different tale from me, my dear. But,"
she shook her head and sighed, "I expect you know what
could 'appen."

"I do," Drusilla groaned. "I do, indeed."

"We will 'ope for the best," Mrs. Griswold said
soothingly, the while her corrugated brow and doubtful
gaze revealed her concern as vividly as if she had voiced
it aloud.

CHAPTER FOUR

"IS IT MUCH further, Katie?" Alethea asked wearily. It had proven to be one of those warm October days, and she had been walking for the better part of three hours.

"'Tisn't much further . . . just over that rise, I'll be bound," Katie said. "May'ap we can sit 'n rest by yon stream." She indicated a brook splashing its way through a small copse.

"Yes," Alethea said eagerly. "And I will wash my face and hands. They are very sticky."

"Me, too." Katie nodded.

A few minutes later, both girls lay back on the grass, rejoicing in the shade from the surrounding trees.

"It be uncommon warm for October," Katie commented.

"Yes . . ."

"Us'll 'ave to leave soon. There'll be a passel a'ead o' us 'n grabbin' the best situations."

"We will be here only a few minutes, no more," Alethea agreed and sighed.

"It be a fair shame," Katie remarked, a few seconds later. "I don't guess ye've ever worked in a dairy."

"I have not," Alethea said. "But I have seen dairy maids at work, and I expect I will have no difficulty in learning how to perform the tasks required of me."

Katie turned to stare at her with wide eyes. "You talk like that 'n they won't know wot to make o' ye." Before

Alethea could comment, she shook her head. "It'll be 'ard for ye, that's a fact. An' ye 'ad such a good position at the big 'ouse."

"Yes," Alethea remarked in a small voice, wishing that Katie had not made mention of that position because it gave rise to the images in the back of her mind—a whole procession of them, inexorably passing before her interior vision. Leading them was Sally Price, who had seen her as she had peered down from Jean-Claude's tower room in her shift. She had stood there only a few seconds but Sally, stubbornly lingering outside, and vainly trying to exhort those remnants of the crowd that had assembled the previous night, had seen. How very quickly that word had passed from mouth to mouth! Those who were there had wasted no time in telling those who were not there, and the gossip mills spewed out the information faster than grain was ever ground into flour. Servants had heard it from friends and had subsequently muttered it to their mistresses and thus it was wafted to the abigail who worked for Lady Dysart.

Alethea shuddered. She had wondered why the gig had not come for her on the day she was expected back. She had walked to the great mansion, where she had been so happily employed and, since she was a governess, had had the privilege of entering through the front door. She had let the great dragon-shaped knocker fall on its plate, and Mr. Wildford, the butler, looking surprised and disapproving, had admitted her. However, when she had started toward the main hall, he had coldly advised her to wait in a small antechamber off that hall.

Alethea winced as her interior vision again began to function, presenting images she would as lief had not contemplated, but inexorably they passed before her. Lady Dysart, coming in, her gaze surprised and cold at the same time.

"Miss Unwin, did you not receive my message?" she had asked.

"No, your ladyship," Alethea had said.

"Very well, it seems that I must render it in person. However, I cannot believe that you are unaware of its contents, given your . . . er connection with Monsieur de Bretigny." Lady Dysart frowned and before Alethea could reply, she had added distastefully, "I might tell you that I hold no brief for him either, foisting his mistress upon this household. It is too, too disgraceful!"

Alethea shuddered as she recalled those words, for it was then and only then that she had become aware of the gossip circulating through the village, the gossip that no one had seen fit to impart to her aunt or to herself. Perhaps they had not believed it. Lady Dysart, however, had believed it. Her belief had been evident in her chill, contemptuous stare and in the freezing cadences of her voice as on hearing Alethea's protests and explanation of that hectic night, she had said, "If you have, indeed, been unjustly accused, Miss Unwin, I am sorry. However, you must understand that the word has spread and, consequently, I cannot retain you in my employ. At all costs it is necessary to avoid the appearance of evil, especially when the innocence of young children is at risk."

"At risk, your ladyship?" Alethea had questioned.

"I am sure you understand my meaning, Miss Unwin." Her ladyship had produced a small purse. "I had intended to send this stipend to you, but since you have decided to present yourself at my door, I will give it to you. I hope it will tide you over while you seek a new position . . . if that is what you have in mind. Unfortunately, in the circumstances, I cannot give you references."

Alethea had longed to throw the money in her ladyship's face. However, with her aunt in mind, she had perforce to accept it and, with Lady Dysart's concluding remarks on the "appearance of evil" ringing in her ears, she had come out of the house. As she had started down the drive to the main gates, she had encountered Lord Dysart and had braced herself in anticipation of a similar rebuff.

He, however, had greeted her cordially and with a warmth she had never heard from him before. He had said, "I will be sorry to see you go, Miss Unwin. Do not imagine that I did not speak in your behalf, but my wife was adamant." He had slipped an arm around her waist. "Jean-Claude's a sly dog, and that's a fact. Still, he's half-French and I understand the French . . . I also understand him. You are very beautiful, Miss Unwin—a feast to the eyes, indeed. I hope that we will have a chance to meet again, if your heart's not wholly given over to Jean-Claude. Meanwhile, have this to—er—tide you over. And there is more in the treasure chest from whence this came. Perhaps you might give me a little treasure from your chest . . . in return." He had produced a golden sovereign and pressed it into her hand. Then, he had dared to lean forward and attempt an embrace.

Alethea exhaled a hissing breath. Sovereigns were not easily come by . . . but it had given her considerable satisfaction to both slap him across the face and let the gold piece fall in the dirt at his feet. She had subdued an impulse to run from him. Instead, lifting her head high, she had walked toward the gates. He had not attempted to follow her, but his laughter had followed her. "I like your spirit, Miss Unwin," he had called.

Alethea, returning to her aunt's cottage, had found Drusilla in receipt of Lady Dysart's letter. She had said apologetically, "I opened it, my love. I guessed its contents. You must not repine, child. You will find another position—you with your schooling and your intelligence. I, with half—less than half your accomplishments—could have held a similar position, had not my father become ill on the eve of the day I was to go."

"You . . . Aunt Drusilla?" Alethea had asked in surprise.

"Yes, I, my dear. The teacher at the village school took a special interest in me. She encouraged me to improve my speech. Have I never told you this?"

"No, you never have," Alethea said wonderingly.

"Well, it is the truth. I expect that because we were separated so long, while you were at Bath, I never thought to mention it. Old Mrs. Blake, my teacher, is dead these many years past—else I am sure she would have given you a reference and it may be—"

"I do not think it will be easy for me to obtain references. Jean-Claude would vouch for me, of course—"

Drusilla had sighed. "He, in common with yourself, is not without the stigma . . . the appearance of evil, but enough. We must consider what we must do, child. It may be that we will have to leave here . . . and go far away. I have a good friend in Scotland."

"But your cottage, Aunt," Alethea had protested.

"I could sell it and—"

"Let us not talk about that yet," Alethea had told her. "I know of a small school . . . not far from here. It may be that I can find a position there."

"Child, you need not look for a position immediately," Drusilla had said gently. "There is the money from Lady Dysart, and I have savings. You are advised to stay here until this tempest in a teapot has blown over—as it undoubtedly will."

Thinking of those valiant words, Alethea smiled fondly and a little sadly. Her aunt had sounded convincing enough, but she could not hide the fear lurking in her eyes. It was true that she did have some money, but not enough to support them both. Alethea could not remain at home longer than a fortnight without causing her aunt great anxiety. She had to find work! On another occasion, she might have consulted Jean-Claude, but the virulent gossip that was circulating through the village had prevented that. She was sure that he was aware of it, too, else he would have come to see them. He had come on the morning she had left and, having been assured by Drusilla that she was safe and sound, sleeping in her room, he had gone back to his tower. He had not emerged from it these last three days.

By now, her aunt would have found her note. She would be distressed, certainly. However, when she calmed down and thought it over, she must see the good sense of her decision. The work might be hard, and she would need to hire herself out for a year and a day, but when that period was over, she might look for a position compatible with her education. The gossip must certainly have died down by that time and . . .

"Us'd better be on our way," Katie said. "An' remember, it won't do puttin' on any airs 'n graces when they start askin' you questions."

"I will follow your lead, Katie," Alethea assured her.

She received a regretful stare. "It ain't right," Katie said hotly. "You oughtn't to be 'avin to come wi' me. That blasted Charlie Denwick! I 'ope 'e filled Sally Price wi' child afore 'e were clapped in jail, 'n I 'ope they keep him in while 'er belly swells."

Alethea was conscious of a similar wish—save that she was of the opinion that Sally Price ought to be sharing poor Charlie's cell. It was only too obvious that she had egged him on to start the riot that had ended with such disaster for herself and for poor Charlie, as well. She had a notion that Sally would escape unscathed. In fact, she might even be on her way back to London at this very moment. Sally, she thought bitterly, would always survive.

"Come on, 'Thea," Katie urged.

Alethea rose to her feet and was conscious of blisters on both heels. It was a long time since she had walked so far. Tonight, she would probably be aching in every limb—and where would she spend this night? She forebore to speculate.

"I wish everythin' wasn't up'ill," Katie moaned as they climbed a rise that had not seemed as steep when they had started. "Oooh," she breathed as they reached its crest. "Look!"

Alethea looked and saw the stretch of fair splashed across a large meadow. Hanging between poles were bright banners blowing in the cool autumn winds. There was a great throng of people already present, and she could see booths full of flimsy but glittering farings and hear the shrieks of those who were on the Up-and-down ride. Yet, despite the color and the gaiety of the crowds, a quotation from Milton rose in her mind: "Long is the way and hard, that out of hell leads up to light . . ."

It seemed to her that she was looking at a portion of

hell, but, resolutely, she dismissed the fancy as Katie walked forward gladly. She was not, she reasoned, visiting hell; she was merely going to find a job that would sustain her for the coming year.

"My dear, what can be amiss?" Jean-Claude came forward as Matt, having answered a frenzied pounding at his door, admitted an anguished Drusilla.

"It's Alethea," she sobbed. "She's gone . . . she's gone with Katie to—to the hiring fair."

"Lord be!" Matt expelled a long whistle.

"To the hiring fair?" Jean-Claude echoed, his dark brows drawing together in a frown. "But I do not understand . . . Why would she wish to go to a hiring fair? She has given up her position with Lady Dysart?"

Drusilla regarded him with a mixture of confusion and actual anger. "Have you not heard from your friends, then? You do not know that she has been dismissed?"

"Dismissed?" he echoed. "Why? I understood that they were most pleased with her."

Drusilla's confusion and anger was replaced by exasperation. "You do not understand," she said. "You actually do not understand, do you, Jean-Claude? What have you been doing these last few days? I mean, since the riot?"

"I have been working. I received papers from a friend in London—a most interesting experiment on the subject of light particles—and we, Matt and I . . ." He broke off, meeting Drusilla's angry and, at the same time, anguished stare. "But Alethea was dismissed? Why . . .?"

Drusilla actually stamped her foot. "You were kind enough to let her remain with you the whole of the night and she was seen in the top of the tower, where it is well-known you sleep. She leaned out of the window in her—her shift and . . . You have heard nothing of this?"

"I have heard nothing." Jean-Claude turned a frowning gaze on Matt. "But you must have heard something," he said accusingly.

Matt flushed. "I 'eard as 'ow she were caught leanin' out the window, but I told anyone wot told me that she were sleepin' up there while you an' me was below."

"And, of course, they believed you!" Jean-Claude said with a fine sarcasm. "Oh, Matt, why did you never tell me or you . . ." He fixed a kindling eye on Drusilla. "You could have come to me, you know that."

"Alethea would not let me trouble you." Drusilla brushed tears from her cheeks. "And now . . . and now . . . She must have arrived there by now and . . . who would not hire her?"

"Lummy," Matt breathed. "Kind o' folks come to those fairs . . . she'll be in the basket for sure."

"How long has she been gone?" Jean-Claude rasped.

"I am not sure, but it's been over an hour—"

"More like two, I'll be bound," Matt said. "They get there early, them wot want to be 'ired."

"Where is it? Do you know?" Jean-Claude demanded, looking from Drusilla to Matt.

"I know where 'tis," Matt said. "In the—"

"Never mind giving me directions, now. I will take the post chaise and you will show me the way," Jean-Claude said determinedly. "You may come with me, if you choose, Drusilla."

"I do choose," she cried. "Let us go at once, I beg you. I am so frightened for her. She's an innocent . . . an innocent!"

They had taken their places in the line of girls all wearing white aprons to signify their wish to work in a dairy. Prospective employers stood in a large tent to interview them. Others, however, strode up and down the line, eyeing the candidates.

The girls, mainly from surrounding farms, giggled at this surveillance, though some bridled and a few, like Alethea, kept their heads down and their eyes firmly fixed on the ground. She was very uncomfortable. Though there was a cool wind blowing, the sun was warm and her gown, an old blue and white calico, clung damply to her body. She had bundled her hair up in a cap, and it, too, was uncomfortable. Furthermore, the noise of the fairgrounds battered at her from all sides. Those in the booths, the merchants and peddlers, all seemed to be hawking their wares at the top of their lungs. In addition, there were the crowds of people, all talking and laughing, and there were children crying and frantic mothers screaming because they had lost one or another tot. In addition, the line was long. Occasionally, there was an outburst of anger as one or another girl was turned down and went her way, screaming her chagrin to anyone who would hear her.

"You . . ." a man said roughly. "Let's 'ave a look at you."

Alethea, startled, found a hand on her shoulder. She glanced to one side and found a tall, husky young man staring at her. His eyes widened as she faced him. "Well, well, well," he said, his gaze wandering over her in a way that caused her to feel singularly uncomfortable. Then, much to her anger, he clutched her arm. "There's not much meat on yer bones . . . but I don't mind that, I don't. An' yer 'ere to be a milkmaid, are you?"

Alethea tried to pull away from him. "I would prefer that you kept your hands to yourself, sir."

He flung his head back and laughed loudly, but he did not release her. "You'd prefer it, would you? Well, I would prefer to keep ahold o' you until it's your turn up there. You're goin' to be mine, girl. I got a good big dairy 'n I need able workers. An' damned if I don't like what I see."

"I do not wish to work for you," Alethea said freezingly as once more she attempted to pull away from him.

"Alethea," Katie protested.

"Oh, ye don't want to work for me, eh, Alethea?" Her captor grinned.

"I have not given you permission to use my name, sir," Alethea said quickly and was immediately regretful as he flung back his head once more, laughing even louder than before.

"Listen to her . . . airs like a fine lady, she 'as. Alethea, mayhap I'm supposed to kiss the 'em of your gown." He clamped his hand on her arm. "You come along with me, lass. I'll have them sign you right off, I will."

Her heart was beating in her throat as she tried to pull

away from him. "I have said that I do not wish to go with you, sir," she said angrily. "I have decided that I do not wish to be hired, after all."

"And I've decided that you'll damned well come with me, whether you work in the dairy or some other part of the house." He rolled his eyes and grinned. "And my name's Harry Smithers . . ."

His eyes roamed over her slight body. "There's lots else you can do . . . lots else, I'd rather have you do, lass."

"You let me go!" she said furiously. "I do not have to work for you, and I will not."

"'Ere, wot's the matter 'ere?" Another young man had joined them. Looking at Alethea, his eyes widened and he emitted a long, low whistle. "Wot's the matter, lass. Is this man botherin' you?"

"Oh, yes, yes, he is," she said. "I do not want to work for him."

"Then, ye don't 'ave to work for 'im," said the stranger with a glare for Mr. Smithers.

"You stay out of this . . . this is none of your concern," growled Alethea's captor.

The second man, staring at Alethea with wide eyes, said menacingly, "An' supposin' I want to make it my business, eh?"

"Cripes," Katie muttered. "There'll be a mill for sure, if the constables don't stop 'em."

Mr. Smithers had finally loosened his hard grip on her arm and, Alethea, backing off, started away quickly only to feel a pair of arms seize her. She struggled against a strong hold.

"Let me go . . . let me go!" she cried.

"Alethea, my dear, come now . . . with me," said a voice in her ear—a voice she knew.

Alethea whirled around and found herself confronting Jean-Claude. "Oh," she cried. "Oh, Jean-Claude!" She clutched his arm. "Oh, please, please, help me to get away. These men—"

"I quite understand, my dear," he said soothingly. Then he added sternly, "But what manner of madness entered into your mind that you would come to such a place?"

"I thought—" she began.

"Hey, where be you going with her?" Harry Smithers strode over to confront Jean-Claude. He was followed by the other young man who was now looking hot, angry, and suspicious.

Jean-Claude eyed Mr. Smithers coolly. "I have come to fetch my niece," he said.

"Your niece?" Mr. Smithers glared at him. "I'd lay a monkey, she's nothin' to you. An' I'll 'ave you know that I mean to hire her for a year and a day. She was here for that, and here she'll stay."

"I will not," Alethea said coldly. "I have not even seen those who preside over these matters."

"And how would you like to know that I am one of them?" he retorted.

"A likely tale," growled the other man.

"And who are you to question it . . . I tell you," Mr. Smithers confronted him, a hamlike hand on the other's slender shoulder.

"Alethea, my dear." Putting his arm around her, Jean-Claude hurried her toward the crowds on the walk. "Let us be gone . . ."

"Here!" He was confronted once more by Mr. Smithers. "Where be you going with her?"

Jean-Claude said icily, "It little concerns you where I am going—save that I am taking my niece back with me. And," he bent a stern eye on Alethea, "I wish to hear no more arguments from you."

"I promise that you will not, Uncle." Alethea bowed her head. "It was very foolish of me, I know that now." She looked back over her shoulder and saw Katie staring at her, open-mouthed. Much to her relief, the girl said nothing. Mr. Smithers, however, was not to be discouraged so easily. As Jean-Claude moved away, he followed him.

"I tell you yet again, she was 'ere to be 'ired, and I was about to 'ire her and you've no right—"

"As her uncle and her next of kin, I have every right,"

Jean-Claude returned coolly. "And I find you most . . . maladroit, sir. I would be pleased if you would take yourself off, at once."

Mr. Smithers showed a pair of large, knotted fists. "Oh, you'd be pleased, eh? Well, supposing I was to say that I'd no intention of doing so, my fine buck. I was about to—"

"I have said that I wish you to leave." Jean-Claude lifted his cane and, with a lightning twist of his wrist to its head, he pulled out a slim sword, placing the narrow blade at a spot just above Mr. Smithers's heart. "I wish," he continued coldly, "for you to take yourself off, at once. I will not repeat my request."

Mr. Smithers, staring down at the weapon, paled. "Damn you," he muttered, but, turning, he strode off and was quickly lost among the crowd. Jean-Claude calmly sheathed his sword and took Alethea's arm again.

She looked at him incredulously. "Your cane is—"

He nodded. "Quite, my dear little Alethea. And now, let us hurry." He was looking at her sternly again. "Your aunt will fear that I have not found you."

"Aunt Drusilla is—here with you?" she gasped.

"Yes, of course, she is here. Did you think she would sit idly at home, while you rushed blindly into peril?" He shook his head. "My poor Alethea, we are not all as foolish as you. Now come, let us leave this wretched place."

A hundred questions trembled on her tongue, but she voiced none of them for his arm was tight about her shoulders as he hurried her through the milling crowds toward a waiting post chaise. As they drew nearer, she saw her aunt's face at the window, her eyes full of anxiety and a burgeoning misery.

"Oh, Aunt Drusilla," Alethea cried and, leaving Jean-Claude, she ran to the post chaise.

"Ah!" Matt, sitting by the driver, yelled, "'Ere she be!"

"Alethea, my love." Drusilla threw open the door. "My dearest, dearest child, I was so afraid."

Jean-Claude had caught up with Alethea. "And you were right to be afraid," he said sternly. "A few more minutes and this foolish, foolish girl . . ." He actually shuddered and stared down at Alethea. "Have you no sense at all?" he demanded angrily.

She did not answer. Her relief was too great. Then Matt, leaping from his seat, pushed the steps against the carriage door, and Alethea climbed inside to safety and to her aunt's heartfelt embrace.

As they put distance between themselves and the fair, a heavy silence fell and prevailed. The combined relief of Jean-Claude and Drusilla was followed by anger, expressed in looks rather than words. Alethea bore this silent disapproval in a similar silence but, as it persisted, she cried finally, "But what was I to do? I did not want to be a burden to anyone, and I thought—"

"What you thought was sheer madness!" Jean-Claude snapped.

"Yes, madness. If we had not come when we did . . ." Drusilla shuddered.

"If we had not come when we did, she would have been at the mercy of those *canaille*," Jean-Claude hissed. "The way that great boor of a farmer looked at you! Have you no notion, child, how very beautiful you are? This loveliness that Marlowe must have envisioned when he wrote, 'Is this the face that launched a thousand ships and burned the topless towers of Ilium?'" He glared at her. "And you would have buried it in a dairy? You'd not have survived a day . . . if, indeed, you'd have survived the fair itself. *Mon dieu!*" He turned to Drusilla. "Where have my wits been wandering that I have so long remained unaware of Alethea's incredible beauty?"

"Jean-Claude!" both ladies protested.

He ignored them as he pursued the subject even further. "It proves only that we can grow used even to an Aphrodite if we have the great good fortune to see her every day. Child," he stared at a blushing Alethea, "you must go to London. Indeed, we must all go to London and see that you are properly launched in society!"

"L—launched in Society," Drusilla echoed. "What can you mean, Jean-Claude? Much as I love my niece, her circumstances—"

"Would preclude it," Alethea finished. "Have you
forgotten that I have no right even to the name I bear?
Unwin is—"

"I know what 'Unwin' is! I know the whole miserable
story," he said brusquely. "And as of this moment, we
will forget it. You are Alethea Unwin, yes! It is a
pseudonym, invented when you and your poor mother
were escaping from France. She was my cousin and you
are my second cousin but—no, no, no—it is better that
the relationship be firmer. You are my niece, the daughter of my poor brother, who died on the guillotine. His
wife escaped and came to live with a cousin in
Marylebone. I knew nothing of your existence. She knew
not how to trace me, but at last she succeeded." He fixed
his eyes on Drusilla. "Alethea was born in your house,
yes?"

"Yes," she said confusedly, "and all here know
that—"

"It does not matter what anyone knows. They will not
connect Alethea Saint Cyr with Alethea Unwin . . . for
suddenly, I have decided that you must not be Unwin.
You must bear with me, ladies. This fiction that I will
invent must be, above all things, believable."

"Jean-Claude," Alethea said on a note of protest.
"There were girls at school who are now living in
London. They all did know—"

"If any of them meet and recognize you," he interrupted impatiently, "we will feed them this tale of fear
and betrayal. You need not imagine that they will disbe-
lieve you." There was a certain sadness in his eyes.
"There are many who have similar tales to tell. And let
me see . . . ah, yes, you are rich. You are an heiress."

"No!" Drusilla protested.

"Yes, I say, yes! I have money to spare, and it will be
gold that was buried in France and brought here by an
old faithful servant."

"No, no, no!" Drusilla protested vehemently. "I will
not agree to any of this . . . this ridiculous plan!"

"Nor I!" Alethea cried.

"We shall see—and before you are much older,"

Jean-Claude said firmly. "Beauty must not go wanting, and you are more than beautiful, Alethea, you are exquisite. Your father may be unknown, but I would lay a thousand pounds on the fact that he was well-born, an aristocrat. And instead of indulging in any such bets, I will include that thousand pounds as a part of your dowry. This is the perfect solution to all your problems . . . and since it will involve a change of heart, a change of mind and a change of milieu, we might even call it . . ." He broke off and smiled affectionately at her. "We may even call it," he repeated, "a chemical solution!"

PART TWO

CHAPTER FIVE

THE POST CHAISE, driven by Matt, now in the green livery with silver buttons and silver epaulets—the colors of Jean-Claude, Comte de Bretigny's house—rolled into London close on seven in the morning.

Alethea, staring out of the window, was amazed and startled by the noise in the streets. They were crowded with drays and carts and occasionally a hackney coach. Even more occasionally, she saw curricles driven by young men, several of whom looked much the worse for wear in fashionable but mud-splattered garments and with pale faces and dark-circled eyes as if, she thought, they had been driving all night.

She hazarded such a comment to Jean-Claude, and he was quick to agree. "Possibly they were racing and on a bet. You will find that wagers are the order of the day among the ton. They will wager upon anything . . . from how fast a turkey will cross a road to whether Lady Such-and-so will be delivered of a boy or a girl. You will find these wagers duly entered in the betting book at White's, which is a famous club."

"I begin to believe you are funning me," Alethea protested.

"Not at all, my dear, and if when you are in one or another drawing room and you should hear mention of such an exploit or bet, you must never appear surprised."

"I promise that I will not," she told him solemnly, the

while her aunt, also looking about her with wide eyes, commented on the height of the buildings. "As your housekeeper, Jean-Claude," she said, "I think that I am allowed to be surprised."

He laughed. "Of course, you are allowed, my dear Drusilla." He sobered quickly. "But as you know, I would much prefer it if you would consent to be Alethea's chaperon."

"Please, Aunt," Alethea begged.

"No, no, and no. I have said that I am far too countrified to undertake such a task. It is enough that I have consented to lend my person to this mad masquerade. Do not try me too far." Drusilla's glance traveled from her niece to Jean-Claude. "And the more I think about it, the more I am convinced that I was entirely mad to let myself be persuaded."

Alethea expelled a long sigh. "I, too," she admitted. "I do not feel right about any of this."

Jean-Claude bent a stern look on her. "It is too late for these cavils—and I assure you, this is the only answer, my dear. I do not know of your entire ancestry, but I do know that such a flower deserves a proper garden."

Drusilla favored him with a long look, and she also sighed. "Much as I dislike and even loathe deception, I must agree. You have no choice, my dearest Alethea. You must marry well, and I can only say that the man who wins you will have nothing to regret."

Alethea grimaced. These were the arguments that had brought her here. No, it had been Jean-Claude, who was solely responsible for her presence in this coach—in this city! There had been no resisting him. Might as well try and resist a tempest at its height! Still, now, faced with London itself, all her fears came rushing back

The city was immense. She did not really like what she had seen of it. From the moment they had invaded its outskirts, it had intimidated her! The people were also intimidating, though some had depressed her, too—those she had seen on the dark, noisome streets where the buildings, sagging with the weariness of the centuries that had passed over them, appeared to be in danger of falling down. She had commented on the ragged children, some of whom ran screaming after the carriage and were threatened with the whip of the young postboy they had hired at a village just before London.

Jean-Claude had not been surprised by her concern. He had said dryly, "Yes, they are wretched, but there is nothing that can be done about it."

She had wanted to argue, and evidently he had anticipated that, for he had added, "My Alethea, I am not hard-hearted, and there are those who do want to alleviate the hardships you find in London's slums. Perhaps, one day, you will be able to help, too. You see, my dear, it remains for you to marry well—perhaps one sympathetic to their cause. I should like to see you the wife of a Member of Parliament, perhaps."

Everything hinged on this hypothetical marriage she was to make, Alethea had thought while listening to his flight of fancy, listening despairingly, realizing that the marriage on which his heart was set would succeed only in breaking her heart.

She could not dwell on that, not yet, because for a brief time, they would be together. That and only that had moved her to consent to his wild plan. As for this future he was constantly mentioning, she would not peer into that dark glass—she would try and drain every drop of happiness from the present. She leaned back in the carriage and dutifully listened to Jean-Claude's identifications of the sights they were presently seeing.

In later years, Alethea, thinking of those first weeks in London, found herself amazed at what they accomplished in so brief a time—no more than a month, in fact! There had been the difficulties attendant on hiring a house for the season and also finding servants to staff it. There had been a need for a chaperon and a quest for a mantua-maker who, in addition to possessing a fine sense of style, must needs be able to work quickly—to turn a country mouse into a city mouse. That last had been her analogy, one sternly contradicted by Jean-Claude, who had commented, "I would say, rather, a princess into a queen, my dear. You must always be cognizant of your assets."

It was Drusilla to whom Jean-Claude deferred in the

matter of house and servants. She had found the tall, thin, half-furnished mansion on Charles Street in fashionable Mayfair. Its bedrooms and drawing room caught the morning sunlight and were spacious above and below. Since it had been vacated early in the season, the papers on the walls were almost new, and such furnishings as remained were in the best of taste. Those pieces Drusilla had needed to add met with Jean-Claude's approval, and he was equally pleased with the small staff of servants she hired.

He himself chose his valet, an émigré who had been in England for some years. As it happened, the valet, Antoine, by name, proved to be married to Marie, an experienced abigail! This stroke of fortune, Jean-Claude had said excitedly, proved that the gods were smiling on them and, despite the protests aunt and niece still voiced from time to time, they could anticipate nothing but success!

Once settled in the house, however, there was still the matter of a chaperon for Alethea, and Jean-Claude confessed himself to be in a quandary. Striding back and forth in the small suite of rooms occupied by Drusilla, he looked from her to Alethea.

"I could inquire among those of my countrymen with whom I have an acquaintance, but I think there might be too many questions asked regarding my cousin, since it is known that my family, one and all, perished during the Terror. No, I think I must speak to some of my colleagues at the Royal Society."

"Aunt Drusilla." Alethea visited a pleading look on her face. "Could you not change your mind?"

"No, no, and no!" came the adamant answer. "I am accepted here as a housekeeper and were I suddenly to doff my apron and join you at one or another art museum or rout or dance or whatever, I would be out of my place. Servants talk . . . the kitchen and the butler's pantry are hotbeds of gossip, my love. We must needs depend on Jean-Claude."

He grimaced. "You may be assured that I will do my best."

On a morning, a week after they were fully settled in the house, Jean-Claude with the air of a prestidigitator, produced the name if not the person of Miss Ludlow.

"She is the elderly sister of a chemist of my acquaintance who—much to the surprise of the Society—has recently married. And after forty years of bachelorhood! When I expressed my need to the members, he fell upon me with loud cries of joy! It seems that Miss Ludlow and the new bride do not agree on the running of his house."

"Oh, how very fortunate, Jean-Claude," Drusilla said. Her sentiments were echoed by her niece, and if either of them entertained any qualms on the subject of Miss Ludlow, they were careful not to voice them.

The fact that the lady might have a quarrelsome disposition had occurred to Drusilla, a fear she did not share with her niece, either. Miss Ludlow was the answer to too many prayers. Her anticipated presence banished all need for Drusilla to fit her small dumpy figure into a garment which would, she thought ruefully, look like a silk gown on a sow. Then, there was the matter of her work-worn hands and a face browned from digging in the garden in all weathers—a condition Alethea had seemingly overlooked. And, in addition to the fact that she did not look like a proper chaperon for her divinely beautiful niece, there was her lurking fear that Alethea, in a moment of excitement or, possibly stress, might slip and address her as "Aunt." That would have spelled disaster for all concerned!

Though Drusilla had had many a private colloquy with herself on the wisdom of Jean-Claude's scheme or, rather, the lack of that necessary ingredient, she had finally convinced herself that it was the one answer to a question that had troubled her since the girl's birth—her future. And, for a brief period of time following her niece's undeserved dismissal, Drusilla had been deeply concerned over a future that looked as black as a winter storm cloud. Now, thanks to Jean-Claude, the sun had broken through that cloud, and she intended that it must continue to shine.

Alethea, too, had thoughts she would not have shared

with anyone in the world. She adored the aunt who had been both mother and father to her, and much as she wished that she might enjoy her comfortable companionship at the routs and the dinners, the dances and the rides through the park to which Jean Claude had said she would be invited, she knew that her chaperon would be ill-received. In her days as governess, she had received ample knowledge concerning the so-called aristocratic attitude toward those who were considered menials. She did not want her adored aunt subjected to the humiliation which might be her portion—which *would have* been her portion. Rather than that, she was prepared to go back and work in a dairy!

She could only hope or, rather, pray that it had not been Miss Ludlow who had instigated the quarrel with her new sister-in-law. It was quite possible that she had. Indeed, it was only natural that she would resent the arrival of one she must needs consider an interloper—upsetting the routine of her brother's house.

Consequently, on the day that Miss Ludlow was expected, Alethea, sitting in the drawing room, wearing a blue kerseymere gown—one of her new ensembles—was on tenterhooks. She had begged her aunt to be with her but, much to her chagrin, Drusilla had refused.

"My dear, a housekeeper attends to her duties," she had said. "To all intents and purposes, you are the lady of the house. That is your duty."

She did not feel like the lady of the house. She felt regrettably like little Alethea Unwin, waiting for her benefactor, one who had no relationship to her, real or assumed. Once again, she was wondering what Miss Ludlow would be like and then, without warning, since the butler hardly needed to announce Jean-Claude, there he was and with him, a fragile doll of a woman.

She was at least a head shorter than Jean-Claude and dressed all in gray. In fact, she seemed gray from her toes to her hair. Her faded eyes were also gray. In stature she was tiny, and there was a timorous look on her face—as if, indeed, she was anticipating a rebuff. Alethea, rising, had an absurd wish to clasp her in her arms and assure her that she had not entered a house populated by dragons. However, she contented herself with a welcoming smile.

Jean-Claude said, "My dear, this is Miss Ludlow. Miss Ludlow, my niece, Miss Alethea de Saint Cyr."

"Oh," Miss Ludlow said in a soft voice. "I did not anticipate . . . one so very, very beautiful!" She blushed. "Oh, dear, you must excuse me, but—"

"I will never excuse you for so kind a compliment," Alethea said gently. "I am very glad to meet you, Miss Ludlow."

"And I, you, my dear." Miss Ludlow extended a small, mitted hand. "I hope—er—that we will suit."

"I see no reason why we should not," Alethea said warmly, giving Miss Ludlow's hand a gentle squeeze before releasing it.

"I knew that you would suit," Jean-Claude said. "I will have your bandbox brought in. We will put you in the east chamber, I think. You will get the morning sun, Miss Ludlow. Will you like that?"

Alethea caught the gleam of tears in the little lady's eyes. "Oh, yes, I should be happy anywhere you choose, my lord."

"Good," he said gently. "But you must not address me as 'my lord,' Miss Ludlow. Despite my English connections, I bear a French title."

"Oh, yes, of course, Monsieur de Bretigny," she amended. "My brother has told me that. I fear I am very forgetful these days."

"There is no harm done, surely," he said soothingly.

After Miss Ludlow had gone, Jean-Claude turned to Alethea, saying, "There, my dear. She is not so intimidating, is she?"

"No, she is not," Alethea said on a note of relief. "Indeed, I am of the opinion that I ought to be her chaperon."

He laughed and then grew serious. "She does seem needful. Though she has not confided in me, I think she sustained a rude shock when her brother wed and was so eager to thrust her from the house."

"Poor thing. I am sure we will deal well together."
Alethea nodded. "And I do thank you for not bringing
me a dragon."

"I would never subject you to a dragon, my dear." His
eyes lingered on her face, and then he said rather
abruptly, "I must go. I am due at Tattersall's to purchase
carriage horses and two for riding. Do you trust me to
choose your mount, Alethea?"

"I trust you with everything, Jean-Claude," she said
softly.

He gave her a long and enigmatic look. "I hope to be
worthy of that trust, my dear," he said and, taking her
hand, he brought it to his lips. Releasing it, he bowed and
quickly left the room.

Tears filled Alethea's eyes as she pressed that kissed
hand to her mouth. Then she, too, hurried out of the
room to find and assure her aunt upon the suitability of
Miss Ludlow.

A week after the arrival of the chaperon, Alethea de
Saint Cyr sat in her dressing room, preparing for her first
ball. It was to be held at the home of the Comtesse de La
Malebranche, an old friend of Jean-Claude's parents,
and excitement warred with trepidation as she stared
into a mirror reflecting an image as unfamiliar as the
name to which she was only gradually becoming accus-
tomed. Marie was pinning a diamond circlet in her
expertly cut and coiffed hair, arranged now in a Psyche
knot with a few curls artfully clustering about her face.

As she watched the abigail at her work, she admired
her deftness. She was learning to appreciate her attentions. They were quite necessary, for though Alethea had
dressed herself nearly the whole of her life, she had never
before dealt with minute buttons, tiny buttonholes, and
equally tiny hooks and eyes. This last, a relatively new
device, meant to abolish the need for buttons, but proved
even more difficult to manipulate. Indeed, Alethea reasoned wryly, she seemed all thumbs these days!

Visiting another glance at her reflection, she smiled.
She was not, however, thinking of her own appearance
but, rather, of the day she had been at Madame de
Fresnay's, the mantua-maker, for the last of several

fittings. Miss Ludlow had been waiting as she tried on the ball gown she was wearing this night. Then, to her surprise, a tall, stylishly garbed, and extremely handsome man had casually strolled into the fitting room! He had spoken familiarly to her, saying, "Ah, my dear, you are indeed a picture in that gown."

Subsequently, he had further shocked her by placing a hand even more familiarly upon her shoulder, as he added, "But I think there must be a necklace . . . pearls, I imagine."

Alethea had given him a chill stare. "I do not believe, sir," she had begun and then, meeting his twinkling gray eyes, she had recognized Jean-Claude, a Jean-Claude shorn of his long hair, and looking amazingly young and attractive! Shock had held her silent a moment and then, she had managed to say, albeit in a rather shaken tone of voice, "Oh, Uncle, you startled me. That is a new suit, I believe."

His gaze and a slight nod of the head complimented her for her quick recovery. He said, "It is, and I must apologize for startling you, *ma belle.*" He had laughed, and the incident had been passed over neatly.

Later, when they reached the house and she was free of Miss Ludlow's presence, she had tried to apologize, but he would not hear of it. "My dear, you should have given me a set-down and you did it like a queen! May I hope that you will be equally regal with the other importunate gallants that must soon surround you."

"I think you exaggerate, Jean-Claude," she had chided.

"My little Alethea," he had said gravely. "You must keep in mind your regrettable experience at the fair. Men, though they be in smocks or tailed coats, are not so different from each other. A beautiful woman is always under siege. You will receive many, many compliments, and it is only right that you should. They are your due. But you must learn to distinquish between them and discourage the men who become too fulsome."

The answer she had longed to give him that day was on her tongue now, but, of course, it would never be uttered aloud. She had longed to say, "I care nothing for compliments from other men, Jean-Claude. I wish only to hear them from you, because you are my world and my love, and I will never, never give my heart to another."

She winced as she envisioned his answer, his reaction to an announcement he would not want to hear from her lips. Despite their supposed relationship and their assumed familiarity, the familiarity that, as a matter of course must needs exist between uncle and niece, Jean-Claude remained as distant from her as a star! Despite her appearance, she was a love child or, in less felicitous terms, the bastard daughter of a woman of no distinction and a man who had loved or, more likely, used her for his pleasure before abandoning her.

Her aunt, pressed to describe her late sister, had reluctantly said that she was lovely and dissatisfied, that she had run away from home to go on the stage and had come back pregnant, bitter, and disillusioned, hating her one-time lover—whose name never passed her lips—and the child he had given her. She had been determined to die.

Despite her curiosity concerning her father's identity, Alethea was glad that her mother had died—even though she had not revealed that identity. She must have been a most unpleasant woman, wanting to affix the bar sinister of bastardy upon her child with the name "Unknown" so reluctantly changed to Unwin at the demand of her older sister and a kindly minister. Yet, the change had not been effected before she had blurted out the damning truth to all who would listen to her. She had, indeed, flaunted her shame like a banner!

And why was she dwelling on these ancient miseries when Jean-Claude would be escorting her to her first ball on this night? And was it not amazing? Whoever would have thought three months ago that she would be present at such an event, she who had watched guests arrive at Dysart Manor on similar occasions, viewing this spectacle from the stairs rather than the ballroom? In those days, she had imagined herself going through the paces of a cotillion or a country dance with some faceless gallant, but never had she expected to actually attend a ball! Now, Jean-Claude had effected his so-called chemical

change, and she would be present as a guest! She would
be Mademoiselle Alethea de Saint Cyr, the daughter of
Jean-Claude's late cousin.

And would she acquit herself well on the dance floor?

She had had instruction in all the popular dances, but
that had been at the school in Bath, and though she had
been receiving further instruction from a dancing master
in the last fortnight, was she really ready? Jean-Claude
had given her an ivory fan, and his name was written on
one of the spokes, suggesting that he, at least, believed
that she was ready.

Oh, she thought unhappily, why had she ever agreed to
this wild plan? Despite the earnest assurances of Jean-
Claude, despite those of her aunt, and despite the
unstinted admiration of little Miss Ludlow, who had no
notion that her charge was, in effect, playing a part,
Alethea feared that she might fail him. The halls of the
rich and the titled were *not* her milieu. Would the other
guests think her gauche and know her for an interloper?
If only her aunt might accompany her, but she, too, was
playing a part—that of a housekeeper—and now that
Miss Ludlow was in residence and there were servants
who could talk, Drusilla kept very much to herself,
allowing her niece to visit her only on one or another
excuse, and these not often.

A tap on her door startled her and, at the same time,
banished her thoughts. "Will you answer the door,
please, Marie?" she said as easily as if she had been
giving such orders to servants all of her life.

"Yes, Mademoiselle." Marie moved to the door and
opened it to little Miss Ludlow, garbed, as usual, in her
favorite gray, but this gown was a handsome silk with a
fall of lace at the throat. Her gray hair was dressed high
beneath a lace cap, and her cheeks were pink with
excitement.

Her eyes widened as Alethea stood up. "Oh, my
dear . . . oh!" She clasped her hands, saying rather sur-
prisingly, "If dearest Papa could only have seen you—he
was an artist, you know. You must have your picture
painted, too. Such beauty must needs be preserved for

the enjoyment of future generations! I do know an
artist—dear, dear Sir James . . . but come, my dear,
your uncle is waiting for you."

Jean-Claude stood at the foot of the long staircase. He
was in full dress. His satin coat, in the fashionable
corbeau shade, was black with the sheen of the raven's
wing for which it was named. His well-fitting breeches
were of cream-colored satin, and he wore white silk
stockings and black leather shoes, polished to a high
shine. His cravat was simply tied above his frilled shirt,
and his hair, cut and dressed a la Brutus, was a most
becoming style. Indeed, he looked even more handsome
than he had on that day at the mantua-maker's and, she
thought privately, far too young to be her uncle. He ought
to be a cousin or . . . but she forebore to follow that
particular thought—or hope—to its ultimate conclusion.

As Alethea reached the middle of the long staircase,
she caught a glimpse of a woman in a neat, black gown.
Leaning over the railing, she saw her aunt standing by the
door that opened into the hall. She was about to greet her
when she received a warning stare and a shake of the
head. Then Drusilla whisked herself into the hall, closing
the door softly behind her. Alethea had a wild impulse to
run down the rest of the stairs and stop her—but that
was impossible. She must needs remember that her aunt,
in common with herself, had a part to play. Lifting her
head high, she went on down the stairs and, moving
toward Jean-Claude, she said, "Uncle, that is a most
becoming suit. I am of the opinion that you will be
mistaken for Beau Brummel."

He laughed. "My dear, you grow far too extravagant. I
myself was about to comment upon a vision of delight. Is
she not, Miss Ludlow?"

The little chaperon appeared rather taken aback at
what she evidently believed to be a rather extravagant
exchange of compliments for an uncle and niece, Alethea
guessed, while at the same time she wondered if she had
been right in reading admiration in Jean-Claude's eyes.
Second thoughts, however, arose to warn her not to

enlarge upon his reaction. He was only being polite.

Compliments, she had always heard, were second nature to the French, and never had she been more aware of Jean-Claude's paternal origins than upon this night. Indeed, she could easily imagine his slim, elegant figure gracing the court of Versailles. All he needed was a powdered wig. No, she corrected herself, he was quite perfect as he was. At that moment, he came forward to bow and to lift her hand to his lips, and then to repeat the gesture with appropriate compliments, to the surprise and delight of Miss Ludlow. In so doing, he managed to bring back Alethea's first impression of the perfect courtier—charming and insincere. She wished that she could keep that thought before her, because it would be easier to dismiss him from her heart. But as she came out into the chill, glittering night, she was only too well aware that she would never be able to do that, not if she were to live a thousand lifetimes!

The Comtesse de La Malebranche lived on Jermyn Street in a house with a magnificent marble facade reminding Alethea of pictures of a Grecian temple. However, if the exterior had proved intimidating in its severe beauty, the interior with its marble floors and curving staircase leading to the upper floor was even more daunting to one who had never before viewed such splendor. Works by Van Dyck, Murillo and Titian hung on the walls, and never had Alethea seen anything as magnificent as the equestrian portrait of the comtesse's father, Lord Runnyford, done by Sir Joshua Reynolds. The portrait graced the wall at the top of the stairs. It was while gazing at these works that little Miss Ludlow dared to approach Jean-Claude, saying that his beautiful niece ought to have her portrait painted by her dear friend, Sir James Carmody.

Alethea felt her cheeks warm with a mixture of embarrassment and annoyance. "I beg you will not consider so unnecessary an expense, Uncle," she whispered.

"But, my dear," he murmured, "I am of the opinion that it is not at all unnecessary. If this Carmody is as expert with the brush as Miss Ludlow appears to believe,

I will certainly commission him to paint your portrait."

She was unable to produce any more arguments on the subject for, at that moment, they came into the ballroom and her burgeoning protests were stilled as she looked about her with a mixture of excitement and wonder.

The ballroom was immense. It would have made two of its counterpart at Dysart Manor, and the latter room did not possess an inlaid floor, or a magnificent chandelier, dripping with crystal and reflected to infinity by two immense, gold-framed mirrors, facing each other across a wide expanse of polished floor.

A double staircase led to that floor, and as the three of them entered, a majordomo bawled their names. "The Comte de Bretigny, Miss Alethea de Saint Cyr and Miss Hermione Ludlow.

A tall, beautiful woman clad in a clinging blue silk gown and with a magnificent diamond necklace sparkling about her throat, came forward. She appeared to be in her late forties. She looked up at Jean-Claude, saying with a trace of sadness, "Ah, my dear Comte . . . it has been so long and you but a child when last I saw you. Your parents and my husband . . ." She let that comment trail away and added quickly, "One day we must meet and exchange memories, but tonight is only for frivolity. I insist."

"Comtesse . . ." He bent over her hand.

"Ah, you do remind me of your father," she murmured, and then smiled graciously as he introduced Alethea and Miss Ludlow to their hostess. In another moment, they had descended to the floor, and Alethea was blinking at the brightness of a room lit by what appeared to be thousands of candles in the chandelier and in sconces along the walls. Of course, she decided, there were not thousands. The hundreds were reflected into thousands by those artfully placed mirrors, which also made it appear as if half of London thronged a floor which could be, she thought, safely described as vast. Music from violins, flutes, horns, and a pianoforte entered her ears. She sent a swift glance around the ballroom but did not see the musicians. However, she did notice baskets of hothouse roses set between the pillars that ascended on either side of the room.

"You must remember, my dear, that you have promised me the first dance. I hope that it will be a cotillion," Jean-Claude said.

"I do, too," she said shyly. She looked about her, a little dazed by the number of people on the floor—women in satins and silks, with diamonds, rubies and emeralds around slender and not-so-slender necks. Some of the gowns were cut shockingly low, at least to her notion, and despite the fact that the fashion for clinging, even dampened silks was gone, there were yet a few of these to be seen. A great number of men had listened to Beau Brummel's dicta and wore black and white for evening. Others appeared in handsome brocades, and one man, she was amused to see, was clad entirely in green—even to his shoes!

"My dearest, such an array," Miss Ludlow murmured breathlessly. "I scarce know where to look!"

"Nor I," Alethea agreed.

"I do see the chairs," Miss Ludlow commented with evident relief. She looked up at Jean-Claude, saying softly, "After the dance, you must bring Alethea to me . . . I shall be sitting with the other chaperons, Monsieur de Bretigny."

His silver eyes appeared to be as bright as the candle flames as he nodded. "I will, Miss Ludlow—but now, I believe our cotillion is about to form."

He led Alethea toward a magnificently garbed group of ladies and gentlemen. "This," he murmured as they joined the other dancers, "I believe, will be our only dance—if I am not careful. I think you must put me down for a country dance later in the evening. May I hope that you will?"

"I would gladly put you down for them all, Jean-Claude," she murmured.

"No, only two, my dear, and I will consider myself twice fortunate."

"Oh, Jean-Claude, you are funning me," she protested.

He smiled down at her and it seemed to Alethea that

she had never seen him look so handsome—even though she was now used to the transformation he had undergone since his arrival in London. He said, "I am not funning you, not at all, my dear little niece. Already, I am envied, and I assure you that when I come to claim my second dance, I will be cordially loathed by any number of these youthful gallants about us."

An argument was lodged on her tongue, but before she could voice it, Jean-Claude had brought her onto the floor, for the cotillion had begun.

She might have guessed, Alethea thought, as they went through the paces of the dance, that Jean-Claude would be grace itself. She watched him when they separated, but she could not always keep her eyes on him, a fact that filled her with regret. His very touch gave her confidence. When they were apart, she remembered the old Greek myth of the giant who received his strength from the earth. Jean-Claude was her earth, she knew. Yet, as the cotillion came to an end, she found him a prophet. Mindful of Miss Ludlow's suggestion, he had started to lead her toward the chairs, but had been forced to stop, as numerous young men formed a circle about Alethea, all begging for dances or, in some instances, demanding them. As Jean-Claude had predicted, the spokes on her ivory fan were soon filled, and she was never off the floor, save for the brief intervals between dances.

Coming to claim his second dance, Jean-Claude smiled down at her, his eyes filled with a pride tempered by amusement. "My dear, as I anticipated, you are the cynosure of all eyes. Was there any one among these gallants who took your fancy?"

"I am hard put to tell one from the other, Jean-Claude," she responded lightly, the while she wished he had not questioned her as to her preferences. Was he so eager to be rid of her?

"Ah," he affected a sigh, "so beautiful and so heartless!"

"I am neither, Jean-Claude," she dared to answer, letting her eyes scan his face. Much to her disappointment, it revealed nothing.

"You must not denigrate yourself, my dear," he reprimanded. "You *are* beautiful, Alethea. There's none in this room can match you."

"Fie, for shame, Jean-Claude," she scolded. "I beg that you, at least, will not mouth these empty compliments!" Then, she blushed, fearing that she had overstepped the boundaries of their friendship.

"My dear little Alethea, my compliments are never empty," he responded gently. "I am half French, yes, but also am I half English, and as half an Englishman, I disdain the meaningless and extravagant phrases of a French courtier. You are beautiful, Alethea, never more than on this night and . . . but do I hear the music of our dance?" He seized her hand. "Come, my dear."

What had he been about to tell her—in a voice that had deepened and a tone that had seemed replete with sincerity? Frustration filled Alethea. She wished that she . . . that they, rather, were a thousands miles distant!

An hour later, Alethea was even more eager to put miles between her and this glittering company. They were at supper in another beautiful apartment with painted walls and a ceiling on which Tritons and sea horses disported. She would have preferred to examine it more closely, but could not because the young man at her side demanded her attention.

She was sitting with Sir Martin Willoughby, who had claimed her for a cotillion and had waxed most unhappy when he found she was not available for a country dance. However, he had managed to bring her into supper, gaining the momentary enmity of several other gallants not as fleet of foot as himself.

Sir Martin was a handsome young man with earnest blue eyes set in a well-shaped and sensitive face. His mouth was firm, and there was a cleft in his chin similar to that of Jean-Claude. She liked him because, in addition to being a good dancer, he did not pay her extravagant compliments—being content only to know that she was from York and, though of French extraction, brought up in England.

She had been glad of the rather dim light in this

chamber, mainly because it did not reveal her blushes. She was also pleased that Miss Ludlow, sitting on her other side, was not attending to the conversation between herself and Sir Martin. It would have made her doubly self-conscious to have the little chaperon hear her glibly reciting the lies she and Jean-Claude had concocted—lies that Sir Martin appeared to accept without question. Occasionally, Alethea glanced about her, trying to find Jean-Claude. Finally, she did see him, sitting next to a beautiful, dark-haired woman, who appeared to be hanging on his every word!

Who was she? Alethea wondered jealously. She hoped devoutly that the woman was merely placed next to him when they came into dinner. Or had Jean-Claude, in common with Sir Martin, made a determined effort to bring her into this chamber and to secure a seat beside her?

"Miss Saint Cyr—" Sir Martin was again demanding her attention and she must, out of courtesy, accord it to him. She listened impatiently to his observations, and a few minutes later, when she was able to look once more in the direction of Jean-Claude, she did not see him. Nor, she realized with a stab of anger, did she see the woman! Where had they gone? She had an impulse to rise and circle that vast chamber until she found them—but, of course, she could do nothing of the kind. She turned her eyes on Sir Martin and favored him with a brilliant smile. If Jean-Claude could immerse himself in these empty flirtations, so could she!

CHAPTER SIX

IN THE DAYS following the ball, Drusilla and Jean-Claude were in agreement that Alethea had enjoyed a great success. The silver salver on the hall table was heavy with invitations to balls, routs, soirees, and to rides in the park on days when the weather permitted such activity. Jean-Claude had gone through the invitations and discarded a great many of them—only a few young men met with his approval and prominent among these was Sir Martin Willoughby, whom he pronounced to be rich and of a fine family.

He was present when Sir Martin came to call the first time and, having presided over several other such calls, he once more lauded him, extending his approval to a ride in the park, during which he, appropriating Miss Ludlow's place as chaperon, waxed even more enthusiastic over the young man's undoubted charm and natural elegance. Meanwhile he, himself, had begun to go about in society. He visited old friends from France, many living in Marylebone—a stone's throw from London proper. On occasion, he took Alethea to meet stranded members of the ancien régime, visits that were often painful since the conversation was all of the past and sprinkled with such names as the dear princess or the divine marquise, met in the Tuilleries or during the course of a grand fete at one or another château. Such entertainments, wistfully remembered and glowingly

described, never failed to remind Alethea of the fairy
tales she had read as a child, save that those had always
ended happily and over these lay the dark, elliptical
shadow of the guillotine.

That Jean-Claude did not limit himself to these visits
was understandable. The social life of London was rich,
and to a man with roots in both France and England, it
was filled with rewards. He was voted a member of
White's, and he was welcomed by the prince regent. He
was also welcomed by an ever-widening acquaintance
among the ton. There were certain evenings which slid
into morning before he came home from one or another
gambling hell, and he had begun to see various ladies—
among whom was the lovely relict of one Sir Harry
Langmore and, on meeting the lady at another ball in
Marylebone, Alethea recognized her as the woman upon
whom Jean-Claude had danced attendance on the night
of her first ball.

Judging from the way they had greeted each other,
Alethea was positive that they had met often, and these
fears were substantiated when, during a ride in the park
one morning with Sir Martin by her side and Miss
Ludlow a few paces behind them, they met Jean-Claude
with Lady Langmore, riding side by side and evidently
on the best of terms. The lady was looking lovely in a
green riding habit, the precise shade of her eyes but,
Alethea was quick to notice, the morning light was less
kind than the candles had been on the night of the ball.
There were fine lines around her eyes and mouth, suggesting that she was certainly past her first youth. However, there seemed no doubt but that Jean-Claude was
extremely taken with her. That the feeling was mutual
was also obvious as her ladyship smiled warmly at him
and coldly at Alethea when he introduced her. Indeed,
Alethea reasoned jealously, he might well be on the way
to falling in love with the lady! Consequently, when after
this brief exchange of greetings and innocuous small talk,
they went their separate ways, she could only be pleased
when Sir Martin observed, "Lady Langmore has been
widowed for quite a few years, I understand. Do you not

think she is quite lovely for one who must be at least thirty-five?"

"Is she really?" Alethea questioned, hoping belatedly that she had not sounded too eager.

"I am sure she is," Sir Martin responded. She is exactly ten years younger than my mother." The second part of his comment did not please Alethea half so much. "It is a long time when I have seen her with one man more than once. She is extremely hard to please, but your uncle seems to have slipped past the barriers. She is, by the way, extremely wealthy."

"Really? Does she go about much in society?" Alethea questioned.

"A very great deal. Of course, she is not accepted everywhere."

"Oh, why would that be?" Alethea asked, hoping that she had not sounded too eager.

"She is known to be . . . rather daring. She puts the backs up of some of our older grande dames, not that she cares a fig for that, I am sure. She is accepted by nearly everyone and her own routs are famous. All London, including the prince regent, can usually be found there. And occasionally, she will invite jockeys and prizefighters, as well. Harriette Wilson once attended. One of her dukes brought her."

"Harriette Wilson . . ." Alethea mused. "She does well for herself, does she not?"

Sir Martin frowned. "Oh, you are acquainted with the name?" he asked coolly.

"Oh, yes." Alethea nodded. "She was often discussed at school."

"Really?" Sir Martin's frown deepened. "That is hardly a subject I would expect to be found in a school for young ladies."

Alethea laughed. "We did not study her, Sir Martin. She was under discussion mainly at midnight gatherings —in one or another room. I expect our teachers would have caned us had they known."

"And so they should have," Sir Martin said stiffly. "She and her sisters—"

"Does she have sisters?" Alethea asked eagerly.

"Yes." He nodded.

"I had not heard about her sisters," Alethea pursued. "Are they also . . . as popular."

"I should not call them precisely popular." Sir Martin frowned. "Except in the sense that . . . easy women are always popular." He added sternly, "I cannot think that your uncle would approve this conversation, Miss Saint Cyr."

"I will not mention it to him," Alethea assured him solemnly. "But you are saying that a duke brought her to one of Lady Langmore's routs?"

"Yes, it was a scandal, of course, and Lady Langmore was most put out . . . she did not speak to the duke for a fortnight, but I understand that they are friends again, now."

"I see . . . I wonder," Alethea continued musingly, "if Lady Langmore and my uncle would suit. He does not really enjoy routs and balls. He prefers his work."

"His work?" Sir Martin echoed, looking surprised. "What manner of work is he engaged in?"

"He is a chemist," Alethea amplified. "He was a pupil of Lavoisier."

"Ah!" Sir Martin said excitedly. "What a privilege to have known that man." He shook his head, adding soberly, "In my opinion, his death at the hands of those monsters in France was even more heinous than that of the poor king and queen!" He flushed. "Though, of course," he added hastily, "I can hardly expect you to agree with me, Miss Saint Cyr, given your own sad loss."

Alethea looked at him in surprise. Then, fortunately, she remembered that her supposed parents had also suffered death at the guillotine. She said, "I do agree with you, Sir Martin. I never knew my parents, but my uncle has spoken so often about Lavoisier that I think sometimes I feel his loss as much as he did. My uncle was much attached to him."

"And so he should have been," Sir Martin said. "I have read a great deal about Lavoisier's singular contributions to chemistry. Oh, I should like to speak to the comte about him. Do you think I might, one day soon?"

"I am sure he would be pleased to tell you as much as he knows about him," Alethea assured Sir Martin.

"My dear," Miss Ludlow called. "The sky is clouding over . . . and there's the smell of rain in the air. I do think we had best return to the stables."

Sir Martin looked regretful. "Must we go so soon?" He glanced upward and visibly sighed as he saw the gray edges on the coalescing clouds. "I will have to yield to Miss Ludlow's suggestion," he said reluctantly. "I would not want you to be drenched, but may I hope that I will be permitted to call upon you tomorrow?"

Alethea hesitated. She had already seen Sir Martin on Monday. Would it not be excessive to see him three times in four days? She did not want to encourage Sir Martin or, indeed, any of the young men whom she occasionally saw and who daily sent her floral tributes. However, if she did not smile on at least one of them, Jean-Claude would be angry and, she thought unhappily, he would have reason! He had done so much for her. Must she, indeed, reward him by making the good marriage that would please him and break her heart? There seemed to be only one answer to that question, and with that in mind, she managed a warm smile as she said, "I would be delighted, Sir Martin. And perhaps at that time you may speak to my uncle about Lavoisier."

"Er—Lavoisier?" Sir Martin appeared confused.

"The chemist . . . the French chemist whom you so admire," Althea said.

"Oh, yes, yes, yes, of course. Lavoisier." Sir Martin nodded. "Yes, I will want to speak to your uncle about him—if there is an opportunity."

"Oh, my dear," Miss Ludlow said when, at last, they had parted from Sir Martin and changed from their riding habits. They were seated in the second drawing room. "I do think young Sir Martin very charming, do not you?"

"Oh, yes," Alethea said absently. "I wonder where my uncle can be?"

"I expect he is still with Lady Langmore—such a very beautiful young woman, do you not agree?"

"She is very beautiful," Alethea said musingly. She

was wishing wholeheartedly that it was possible to seek out her aunt in her small room on the third floor which, against Jean-Claude's wishes, she had insisted upon appropriating for herself. "It receives the morning sunshine, my dears," she had explained. "And it is exactly what a housekeeper would choose."

"Would it not be lovely were your uncle and Lady Langmore to marry . . . there could be a double wedding," Miss Ludlow murmured.

"A . . . double wedding?" Alethea repeated tensely. "My uncle has only just met Lady Langmore, and whom have you in mind for me, pray?"

"Why, young Sir Martin Willoughby, of course. It is easy to see that he has been pricked by cupid's arrow, my dear."

"Miss Ludlow." Alethea gave her an affronted stare. "I have yet to feel the sting of that arrow."

Miss Ludlow regarded her, wide-eyed. "But, my dear, Sir Martin is a most eligible young man, and it is easy to see that he is in love."

"In love, is he?" Jean-Claude strolled in, peeling off his gauntlets. "And with whom is whomever you are mentioning, in love?" He put his gloves on a nearby table and stared down at Miss Ludlow.

"No one!" Alethea snapped. "It is the most arrant nonsense!"

Miss Ludlow paled and rose swiftly. "I must ask," she said in a hurt voice, "that you excuse me."

"Oh, dear." Alethea also rose. "Pray accept my apologies, Miss Ludlow. I did not mean to snap at you. It is only that I have been in London such a short time. I . . . I am not yet ready to think of marriage, even though it is the reason I am here."

"I understand, dear." Miss Ludlow smiled.

"Marriage . . . with whom, pray?" Jean-Claude asked.

There being no help for it, Alethea said sulkily, "Miss Ludlow appears to believe that Sir Martin Willoughby has a penchant for me."

"Indeed." A frown flickered in Jean-Claude's eyes and passed so swiftly that Alethea, whose heart had risen at the sight, was not even sure she had actually seen it. He said, "Has he already given signs of offering for you?"

"No," Alethea assured him. "Of course, he has not. We have met only a few times."

"My brother . . ." Miss Ludlow sighed, "met Milicent, his wife, when she came with her brother while he attended a meeting of the Royal Society. Within a fortnight, they were wed."

"Yes, so I understand." Jean-Claude nodded. "However, though I have never been wed, I have observed that love does not generally follow a prescribed pattern." He smiled at Alethea. "To change the subject, my dear, I have decided to take Miss Ludlow's advice and have your portrait painted. I have made an appointment with Sir James Carmody, and tomorrow we will visit him at his studio."

"A portrait, Jean-Claude—" Alethea began.

"Oh, my dear, how very delightful!" Miss Ludlow's usual shyness deserted her in her obvious admiration for the artist. "Sir James is the most charming man—well connected, too. So many artists tend to be . . . members of the lower classes, but Sir James is quite exceptional! I do feel perfectly safe in recommending him."

Jean-Claude said earnestly, "I hope that in addition to these assets, he will do justice to my niece."

"Oh, I think you can have no worries on that count. The dear prince regent has, I understand, complimented him on his work and he, as you know, is quite a connoisseur. Furthermore, it will be lovely for you to have one of his works. I quite forgot to say that since his circumstances are quite comfortable, he does not accept everyone who wishes a portrait. However, I think there will be no difficulty in persuading him to paint Miss Saint Cyr."

"I should hope there were not," Jean-Claude said. "I cannot imagine that he would refuse her."

Alethea was not so sanguine. Painters had sharp eyes; would Sir James be able to see beneath the face of fine clothes to the imposter beneath? Once again, she felt at odds with her chaperon. Indeed, she could see, she decided bitterly, why her sister-in-law wanted her out of the house. Beneath that shyness, that demure facade, lurked a determination to manipulate and control! She would, she thought, discuss that with her aunt—and soon!

"Oh, no, dearest, no, no, no," Drusilla said emphatically. "You have misinterpreted Miss Ludlow entirely. She admires you, and I am quite sure that she does not have a notion in her head such as you imagine." She gave her niece a long, penetrating look. "I have a feeling that, for some reason, you are afraid of this artist. Why?"

Alethea took a nervous turn around the little parlor. "Suppose he does not want to paint me, Aunt?"

"I cannot imagine that he would refuse, my dearest. I loathe women who spend their time staring into every mirror that catches their eye but, on the other hand, I am no admirer of false humility."

"False humility, Aunt?" Alethea echoed indignantly. "I do not understand you, not in the least."

"Surely you know you are beautiful."

Alethea sighed. "I know that I am not ill-looking, but if this artist is . . . so discerning, will he not know me for what I really am—a governess in . . . in sheep's clothing?"

"Not unless you display your fangs, my love." Drusilla laughed. "Oh, Alethea, my dear child, you need not repine. You are beautiful, and there is nothing in your manner to lead anyone to imagine you are not what you seem! You are and you have always been a lady to your fingertips." Drusilla hesitated and then added slowly, "Indeed, I think I must tell you something else. Your poor mother, my love, was only my . . . half sister."

Alethea looked at her in surprise. "Your . . . half sister, Aunt? I was not aware that Grandfather was married twice."

"He was not. You have seen a likeness of your mother. Though it is only a crayon portrait and indifferently done, has it not led you to wonder at the great difference in our appearance?"

Alethea shook her head. "I never thought about it."

Drusilla sighed. "There was a time, my love, when we were very poor. Your grandfather's blacksmith shop was partially destroyed by fire, and while he was able to rebuild it, many of his customers had changed to another blacksmith across town. Money was wanting and your grandmother, in order to help defray expenses, went to work at the Golden Anchor as a chambermaid. She was very pretty, our mother. And she caught the eye of a gentleman—a young viscount, who came to the inn during a rainstorm. She was sent to make up his room, and he saw to it that she remained for other purposes . . ."

"Aunt!" Alethea gasped.

"It was much against her will, I might add," Drusilla sighed.

"He ravished her, then?" Alethea demanded bluntly.

"Yes . . . and when she complained to the landlord, she was dismissed. Your mother, my dearest, was born nine months to the day of that dismissal. And that is why we were so different in appearance . . . and that is also why she ran away to London. She was so beautiful and so miserably unhappy."

"Did she know the circumstances surrounding her birth?" Alethea demanded.

"Yes, she knew . . . even though my mother died shortly after Dorinda was born."

"You mean, I expect," Alethea said in a hard little voice, "that Grandfather was aware that a cuckoo had entered his nest and did not scruple to inform his so-called daughter of that fact."

"Yes, God rest his soul, he knew. Mother told him. He tried very hard to forgive her, but—"

"*He* tried very hard to forgive *her?*" Alethea interrupted. "Because she was ravished?"

"Most men, my dear, are born suspicious. He accused her of inviting the . . . attack. I was very little at the time, but I remember their quarrels, quarrels that usually ended with my father striking my mother. They had been happy . . . but they were never happy again after she came back from the inn. I think she was actually glad to

die. And, of course, my father resented Dorrie . . . he
never ceased throwing her birth in her face. It was why
she ran away from home."

"Oh, God," Alethea groaned. "And I have hated her
all these years. Why did you never tell me this before?"

"I did not see where it would serve any purpose, my
love, but I think it only right for you to know that on your
mother's side as well as on the side of your father, you
have every claim to this world of which you are now a
part—that, in fact, is one of the reasons I was willing to
go along with this so-called deception."

Alethea was silent a long moment, staring at the floor.
When, at last she raised her head, she looked drained and
angry. "You mean, Aunt Drusilla, that I am the descendant of two venal, so-called aristocrats, who, between
them, ravished a chambermaid and an actress—and
consequently, I am supposed to be confident of my
passport into their world and also proud of that heritage?
Well, Aunt Drusilla, I am not. If all doors were not closed
against me, I would prefer to be a governess! That, at
least is honest work." She laughed mirthlessly. "But
since, in effect, I am disgraced because I was given a
lodging for the night—alone in a tower room, unmo-
lested by a real gentleman—it behooves me to revenge
myself upon that society that did not hesitate to con-
demn me by making a good marriage with one of their
number! It is truly ironic, is it not, Aunt Drusilla . . . or
must I address you as Half Aunt Drusilla?"

Drusilla said unhappily, "Oh, my poor child, I think
that after all I was unwise in burdening you with these
confidences."

"I do not agree," Alethea responded in a hard little
voice. "You have at least given me a reason to have my
portrait painted—I do not look like you. I expect I do
resemble my paternal forebears. I am sure that my poor
grandmother, dying in shame and disgrace, and her
daughter, after her, would be pleased to know that their
descendant was living in luxury and in the supposed
sanctity of yet another aristocratic household—to the
point that she is about to crown that glory by being

painted by the esteemed Sir James Carmody!

"And whom shall I marry, Aunt Drusilla? Will it be Sir Martin Willoughby or . . . but no, I will not cite others. A bird in the hand, as they say." Before Drusilla could answer her, she had moved out of the room, shutting the door softly behind her.

Sir James Carmody's studio was located on a narrow street not far from the British Museum. The building in which it lay was old and run-down. However, the artist utterly refused to come to the homes of those who sought his services. Citing the remarkable north light that seeped through the windows of his studio, located three flights up, he merely advised the ladies to bring an abigail or better yet, a husband or, on occasion, a lover, lest they run into some of the undesirable elements that frequented the neighborhood.

In the case of Alethea, Jean-Claude had accompanied her the first time when the artist, obviously taken by her beauty, had quickly agreed that he would paint her. Jean-Claude had also accompanied her a second time, and on the third occasion, it had been Miss Ludlow and Sir Martin. Today, a momentous day, in fact—though that, of course, was known neither to Miss Ludlow nor the artist—Sir Martin and the little chaperon were once more accompanying Alethea.

The painting was going well—for once he was inspired, Sir James worked quickly. And today, he was willing to allow his visitors to view the work.

Sir Martin, obviously impressed, turned adoring eyes on the subject. "It is you, my dear. Even at this stage in the painting, I can see he has captured your very essence. I will buy it, of course."

Alethea, who was in her rest period, smiled at him. "You will need to discuss that with my uncle, I think."

"I most certainly will." Sir Martin's eyes were now resting on the portrait and shining with adoration. "I will do so directly when I take you home."

"I do not believe my uncle will be at home this afternoon," Alethea said. "I believe he is waiting on Lady Langmore."

Sir Martin's face fell. "But," he said in a complaining tone of voice, "he will be seeing her this night at the opera in my box."

"And you will be seeing him this night at the opera in your box," Alethea reminded him.

He visited a regretful look on her face. "But I had particularly wanted to speak to him in person."

"You will need to make an appointment for that, my dear," Alethea responded. "He is rarely home these days." She turned toward Sir James. "Have you ever painted Lady Langmore?" she asked.

The artist shook his head. "The late Sir Harry Langmore commissioned a portrait from Sir Thomas Lawrence."

"Oh, I have seen his work at the Royal Academy," She looked at Sir Martin. "Last week, I think it was."

"Yes, last week, my dear," Sir Martin corroborated. "I hope," he continued, "that your uncle will allow me to purchase Sir James's painting."

"I think he might even give it to you," Alethea said. "I doubt that his bride will want it in her house."

"His bride . . . ?" Sir Martin repeated in some surprise.

"My dear—" Miss Ludlow, an interested listener to this conversation, suddenly stiffened. "Until the announcement is in *The Morning Post,* you cannot speak of brides or . . . grooms." She had a nervous glance for Sir James. "I hope, sir—" she began.

"You need not hope, Hermione," the artist said, looking fondly at her. "Have you not known me long enough to be assured that the conversation that is heard in my studio remains in my studio—but rarely in my head?"

"I do know that," she said shyly and apologetically.

"And now," Sir James glanced at Alethea, "it is time that conversation ceased and painting began."

Sir Martin, looking at Alethea, his eyes filled with excitement and frustration, sighed. As plainly as if he had spoken the words aloud, he was telling her that he wanted to be out of the studio and away so that he could realize to the fullest the feelings of a man who has just managed to tell the girl he loves that he wishes to marry her and has received an affirmative reply.

Alethea, her own expression enigmatic, sat quietly in her chair, holding her head in the position the artist had demanded. She, too, was deep in thought. She wondered how Jean-Claude would react to the offer that Sir Martin, ignoring the proprieties, had put to her a scant two hours ago. They had been walking in the park, and they had managed to elude Miss Ludlow. The offer was not a surprise. In the fortnight that had passed since her aunt's revelations, she had been, at first, angry and hurt. Then, both these emotions had given way to an overpowering desire for revenge upon those who had so blithely ruined the lives of her grandmother and her mother, her poor, confused, unhappy mother, growing to maturity under the taunts of the man she called father—but who, to all intents and purposes, was her stepfather! And she, too, she had discovered, craved revenge upon the persons who had thought nothing of dismissing her—this without even the grace of giving her a chance to explain! Probably, her background had not been unknown to them, and they had summarily coupled her with her mother!

In the few minutes that it had taken her aunt to recount the miseries of her immediate female forebears, it seemed to her that she had changed—and one of the most important aspects of this change was the fact that her foolish hopes and dreams had been summarily obliterated. She shuddered slightly, realizing how very near she had come to falling into the same error that her mother had. She must have come to London, hoping that she—with the blood for which her "foster" father had reviled her—might use this nectar to her advantage. She had not realized that there was no such advantage to be had for girls who displayed their charms upon the stage, not to mention being born on the wrong side of the blanket!

Alethea herself was more fortunate. She had won the pity if not the love of Jean-Claude. How stupid to imagine that a gentleman would want to ally himself with such a one as Alethea Unknown. No, when it came to marriage, there was Lady Langmore of the impeccable, *legitimate* background.

Her ladyship was a little racy in her ways, but there were boundaries across which she did not step. While Alethea, loving Jean-Claude as she did, had actually dared to dream of his returning that love one day. She had been, she realized, prepared to give of herself wholly—and devil take the consequences! But in her naiveté, she had not believed there would be consequences. She had actually imagined that, seeing her in this new setting, the scales would fall from Jean-Claude's eyes, and upon realizing that he cared for her . . . What utter, utter nonsense! Indeed, it was worse than nonsense —it was sheer lunacy. The likes of Jean-Claude, with his mixture of French and English nobility, would never ally himself with a young woman whose background was a series of furtive couplings. Sir Martin was different . . . no, not different, only uninformed, she thought bitterly.

He knew nothing of her heritage. He believed the tale that Jean-Claude had created, and he was only too willing to ally himself with her—sole representative of the defunct Saint Cyrs. In the beginning, there had been an attraction. She had managed to change that to infatuation, using some of the tricks she had seen Lady Langmore employ. Seemingly, these had come naturally to her, the direct descendant of two women to whom virtue was a stranger. No, she was being unkind when it came to her poor grandmother. Unlike her so-called grandfather, she was quite sure that his wife had been a victim. Her mother had, in a sense, also been a victim, but she, Alethea de Saint Cyr, would be a victor. She was already crowned with those laurel leaves, for she'd won the approval not only of Sir Martin, but also of his mother and his stodgy uncle, a vicar. Coming to town especially to meet her, they had effected that meeting at a dinner given by Jean-Claude. They had found her "entirely charming," so had said a delighted Sir Martin.

Consequently, all that Jean-Claude had wanted for her

had come to pass—and in a mere two months! That was a victory in itself—and soon the descendant of the chambermaid and the actress would be Lady Willoughby. In short, she had ably aided Jean-Claude in realizing his ambitions for her and, much to his surprise, he had realized some of his own, as well. She had no doubt that his betrothal would soon be announced in *The Morning Post,* indeed, one might follow the other in the same column.

She would be a good wife to Martin; she was fond of him, and he would not be the loser, she would see to that. There remained but one lurking fear: if she should happen to meet one of the girls she had known at school. She had discussed this possibility with Jean-Claude, and he had assured her that she was much changed. He had added, "I do not imagine that anyone would care to challenge me on that count. I have said you are my niece, and that should suffice."

She smiled wryly. That was one more instance of the pride which had would forever keep him at a distance from the likes of Alethea Unknown. Meanwhile, Martin would approach him tonight at the opera—with the request that he see him on the morrow, and Jean-Claude could congratulate himself that his plans for her future had, at last, borne fruit.

CHAPTER SEVEN

"AH, YOU DO look lovely, my dear child," Drusilla said as she surveyed the shining vision who had come to display her new gown, a white silk, classically simple, and having a matching overdress swept back from the skirt and edged with the popular Greek key design in gold. The neckline, in contrast to some of the prevailing styles, was cut low but filled in with a small square of delicate lace. The mantua-maker had disdained ruffles, saying that they quite spoiled the contour of the gown. She wore new kid slippers, also in white, and she had pulled up her gown to show her aunt white silk stockings with little gold clocks. Her hair was arranged in the Psyche Knot, and a band of gold leaves encircled her head. She was also wearing a gold armband, given to her by Jean-Claude to complete her costume, he had said. Once she might have believed that there was another, more felicitous reason for that gift, but that was before wisdom had replaced naiveté. Jean-Claude had also given her the long white kid gloves that reached a spot just below the bracelet.

"It is a pity that Miss Ludlow should have been taken ill," Drusilla commented in some distress. "Jean-Claude might cavil at my allowing Martin to take you to the opera in his post chaise, but—"

"I will explain the situation, Aunt. And since Martin intends to ask Jean-Claude if he can see him tomorrow, I think my reputation will not suffer, for I doubt that he wishes to discuss the latest horse race or whether he should invest—"

"That is enough," Drusilla interrupted. "I am quite aware that young Martin intends to offer for you—but you, how do you feel about that, Alethea?"

"How should I feel, but utterly, utterly, elated?" Alethea asked airly. She whirled around the small room as if dancing to the strains of an invisible orchestra. "Have I not accomplished all that you and Jean-Claude desired for me? I *will* make a good marriage—not a brilliant marriage, to be sure—but I do feel more comfortable with Martin than the others who have done me the great favor to glance in my direction. And just think, I might have been a countess, had not his ancestor chosen to fight for Cromwell—a decision that cost him his earldom. But enough of ancient history, Aunt. My children will not need to add a bar sinister to their coats of arms, and they will be born in wedlock and will grow up enjoying one of those beautiful nurseries and—"

"Alethea," Drusilla interrupted sharply. "Why do I feel that you are not happy?"

Alethea gazed at her with a surprise that was patently assumed. "I cannot imagine, Aunt," she said softly. "Especially when I have been detailing the glories that await me when I enter into marital heaven."

"I should not have told you," Drusilla said in some distress. "What I said was to give you a sense of your own value, your passport to a world that is not as remote as you appeared to imagine."

She winced at the mirthless smile that curled her niece's lips as the girl responded, "That is to say that a sense of value must needs be predicated on blood rather than accomplishment or that elusive ingredient known as character?"

Drusilla hesitated and then said, "Yes, I fear that is true of our world, child."

"I beg you will not call me a child, Aunt. I have turned twenty, if you will remember. Jean-Claude toasted me in champagne and gave me this gold bracelet." She touched her armband. "To be a child, Aunt, one must needs have illusions, illusions which I can no longer entertain. I

hope you will not believe me ungrateful for all that has
been done for me. I am not. Certainly, it will be infinitely
preferable to be Lady Willoughby rather than Alethea
Unknown. I will be a good wife to Martin, I promise you.
In that way, perhaps I may raise our banners from the
dust even if, in essence, I will still be living a lie."

Drusilla found herself close to despair. Words
thronged her tongue. They seemed actually to urge
expulsion and expression, but she ruthlessly swallowed
them. The girl before her was totally unlike the Alethea
who had come so joyously to London—joyously, she
suddenly realized, because she was in love with Jean-
Claude and might even have hoped . . . but it was useless
to follow that thought to its conclusion. She looked at her
niece and had no idea what to say to her, save a pallid
wish: "I hope that you will find some happiness from this
life you are contemplating, my dear. Meanwhile, do
enjoy the opera. *Cosi Fan Tutte* is, I understand, a most
beautiful work."

"I have every intention of enjoying the evening, Aunt."
Alethea's kiss, as different from her exuberant embraces
as night from day, chilled Drusilla, and after the door
had closed on her, the tears the older woman had been
restraining with difficulty flooded her eyes. "Oh, God,
God, God! Why did I tell her, why?" she moaned.

The answer eluded her. She had thought at the time
that she would be doing the girl a service—or had she
thought that? Had something deep inside her urged those
revelations out of an anger she had thought buried these
many years?

"I never should have . . ." she whispered. "Oh, God, I
am so confused." But actually, she decided when she
finally calmed down, Alethea's future, happy or not, was
finally settled. She had nothing more to worry about . . .
she stood to be accepted by the world her blood entitled
her to enter!

The King's Theatre in the Haymarket, stretched almost the length of a street and rose three stories high. On
this late December night, it was ablaze with lights and a
vast crowd pushed past coach doors open to let patrons

descend and go in at one or another arched entrance. Inside, it was even more brilliantly lighted—with crystal sconces on each box and an immense chandelier in the center of the high ceiling, its crystal drops catching the gleam of candle glow and turning it into rainbowed brilliance. Five tiers of boxes rose up from the crowded and glittering pit. The boxes in the first and second tiers were thronged with members of the ton and, much to the annoyance of some high-bred ladies, groups of bedizened females, whose manners and appearance was more than indicative of their calling.

Despite the confusion and the unhappiness so evident to her aunt, Alethea could not help but be thrilled by the spectacle about her. Sir Martin, in his usual faultless evening apparel, looked very handsome, and his eyes were alight with an excitement enhanced by happiness. He had guided her through the throng below, expertly, and now, as they sat in the box, he looked at her as if he could not believe his good fortune. Indeed, meeting his adoring gaze, something much akin to compunction struck Alethea, and she knew a moment of regret for the naive girl she had been until her aunt's revelations. She could not dwell on that or on her passion for Jean-Claude, who was yet to arrive. It would quite spoil an evening she was determined to enjoy—if only because she was soon due to see her very first opera!

She was passionately fond of music and, at school, she had seized every opportunity to pass by the rooms where one or another pupil was practicing the pianoforte or the harp. She had a smattering of both, but could not actually count herself a musician. As one teacher had told her, she would have had to have begun earlier—at the age of four or five. She remembered now that Mozart, the composer of the opera they were about to see, had started playing the pianoforte at three and was composing by the age of five! Jean-Claude had told her that, she recalled. She also remembered that Jean-Claude had journeyed to Vienna at the age of twelve to see the city and to hear *Don Giovanni* conducted by its composer! That had been in 1788 and, she also remembered him saying that after that time, his family did no more traveling.

Poor Jean-Claude! But she did not want to dwell on him because then the memories would come flooding back, and she was here to enjoy herself!

"Damn and blast them," Sir Martin suddenly growled.

"What is the matter?" Alethea asked, shocked by his unusual vehemence.

"Those quizzing glasses." He pointed across the house, and then pointed downward. "Above and below . . . we might be Punch and Judy at a Bartholomew Fair sideshow! But why do I include myself—the attention is all on you. Have I told you how very beautiful you look tonight?"

"Quite a few times." She smiled at him and, glancing down, she blushed as she saw the upraised quizzing glasses to which he had been referring. Yes, they did appear to be directed at this box. She glanced to one side and then to the other, seeing only a solitary gentleman in one box and in the other, a lady and her escort. He, too, was looking in her direction. He smiled as their glances met, and she hastily turned aside.

"Alethea!" Sir Martin whispered. "Why did you deliberately smile at that importunate—"

"I did not smile at him," she said in some surprise. "He smiled at me. I only wanted to see—"

"You only wanted to bask in his admiration," Sir Martin said crossly. "Is it not enough that I love you?"

"Sir Martin," she said in a low, surprised, and affronted tone of voice, "I did nothing of the kind. And if you are to resent my every glance, I do not see—"

He looked almost frightened. "I am sorry, my love." He lifted her hand to his lips.

Before she had an opportunity to respond, the curtains of the box were pulled back by the attendant, and Jean-Claude entered with Lady Langmore, a vision in a dark red satin gown cut beguillingly low, the décolletage enhanced by a diamond and ruby pin between her full breasts. She wore a small tiara, also sparkling with diamonds and rubies, and she carried herself with the air of one who knows herself to be as extraordinarily beautiful as, indeed, she appeared.

Sir Martin rose immediately and bowed over the lady's slender hand. Alethea noticed as he sat down that Lady Langmore was wearing a huge ruby which, again, was surrounded by diamonds on her third finger—but it was, she saw with considerable relief, on her right hand.

Greetings were reserved on the part of her ladyship and exuberant from Jean-Claude, whose eyes lingered on Alethea's slender figure and then traveled to her face. "Ah," he said. "We are indeed fortunate, are we not, Sir Martin, to have before us Venus and Aphrodite."

"But my dear Comte," Lady Langmore spoke before Sir Martin could reply. "Are not Venus and Aphrodite one and the same?"

"No, my dear Lady Langmore," Jean-Claude said. "Aphrodite is a Greek diety and Venus, a Roman."

"And which of us is to be the Roman, pray?" Lady Langmore's smile was a trifle forced as if, indeed, Alethea thought, she anticipated an answer that might not be to her liking.

"My dear, I can think of you only as Venus," Jean-Claude said lightly.

"Well, I expect I am complimented," Lady Langmore said coolly. "And you, my dear Miss Saint Cyr, are you pleased to be Aphrodite?"

"Aphrodite, born in the sea," Sir Martin said. "I think it a most apt description . . . When I was in Rome, I had the pleasure of viewing Botticelli's *Venus Rising from the Sea.*"

"Ah, Venus and not Aphrodite." Lady Langmore smiled at him. "I do thank you for your compliment, Sir Martin."

He flushed. "Your ladyship is most welcome." He bowed, but his gaze, mirroring an apology, slid to Alethea.

"Gracious, it is uncommonly warm in here tonight," Lady Langmore observed. She glanced into the pit. "Oh, dear, I am half-blinded by the gleam on those upraised quizzing glasses! Indeed, I often feel as if I were one of the denizens of the royal menagerie—but I suppose one must take it as a compliment?"

"Indeed, you must, my dear." Jean-Claude smiled at her.

Alethea, who had been staring across the auditorium at the other boxes, said suddenly, "I wonder who all those women are . . . they do seem very fidgety."

"Alethea!" Sir Martin protested in shocked tones, while Lady Langmore glanced at Jean-Claude and laughed lightly.

"My dear," she turned to Alethea, "you will surely not tell me that you do not recognize that fair sisterhood?"

"How might she recognize them?" Jean-Claude demanded. "My niece has never been to the opera. She has not been long in London, as you know."

"Oh, then I must beg your pardon, Miss Saint Cyr," Lady Langmore said coolly. "Those women are . . . if I might use a Grecian analogy, of the class of say a Phyrne or an Aspasia . . . the modern equivalent of, let us say, the Hetairae, my dear, but much, much less intelligent or accomplished if, of course, one discounts Harriette Wilson, whom you may see fanning herself in the box directly across from her and—"

"If you will pardon me," Jean-Claude interrupted. "I do not believe that my niece needs any more enlightenment than you have already so graciously given her." He smiled at Lady Langmore and then at Alethea, thus softening what might easily have been construed as a gentle set-down.

Lady Langmore stared at him through narrowed eyes, her manner suggesting that his veiled protest had annoyed her, but then she smiled. "It is, indeed, refreshing to meet with innocence in this jaded city. And—" Whatever else she might have said was cut off by the wild burst of applause and the cheers that greeted the orchestra, now with its bows in readiness as the harpsichordist, who would act as conductor, sounded the first note.

The music was beautiful, and Alethea, who had heard some of it played on the harpsichord at school, was thrilled by the difference a full orchestra made. However, she was slightly taken aback when an immense woman appeared in a white muslin gown that made her seem even larger. Furthermore, she had tripped in with a girlish smile looking ludicrous on her broad, if very lovely face with its several chins. Alethea was even more astonished as the house appeared to go mad. Then, as the applause and the cheers and the whistles finally died down, Lady Langmore hissed, "Ah, the divine Catalani —her Fiordiligi never fails to be utterly enchanting."

And so it proved true, even in such moments when the singer playing the role of her lover endeavored to embrace her—no small feat, considering that his arms could not encompass her immense shape.

It was during one of these moments when Alethea, striving to keep a straight face, heard a very audible giggle from across the house, followed by a battering of angry "Shhh's." She tensed. The sound had been familiar. She had heard it before, but as she tried to place it, Catalani was singing again, and she gave herself up to the enjoyment of that sprightly and beautiful music. She was sorry to see the act end, and though she was invited to stroll with Jean-Claude and Lady Langmore during the interval, she refused, with Martin in mind. The giggle still resounded in her mind's ears, as it were, and she scanned the boxes across from them, but for the most part they were empty. That glittering bevy of females had departed to stroll in the corridors and partake of refreshments, she guessed.

"Why are you so interested in them?" Sir Martin suddenly demanded.

Alethea turned to him in confusion. "In whom?" she asked and, to her surprise, read anger in his gaze.

"Those women," he muttered. "As Lady Langmore was pleased to tell you, they are whores, all of them. I begin to believe that the opera is no place for a gently bred young female."

For the second time that evening, Alethea was shocked by a side of Sir Martin she had never seen before. "But the music," she breathed. "Do you not think it heavenly?"

"It has very little to do with heaven, I assure you," he snapped. "It is a straightforward tale of deceit, of seduction and betrayal. When we are wed, my love, I will take you to concerts—but I fear that the opera must be avoided."

A number of retorts rose to Alethea's lips, but she decided against uttering any of them. She said only, "I cannot see that the plot differs much from a novel. Or do you disdain novel-reading as well?"

"I have not read many novels. My father did not purchase them for his library. Do you enjoy them?" There was surprise and, again, a vague displeasure reflected in his tone.

Alethea was spared from answering by the fortuitous return of Jean-Claude and Lady Langmore. Shortly after they had taken their places, the second act commenced and once more Alethea was engulfed by that sprightly music as Fiordiligi and Dorabella flirted with the pair of strangers who were, actually, their jealous lovers disguised in an effort to test the virtue of their sweethearts.

It was a charming bit of buffoonery and, again, she was much moved and excited by the beauty of the music and by the singing. As the curtain came down on the final act, her palms stung from applauding, and she was distressed to hear Sir Martin observe that, for his part, he preferred the orchestra in concert rather than the caterwauling of those two fat, ugly women on stage.

"Have you seen many operas, Sir Martin?" she asked as he was draping her cloak about her.

"Not many," he said stiffly. "My father was of the opinion that they did not improve the mind and, judging from this piece that we have just seen, I must agree with him."

"It is not to the mind but to the heart that an opera must needs appeal." Jean-Claude, who had been helping Lady Langmore with her long, furred cloak, turned to address Sir Martin. Before the young man could respond, he added, his eyes on Alethea, "I am sure you must agree, my dear."

"Oh, I do," she breathed. "I was quite . . . quite transported."

"I thought you might be. That is why I chose a Mozart opera. He is, by far, the most sublime of composers, at least to my way of thinking."

"And to mine," Lady Langmore said. *"Cosi Fan Tutte* is an ideal introduction to the art for one who has not been exposed to it at an earlier age." She glanced at Alethea, and then went on to say, "I hope that you will join Monsieur de Bretigny and myself at supper."

"Of course, they will," Jean-Claude said before Martin had had a chance to reply. He smiled at the young man. "Come, we insist," he added.

Alethea, who was holding Martin's arm, felt it tense and, at the same time, saw a look of annoyance pass swiftly over Lady Langmore's face. She guessed that the lady had hoped her invitation would be respectfully declined. She was very grateful to Jean-Claude for preventing that. At this particular moment, she was not in sympathy with Sir Martin, and she guessed that had they been left together, it was quite likely she must have been treated to a diatribe on the subject of immorality on stage. Indeed, they might even have quarreled. However, those proprieties at which she had often chafed, precluded that they be left alone together for longer than the time it took to go to and from the opera, she suddenly realized. She was momentarily disappointed. Jean-Claude must have had etiquette in mind when he seconded Lady Langmore's invitation. He had made a concession in allowing Sir Martin to escort her to the opera, and another in allowing him to take her home, but further than that he was not prepared to go.

Doubtlessly, he feared that Sir Martin might take advantage of the situation, were he permitted to drive her home at a relatively early hour when Jean-Claude himself would not be leaving Lady Langmore's house for quite some time. In other words, she reasoned bitterly, he was thinking not of enjoying her company but of observing the proprieties.

Lady Langmore's house, a tall, oblong mansion, faced Berkeley Square and was fashioned from brick. Deceptively simple from the outside, its interior bordered on the palatial. A long staircase led to the first floor, and the furnishings—as much as could be seen of them in the dim candlelight—were luxurious. The library, where supper would be served, caused Alethea to catch her breath.

Tall shelves of books reached up to a painted ceiling depicting a mythological scene—Venus parting from Adonis, while numerous nymphs and satyrs sadly observed that melancholy moment. There was a magnificent chandelier in the center, with only a small circle of candles lighted. They cast a pleasant glow over the room—one enhanced by the fire in a huge, sculptured fireplace. On either side of it were caryatids holding up a marble mantelpiece, and over it hung the Lawrence portrait.

It must have been painted when Lady Langmore was still in her twenties, Alethea decided or, possibly, she might have been even younger if one were to judge by the gown, a figure-outlining muslin of the type popular during the French Revolution. Sir Thomas had elected to paint his subject in a classical pose, a rather unusual one, since he had chosen as his subject Andromeda chained to her rock, with the head of the monster just rising from the waves.

Catching Alethea staring at it, Lady Langmore said lightly, "'Twas a conceit of my late husband to have me painted thus. It was meant as a warning."

"A warning?" Sir Martin had come up behind Alethea at that moment. "What manner of warning?"

Lady Langmore favored him with a provocative smile. "In those days, I was known as . . . shall we say 'daring,' and my husband thought I must be reminded that monsters are apt to lurk in unexpected places."

"Indeed, I hope you have not encountered many of that species." Jean-Claude moved to her side.

"No, I took the warning to heart." She favored him with another of her charming smiles. "Though I still do have a reputation for being . . . daring?" she added teasingly and laughed.

Alethea, hearing that laugh, was once more reminded of that tantalizing giggle she had heard in the opera house, tantalizing because she was positive she had heard it before. She did not know why she should remember it . . . Perhaps it would come to her when she was alone. She wished that she were alone at this moment—alone and in her own chamber. She also had the distinct feeling that Lady Langmore would have shared that wish had she been privy to it.

Though she smiled graciously at both gentlemen, that same smile hardened whenever her ladyship glanced in her direction which, she realized, was not often. She had addressed a few remarks to Alethea, as her attention naturally was centered on Jean-Claude. However, she did have some pleasant observations to make to Sir Martin, as well. He, Alethea, noticed, was reserved in his manner with both his hostess and Jean-Claude. In fact, she had surprised a disapproving look in his eyes as he scanned the portrait, and she was uncomfortably reminded of his pointed remarks regarding the opera and its audience. It was quite likely that he held Lady Langmore in anathema, as well, because of her blithe explanations concerning the reasons for the portrait.

Thinking of them, she felt a certain sympathy for her hostess. She must have suffered under her husband's disapproval. She herself resented Sir Martin's attitude— indeed, it had been quite daunting to hear him expound on the immorality of the opera. She remembered his regretful explanation of how his family had lost its title, and she had received the distinct impression that he, at least, regretted the fact that his ancestor had elected to side with Sir Oliver Cromwell. Now, she was not so sure. It was more than possible that he had inherited that same Puritanical streak, and if that were true, she was certainly not the wife for him. If ever he discovered the truth of her situation . . . but again, who could possibly tell him?

"My dear, you have grown very pensive," Sir Martin murmured. "Is there something troubling you?"

She forced a smile. "No, nothing, save that it is late and I find myself rather weary."

"I, too," he agreed. "I expect that since your uncle was kind enough to entrust me to bring you to the opera, he will not cavil at my taking you home?"

In that same moment, Lady Langmore, who had been

conversing with Jean-Claude in a low voice, said in some surprise, "You wish to attend the opera on Saturday, next? But that would be lovely. You know that Gluck is a favorite of mine."

"Yes, I remember you telling me so . . . He is also a favorite of mine, and I believe my niece would appreciate his work. You do know some of the music from *Alceste,* do you not, Alethea?"

"Yes, oh, yes," she said excitedly. "I have heard the 'Divinites du Styx' sung in concert, but I can imagine that it would sound very much better if heard in the context of the opera," she observed and, in facing Jean-Claude, read annoyance in the eyes of Lady Langmore.

"Then," Jean-Claude pursued, "perhaps you and Sir Martin would join us at the opera this Saturday."

Alethea, glancing quickly at Sir Martin, saw a slight frown in his eyes and guessed that he was about to demur. She said quickly, "Oh, I should love that, Uncle. Should you not, Sir Martin?"

He hesitated briefly before saying with a rather forced smile, "If you are anxious to go, my dear, how may I refuse." He turned to Jean-Claude. "It is kind of you to invite us, sir."

"I am delighted that you have agreed to come," Jean-Claude said courteously. "Gluck is also a feast to the ears, do you not agree, Sir Martin?"

"I have not had the opportunity of hearing his music," Sir Martin responded diffidently. "But I shall look forward to it." He added, "Sir, is . . . it possible that I might wait on you tomorrow—at eleven?"

"Ah," Lady Langmore said teasingly, looking from Sir Martin to Alethea. "It has come to that, has it, Sir Martin?"

He was obviously embarrassed and possibly even shocked at her frankness, Alethea thought. He said, "I . . . uh . . . yes."

Lady Langmore gave him an arch look. "I was sure that it must." She smiled at Alethea in a way that the latter, even in her current state of confusion, was quick to divine as relief. Or could she be mistaken? Why would Lady Langmore be relieved?

Before she could devote any more thought to that subject, Jean-Claude, visiting a regretful look on Martin's face said, "Unfortunately, my day is given over to the Royal Society . . . or at least to one of its members, who has invited me to view a most interesting experiment." He appeared to be unaware of the young man's crestfallen expression as he continued, "Perhaps you will come to see me on Thursday."

Sir Martin said stiffly, "Unfortunately, sir, I am briefly called out of town on that day. I will not return until Saturday. Might I see you on Monday next?"

"Next Monday . . . ah, that is the day or, rather the evening, when I shall be giving a rout." Lady Langmore interrupted. "May I hope that you and Alethea will be present?" She bestowed a warm smile on Sir Martin and also glanced briefly at Alethea.

"Yes, I will be able to see you on Monday. Shall we say two in the afternoon?" Jean-Claude asked.

Sir Martin said eagerly, "Yes, sir, that would be an excellent time." The look he visited on Alethea was one of relief as if, indeed, he had feared that Jean-Claude might refuse him entirely.

She, in turn, wondered why Jean-Claude, who obviously must be aware of why Martin was so eager to see him, was being elusive. A vagrant wish arose in her mind and was summarily banished. Undoubtedly, the excuse he had proffered was valid. He had something else to do and, in spite of the reason they had come to London, it must take precedence over all other considerations, even including her pending betrothal.

Her ruminations were put to flight as a servant brought in a supper consisting of cold chicken, ham, and pickled salmon. Subsequently, they were served potatoes, fresh greens and poached eggs. A delicious custard and a lemon tart finished the meal, which was accompanied by champagne.

Confronted by this array of food, Alethea found she could barely eat more than a slice or two of chicken and a few greens. She eschewed the tart in favor of the custard and drank no more than a glass of champagne.

Sir Martin, on the other hand, sampled every dish and had two helpings of chicken and two of ham. It was near midnight before he grew restive and asked if he might have the privilege of taking Alethea home.

Jean-Claude hesitated and then, glancing at his hostess, he appeared to make up his mind. "Yes, you may, but . . ." he added with another glance at Lady Langmore, "I will be joining you presently.

After a smiling exchange of farewells, Sir Martin, assisting Alethea into his post chaise, climbed in beside her, saying in an aggrieved tone of voice, "I had hoped to wait upon your uncle tomorrow—and I am sure he knows the reason why. There can be no doubt of that."

"I am sure that there is not," Alethea said. "But the Royal Society must needs take precedence over all other considerations—at least to my uncle's way of thinking. He is a chemist, you know."

"Yes, I do know . . . but still." Sir Martin sighed. "I am going to the country to fetch my mother and my uncle. I should like to inform them that all is settled."

"I had hoped it might be." Alethea felt it incumbent upon her to say. "And—"

"Alethea!" Sir Martin exclaimed and, taking her in his arms, he kissed her passionately. At length, he let her go, saying, "Sometimes I have feared that you did not really wish to wed me." His arm tightened about her once again.

Fearing another embrace was imminent, Alethea said hastily, "But I have agreed . . ."

"I know," he broke in, "but there have been times—" He paused as the vehicle drew to a stop. "Alas, we have arrived, I believe."

"Yes." Alethea nodded and stifled a sigh as Sir Martin embraced her again. As he released her, she said quickly, "I think I must go in . . . The footman at the door will have seen us arrive. He will wonder why your post chaise remains here so long."

"I am of the opinion that he will not wonder at all." Sir

Martin gave her a tender look. "I wish I were as
privileged as your footman, seeing you every day and all
through the day. "'Oh, that I were a glove upon thy
hand . . .'"

Alethea laughed. "I am very glad that you are not a
glove, Sir Martin."

"Alethea," he breathed, embracing her yet again and
more passionately than all the other times combined.
Then he signaled to his footman, who opened the door of
the post chaise. Reluctantly, Sir Martin accompanied her
to her door and waited until she went in. Much to her
relief, he did not attempt another embrace.

As she was lighted up the stairs by the footman,
Alethea discovered that she did not yet want to go to bed.
"I think, Thomas, that I should like to go to the library. I
hope there is a fire in there."

"There is, Miss Saint Cyr," he returned and ushered
her into the vast book-lined room. The moon, shining
through the windows, made it look even larger. At her
request, the man lighted the candelabra on the mantelshelf and courteously withdrew.

She was conscious of a sudden feeling of pleasure—at
being alone in the stillness. She had loved the opera, but
she had not loved the aftermath, the discomfort she had
sustained at Lady Langmore's house, and the subsequent
discomfort of Sir Martin's impassioned embraces. The
memory of his kisses did not arouse her any more than
they had at the time they had been pressed on her lips.
She frowned, wondering if she ought to have allowed
such familiarities—probably not. Yet, to have rejected
them would have been missish, especially when, to all
intents and purposes, she was nearly betrothed.

Well brought-up young ladies, however, were expected
to be circumspect. Ostensibly, they never exchanged
more than a handshake or received more than a kiss on
the hand until their wedding day. Still, judging from the
gossip at school, these expectations often stopped short
of reality. Girls not yet sixteen giggled over embraces in
sequestered spots—a grove of trees, a shattered ruin.
And one young lady, the daughter of a marquis, had

described in salacious and—to the innocent Alethea's ears—shocking detail, an encounter with one youthful lord, her sister's fiancé, during a Christmas game of hide-and-seek in the family castle. It had taken place in the unused wing of that vast pile, and she had narrowly escaped being ravished! Still, there had been no doubt but that she had enjoyed every minute of it. Other girls, listening to this account, gleefully responded with experiences of their own. Consequently, since she knew that such encounters occurred in the most aristocratic of households, she could comfort herself with the fact that she was not revealing her so-called plebeian origins. Yet, she wished that she need not submit to Sir Martin's embraces. Quite truthfully, she felt none of the excitement so graphically detailed by Lady Marianne and her friends. Unlike Marianne, she had not wished that he might become even more passionate.

On the contrary, this path that she had decided she must tread, given her aunt's revelations, seemed ever more thorny and uphill to boot!

The flames in the fireplace startled her as they suddenly shot higher. Someone had opened the door. She looked around and found Jean-Claude standing in the doorway.

"Did I frighten you, then?" Closing the door softly behind him, he moved to her side and put an arm around her shoulders. "I did not mean to do so. Indeed, until I was told you were here, I had thought you must be asleep and dreaming by now."

A little thrill went through her at his touch. Her voice was not quite steady as she explained, "I . . . I was not ready to sleep." Her heart was beating very heavily, mainly, she knew, because he had not yet removed his arm. "You are home earlier than I had anticipated."

"Yes." He moved away from her. "I will need to rise early tomorrow . . . so I did not wish to burn the midnight oil, as they say."

"Ah, the meeting of the Royal Society—" she began.

"It is not precisely a meeting," he interrupted. "And I am glad you are here, my dear. I would like you to come with me. I am sure you would find this particular experiment to your taste."

"I know I would," she said quickly.

"Do you?" He smiled at her. "Then, you must be of that ilk that will buy a pig in a poke. But I will relieve your curiosity. I am going to watch a balloon ascension. Should you like to come with me—now that I have explained it?"

"Oh, Jean-Claude," she breathed. "I would like it above all things."

He was silent a moment. Then he said, "Would you? Above all things, really?"

There was such a huskiness to his voice that she did not understand the question. She said softly, "Yes, oh, yes. It would make me very happy to . . . be with you." She paused, fearing that she might have been too frank. "You could tell me so much about it."

His face was in shadow, but she seemed somehow to be aware of the intensity of his stare. "Are you pleased . . . are you happy with young Martin?"

She was not surprised at this swift change of subject. In fact, she realized, she had been expecting it. "He is very pleasant—"

"Is he pleasant enough . . ." He paused. "I mean, will you want to spend your life with him?"

A vehement series of denials demanded egress, but she clamped her lips against them and swallowed convulsively as if, indeed, she were swallowing hard-edged stones. She said, "He has not yet asked for my hand, Jean-Claude."

"Have you any doubt that he will?"

She shook her head. "I know that he was disappointed because you would not see him tomorrow." Against her will, a little smile curled her lips. "He would be even more disappointed were he to know the reason for your refusal."

"But you . . . you are not disappointed?" he pursued.

"No," she said, and at that moment, her aunt's revelations came rushing back into her mind, bringing with them the knowledge that Jean-Claude wanted her to marry Sir Martin. Consequently, why was he putting this question to her? What did he have in mind? The hope that had, for a moment, risen in her breast, flickered and died. She said, "We will have a lifetime together, after all."

There was a pause before he said, "Yes, that is true, you will have a lifetime together. And, now, if we are to rise early, I suggest that we both retire."

"Very well, Jean-Claude. At what hour shall I ask Marie to rouse me?"

"Shall we say eight? Would that be too early?"

"No, eight it will be," she responded, hoping that the excitement of spending a day with him, the excitement she could not quite suppress, however hard she tried, did not show in her voice.

Jean-Claude did not call a footman to light the way up the stairs. He himself, walking behind her, bore the single candle appropriated from the mantelshelf in the library. He bade a good night to her at her door, and it was all she could do not to stand there and watch him walk down the hall. But poor Marie was waiting to undress her and, besides, there was the off chance that he might look back.

It was totally ridiculous, she told herself some thirty-odd minutes later, to be weeping into her pillow over a man who was soon to make an offer to a woman of his own class, but the tears came. It was another thirty minutes before sleep finally banished them.

CHAPTER EIGHT

THE WINDS WERE COOL, but it was a sunny day with only a few puffy white clouds in the sky. One cloud, Alethea thought, looked like a fish and the other had, at first, reminded her of a camel, but now it appeared to resemble the craggy profile of an old man. She stood with Jean-Claude on a small rise on Hampstead Heath, once, she had been told, a place where highwaymen had been wont to lurk. Now, however, an immense red, orange, and blue balloon anchored to the ground by a series of ropes all around its wide circumference, was being readied for flight.

The structure, Jean-Claude had told her with pride, was almost an exact replica of the balloon in which a brave and enterprising Frenchman named Jean-Pierre Blanchard and an American, Dr. Jeffries, had crossed the English channel!

"Without injury?" she had asked in amazement.

"Yes, but not without a few frightening moments, I understand. I had it from Pierre Jardin, a friend of Blanchard's, that when they approached the English channel, the balloon gave signs of descending and into the water, they feared."

"My gracious," Alethea said with a little shudder. "What did they do?"

"They threw out anything that they believed to be weighing down the craft and then they soared aloft again." Jean-Claude looked up, almost as if he were seeing that historic flight at this very moment.

"And did anything go wrong after that?"

"Oh, yes, they started to descend when they were halfway across, and then they threw out everything else that remained in the car—including the anchor. They were even contemplating throwing out their basket and clinging to the ropes."

"No!" Alethea gasped.

"No," Jean-Claude said. "Fortunately, they did not need to resort to that last measure . . . The balloon ascended again, and they came down in the Forest of Guinnes."

"Ah!" Alethea clasped her hands. "How exciting."

"Yes . . . it can be." Jean-Claude smiled at her. "If one remains aloft."

"Have there been many accidents?" she asked nervously, her eyes on the balloon in the field.

"A few . . . one Philatre de Rozier, who with a Monsieur Romains decided to duplicate the feat of Jean-Pierre Blanchard and his partner—but flying from France to England. They started at Boulogne and in order to assure their safety, they used a double balloon—one filled with gas and the other, a fire balloon. It seemed as if they had nothing to fear . . . The balloons soared high and then one of them caught fire."

"Oh." Alethea shuddered. "The poor men. I expect they must have been killed!"

"Yes," Jean-Claude said solemnly. "They fell three-thousand feet."

"Oh, dear . . ." She was silent a moment and then she said, "But you told me this was a chemical experiment."

"And so it is, my dear. The balloon is filled with hydrogen gas which comes—"

"From a chemical laboratory!" she finished. "Of course."

"Yes, of course," he echoed. "Chemistry, my dear, is a science of the future, but come . . . I think they are ready."

There were two men in the basket of the balloon, and

several others were making various adjustments to the ropes. Finally, the ropes were released and slowly, at first, the immense balloon began to rise.

"Oh," Alethea breathed. "I hope they will be safe."

Jean-Claude put his arm around her waist. "But, of course, they will be . . . and it is a fine day for flying."

"Flying . . ." Alethea echoed. "Oh, they are flying, are they not? I wish I might go up in a balloon sometime."

"Do you, my dear?" Jean-Claude smiled at her. "You are not put off by the sad experience of the late Monsieur de Rozier?"

"I expect he was not very cautious. He was too intent on bettering the record of Jean-Pierre Blanchard. At least, that is the feeling I had when you told me the story."

"You are quite right." Jean-Claude nodded. "Even to the double balloons." He gave her a little squeeze. "And so, my dear, you would brave the skies?"

"Would not you?" she demanded.

"Yes . . . I have been thinking about it for quite a long time."

"And will you take me with you?" she asked.

"Of course, I will take you if . . . it is possible to do so." He smiled down at her and then his smile faded. He said almost brusquely, "But come, my dear, let us watch them. That is why we are here, after all."

At his words, the joy she had been feeling fled. Once such an excursion might have been possible, but now, there was Sir Martin, who would surely frown on it. And, too, there was Lady Langmore. But, she told herself, they were neither of them here now . . . For this day, for possibly the last time, they needed to think of neither. She smiled up at him and daringly seized his hand. "Come, Jean-Claude," she said gaily. "Let us follow them a short ways . . . as those other men are doing."

He was smiling again, and he removed his hand from her grasp only to put his arm around her shoulders. "Very well, my dear, why should we not?"

Late that afternoon, Alethea, standing in her aunt's room, was excitedly telling her of the balloon ascension.

"Oh, it was enjoyable. I do wish you might have been with us!"

"I expect I will see it one day—when Jean-Claude is back in his tower," Drusilla responded and immediately wished she had not unleashed that particular remark. All the animation faded from Alethea's face.

She said, "I do not think Jean-Claude will ever return to his tower, Aunt. Do not forget Lady Langmore. I doubt if she would find the tower to her liking and even were she to visit it, I cannot imagine her wanting him to take her up in a balloon."

"Not if there were no members of the ton to observe her flight," Drusilla commented dryly.

"Oh, Aunt." Alethea giggled. "But, of course, you are right. I have a feeling that she loves to shock her friends." She tossed her head. "But I will not think of her. I do not wish to spoil the remainder of the day." She glanced out the window. "Oh, dear, it's nearly dark. Why must happy days end so quickly?"

"There will be other happy days, child."

"Yes." Alethea sighed. She did not utter the words hovering at the tip of her tongue, but afterwards, when she was in her own room, she lay in her bed thinking of Jean-Claude, looking so young, so eager and excited that she had hardly recognized him.

It had occurred to her during those moments when he was watching that soaring balloon and she was surreptitiously scanning his face, that she was, in effect, seeing an image of his younger self when he, still living in France, was working with the great Antoine Lavoisier and visiting his parents in their one-time fastness of Normandy. And had there been someone else whom he had visited? A girl?

She was suddenly positive that there had been—one who had perished as his family had perished, and in so doing had taken all his capacity for loving with her? She was also positive that he did not love Lady Langmore but, she thought with a return of bitterness, he might marry her all the same. The Revolution was ended and with it Jean-Claude's world, but he was still alive and what a father he would be . . . instructing his son as once he had instructed her. At that moment, she suddenly wanted to hate him because he did not believe her worthy enough to give him that son—and so he would settle for the likes of Lady Langmore, who had, she understood, two children from her first marriage. These remained on the top floor of her house with their governess and were seen by no one. A son born to Jean-Claude would be equally sequestered and . . . Alethea suddenly laughed. She might be a novelist from the Minerva Press, spinning out these romances, as she was presently doing. However, she decided bitterly, she would not be a very good novelist because she did not really believe in romance.

"Oh, God, why, why, why did he take me with him today?" she asked herself unhappily. "Was it only to torture me?"

That, of course, was ridiculous. He had taken her with him because he thought she might find pleasure in watching the balloon ascension, a private ascension without a thousand people looking on, pushing and shoving, screaming and laughing. He might, of course, even enjoy her company. He was fond of her, had proved that already, and would continue to prove it until her future was assured—and it soon would be, she reminded herself. Sir Martin would be seeing Jean-Claude on Monday next.

The weather had suddenly changed, growing colder. On Saturday night, there was a thin, gray snow on the ground, a snow which, in the vicinity of the King's Theatre, was marked by the passage of many feet. Nothing, Alethea thought as she clung to Sir Martin's arm, kept the aficionados from the opera! The street was thronged with vehicles. More than one coach had slammed into another as drivers jockeyed for positions as close to the arched doors of the theatre as possible. In spite of the angry exhortations of the coachmen, the horses moved more like snails than steeds. Their passengers crossly descended, some of the men loudly cursing the slippery ground. A great many pushed and shoved their way inside, and among these was Sir Martin, almost ruthlessly hurrying Alethea toward one of the portals.

Though he had been delighted at seeing her again, he had not been delighted to discover that Miss Ludlow, quite herself again after her brief illness, was able to take up her duties that night. Perhaps it was her restraining presence that had moved him to describe his journey from the country, marred by the weather, which had forced him to remain inside the family coach.

Consequently, he had been forced to endure the continual carping of his mother, who had seemed to imagine herself within imminent danger of being thrown from the coach onto an adjacent snowbank. His uncle had suffered her complaints in a martyred silence punctuated by complaints of his own—regarding the skill of the driver or, rather, the lack of it, at least in his estimation. Martin had reached London weary and out of sorts and then, he had sustained a shock to which he had referred several times during the course of their drive to the theatre.

He had taken his family to view the portrait of Alethea, now completed, only to be told by Sir James that the work had mysteriously vanished! He had been very apologetic about that, insisting that he had no idea who could have removed it from his studio. What had made the matter even more mysterious was that nothing else was missing. "I," Sir Martin, had informed Alethea, "do not, for a moment, believe him. I am of the opinion that he has sold it to someone for a sum exceeding that which I was prepared to pay."

It was with great relief that Alethea came into the opera house. In a short time, the overture would begin and Sir Martin would be unable to regale her with any more of the problems he had encountered since leaving London. And, for herself, she was pleased that Miss Ludlow had recovered. She had remarked more than once on her delight at being able to hear *Alceste* and had highly praised the composer's other works, in the process, displaying quite an extensive knowledge of music. However, aside from the pleasure of hearing much about music, Alethea was contemplating her return to her house. With Miss Ludlow present, Sir Martin would not be able to take advantage of the situation as he had before.

Shortly after Sir Martin, Alethea, and Miss Ludlow had taken their places in the box, Jean-Claude and Lady Langmore, the latter looking extremely annoyed, joined them. They, too, had their stories to tell about the crush of traffic outside the opera house, and Lady Langmore commented upon the astonishing rudeness of a young woman, one of the *filles de joie* who graced or, in her opinion, disgraced the boxes around and across from them.

"She put herself forward and stared up at me in the most bold way!" her ladyship complained.

Jean-Claude said quickly, "I beg you will not think on it, my dear Lady Langmore. It is possible that she mistook you for someone she knew—"

"I know one of those . . . creatures?" Lady Langmore glared at him.

Alethea, looking at him, saw that Jean-Claude's face was flushed, and she guessed he might be upset at the fair Lady Langmore's angry set-down. She was sure of it when he said placatingly, "You do mistake me, Felicia, I did not suggest—"

"Oh." She smiled at him now. "I know you did not, my dear Jean-Claude. You must forgive me. It has been such a chore getting into the opera house tonight. London becomes an entirely different city when it snows."

"I must agree with you," Sir Martin said feelingly.

Alethea exhaled a long breath. She had been trying to distance herself both from Sir Martin's carping comments and those of Lady Langmore, but she could not distance herself from one glaring fact. Jean-Claude had called Lady Langmore by her given name—Felicia. And what did that mean? She sighed and stared out across the house, finding that meaning only too clear. He was on terms of even greater intimacy with the woman whom she was quite sure he meant to marry!

"Lord love a duck!" One of the bedizened young

females in a box across the house grabbed the quizzing glass of the young man sitting next to her and put it to her eye. "Lord love a duck!" she repeated in wonder.

"Sally," her escort, a plump, but not ill-looking young man, gave her a long-suffering stare. "These expressions of yours—"

"Oh, do not look down yer nose at me, yer Lordship," his companion retorted pertly. "You like a bit o' gossip as well as the next, an' it might be that I'll 'ave a choice bit . . . Where's 'Arriette sittin'?"

His lordship gave her a curious stare. "What deviltry'd you be up to now?" he inquired, his eyes narrowing.

"No matter, where be 'Arriette? She 'as everythin' at 'er fingertips, she do." She handed him back his quizzing glass.

"She's in that box—third from the left." His lordship pointed.

"Ah, so she is," Sally positively purred. "'Ave I got time afore the curtain goes up?"

"I would say you had about five minutes," his lordship commented. "Are you not going to tell me what's going on in that little head of yours?"

Sally giggled. "Not until I've talked to 'Arriette . . . I won't be a minute, luv."

He grinned at her knowingly. "I'd give a monkey to know what you're hatching, you little devil."

"You'll know, Tommy, and afore yer much older— that's a fact." Sally rose and, seeing that Harriette Wilson was for the moment sitting alone, she hurried out of her box and down the carpeted aisle that ran behind it. As she walked, the smiles she had visited upon her escort faded, and her eyes glittered with anger. Tuesday, last, she had been sure she had seen Jean-Claude—well, almost sure. And the blond young woman in his box had certainly reminded her of Alethea. But Alethea could not be in London with Jean-Claude, unless she were really his mistress, which she did not believe for a second! Even given Alethea's all-night stay in the tower, Sally had not believed that Jean-Claude could have taken a namby-pamby creature like that into his bed. It had undoubtedly happened the way Matt, damn him, said it had—but it was useless to speculate, and at least she was not drunk or dreaming, as she had believed on Tuesday.

No, she was not mistaken. The beautiful young woman, dressed to the nines, was Alethea, and sitting behind her with another young man was Jean-Claude. And who was the very attractive older woman beside her? And who was the little lady in gray?

Harriette would know. Harriette, in common with the red Indians of the New World, had an ear to the ground. She knew everything. There was not an on-dit did not reach her ears from one or another of her lovers.

Sally loosed a sigh of pure envy. It would be delightful to have a marquess by the leading strings, as it were. Tommy was well enough. He was a viscount, after all, and he had set her up in a very nice little boite in the Village of Chelsea. He had also seen to it that she had money for clothes and a servant. She did enjoy having an abigail, and being kept by Tommy was ever so much nicer than sewing until her fingers ached or modeling hats for cross females who, like as not, ratted on her to the milliner, saying that she was casting an eye at one or another of their escorts when it was quite the other way around!

Still, every so often she was wracked by memories of that moment when she had flung herself at Jean-Claude and had been rejected . . . She winced at her memories of the aftermath. *Charlie.*

He had broken one of her teeth before she was able to get away from him. She could blame that on Jean-Claude, too. She had, in fact, wanted to kill Jean-Claude and, indeed, she had done her best—and she had believed that she had destroyed the reputation of Alethea Nobody forever. Yet, here they all were, sitting in a box at the opera, if you please, as if they were on top of the world. Well, there was no saying they would remain there—not if she had anything to do about it.

"I say, Sally, you are in a rare taking." Harriette Wilson looked up at the seething Sally with a touch of hauteur. She was not fond of Tommy's latest flame. She

was too common by half, and Harriette doubted that the
creature would long remain in Tommy's keeping.

In the scant two years she had known the viscount, he
had kept a score of doxies, and God knows what happened to them after he tired of them. She could have
dropped a word to the wise in Sally's ear, but she did not
like her enough to share such confidences. Let Tommy
have his fling and let Sally seek her own level. She would,
soon enough. Mayhap she would end up among the
whores that thronged the alleys behind Covent Garden.
Plenty of her sort had. However, she had been asked a
question, and she was not loathe to answer it.

She said, "The young man is Sir Martin Willoughby,
good family, estate in Lincolnshire. The older woman is
Lady Langmore, rich, well-connected, widowed . . . "
An imp of mischief stirred Harriette to add, "Her
ladyship is known for her routs. She's not choosy as to
whom she finds amongst her guests, as long as they are
amusing and even if they are not. The marquess has
promised to take me, and I am sure that Tommy could
command an invitation, were he to ask . . . Perhaps, he
has received one already. Lady Langmore enjoys variety.
I can remember a time when she had a Newgate winner
as a guest of honor—I am speaking about a horse, my
dear. And she also had a magician from Bartholomew
Fair, who magicked away some choice bits of jewelry. At
any rate, her routs are never dull. Perhaps we should
make up a group and attend the one on Thursday, next."

Sally said lightly, but with an undertone of intensity,
"I should quite enjoy that, I think."

Miss Wilson, looking up at her, surprised an expression on her face that inadvertently produced a shudder.
As she later remarked to her sometime friend and
occasional rival Julia Johnstone, "I have finally looked
upon the evil eye tonight and, of all things wonderful, I
found it blinking at me from Sally Price's countenance."

"That little slut. She quite offends me," Miss
Johnstone said coldly. "She is so entirely of the country."

"I will not deny it," Miss Wilson returned, "but I
thought her a harmless enough wanton until this evening.

The chit is out for blood. It was possibly a mistake to suggest that she come with us to the Langmore rout . . . but I could not resist it."

Miss Johnstone raised thin eyebrows. "That is unlike you, Harriette. The little Price is not of the ilk you generally wish to fly with—"

"Quite true . . . and I shall not repine if she loses a few feathers in this flight, but I must admit, I find myself very curious as to what might take place."

"Can you imagine that it might embarrass the Langmore?" Miss Johnstone inquired with a lift of her eyebrow.

"I have not devoted much thought to it," Miss Wilson began. "Indeed—"

"Harriette," Miss Johnstone interrupted. "You are speaking to me, not the marquess."

Miss Wilson pretended to pout. Then, she suddenly laughed. "Very well, Julia. I should not mind seeing Lady Langmore's nose put out of joint . . . How she did look down that same nose—not her best feature, I might add—when I came with the marquess last year. Besides, these great ladies who enjoy playing with fire deserve a little singeing. Do you not agree?"

"What might the Price have against Lady Langmore?" Miss Johnstone wondered. "I am quite sure that they have never moved in the same circles."

"Do you know," Miss Wilson mused, "I am of the opinion that Sally's rage is not directed at the Langmore witch. I would think it is turned on that divinely beautiful young creature that her ladyship has, amazingly, invited to sit in her box. It is truly odd. I cannot remember when La Langmore allowed herself to be seen with any female under the age of fifty."

"And what could Sally have against that girl?" Julia asked.

"I do not know . . . but I should like to know," Miss Wilson murmured.

"As would I—indeed, I am all agog to hear the reasons. By all means, Harriette, do let us go to the rout."

"But I thought that we had already agreed we would. I

will bring the marquess, of course," Miss Wilson said decisively. "or perhaps Beau Brummel."

"Bring Brummel," Miss Johnstone begged. "He will be much more amusing."

"I think," Miss Wilson said thoughtfully, "that there will be amusement a-plenty, even without the dear Beau."

"Shhh . . ." someone said from an adjoining box.

"My dear," Miss Johnstone murmured, "I think it is time we enjoyed the opera. The second act is about to commence."

"My dear, you look entirely charming," Drusilla said as Alethea came to see her, a short time before she was due to leave for the Langmore rout. "That is another new gown, is it not?" As Alethea nodded, she continued, "Gold is so becoming to your coloring. Has Jean-Claude seen it?"

"No," Alethea said. "It was just finished this afternoon."

"Certainly it suits you. It is so artfully draped and . . ." Drusilla ran her hand lightly over the material. "It is a really fine satin."

"Yes, I fear it was a trifle dear." Alethea frowned.

"Never you mind. Jean-Claude will not complain. He is most generous, and I think he is very happy over your betrothal."

"Yes, he does appear to be." Alethea turned away from her aunt, looking out the window at a darkening sky. "Sir Martin has told me that Jean-Claude was extremely gracious when he asked for my hand. It is Sir Martin's opinion that Jean-Claude himself will soon be betrothed."

"To Lady Langmore, of course."

Alethea nodded. "Of course." She added, "Oh, Aunt, I do not like her—and she feels the same about me."

Drusilla regarded her with some consternation. "I think you must be mistaken, child. Hermione tells me that Lady Langmore has been most gracious to you."

"Miss Ludlow is not particularly observant, Aunt, and she has been ill. Consequently, she has not been treated to as much of Lady Langmore's society as myself. And I tell you that she does not like me. It is evident in her every look, her every gesture. She resents it when Jean- Claude so much as glances at me and, since he is supposed to be my uncle, I do find that very strange."

"My dear, it is not strange. You are young. You are beautiful—"

"Aunt, whether I am well-looking or not—and I think you refine upon my appearance far too much—I repeat, Jean-Claude is supposed to be my uncle." Alethea emphasized this with a touch of ire.

"I have not moved in these circles, my love, but I cannot think women are much different from each other whether they wear a sacking apron or a fine satin gown. There are some females who imagine that every other female is a potential rival, especially when she has the good fortune to be beautiful."

"I do not entertain such thoughts," Alethea said.

"No, child, but you are quite unusual. When, by the way, will the announcement be released to *The Morning Post?*"

Alethea stifled a sigh. "I think it will be in the next edition. Perhaps there will also be an announcement concerning the wedding of Jean-Claude and Lady Langmore."

"Oh, dear, I do hope that he will be happy," Drusilla said. "He needs a little happiness after his great loss."

"His . . . great loss?" Alethea stared at her in surprise. "What great loss, Aunt?"

Drusilla looked down. "Oh, dear, I fear I have said too much."

"Too much about what?" Alethea pursued. "I know Jean-Claude confides in you—"

"Yes, he has from time to time . . . Also he has confidence in my silence, where his affairs are concerned."

"Aunt Drusilla, you may have the same confidence in me," Alethea said earnestly.

Drusilla stared at her in silence for a moment. Then she said slowly, "I should not tell you . . . but, of course, you will say nothing."

"No," Alethea said eagerly. "You have my solemn word on that, Aunt."

"Very well . . . I tell you this because I have always felt that if he had ever given you any encouragement, and though he is fully sixteen years your senior, you might have cared for him greatly. That, my dear, would have been most unfortunate."

"Because of my birth?" Alethea asked.

"No, child, because of a poor girl named Denise."

"Denise?" Alethea echoed. "Who is Denise?"

Drusilla sighed. "Rather ask me, who she was . . . They had loved each other since they were children. He was eighteen and she was seventeen, and they were betrothed—when his teacher, Lavoisier, sent him to England with a message to a fellow chemist. As Jean-Claude was half English, he traveled with another Englishman from the diplomatic corps. He reached England safely enough . . . but before he could return—"

"Oh, dear, I can guess the rest." Alethea's eyes filled with tears. "That does explain much that . . . that I had wondered about. I do not imagine he has ever recovered from losing her in that dreadful way?"

"I do not believe he has, my dear. Indeed, if he ever does marry, it will be solely for an heir. He does have his share of family pride. It is an old family, my dear, old and aristocratic—on both sides."

"I see," Alethea said dully. "And to ally himself with anyone not of that heritage . . . would be a mésalliance."

"Yes, my child, there's no doubt about that."

Alethea took a turn around the room and came back to face her aunt. "I have heard that Lady Langmore is very well-connected. She can trace her lineage back to the dukes of Aquitaine. Sir Martin, too, is well-connected, but his coat of arms does not boast such quarterings."

"And you, also, child, if we but knew—" Drusilla began.

"But we do not, Aunt," Alethea reminded her rather brusquely. "And . . ." she said more gently, "it is enough to know that I am related to you, and that is the truth."

"Oh, my dear child," Drusilla said warmly. She put

her arms around Alethea and kissed her. "You have given me the greatest happiness—all my life."

"And you, me," Alethea said. "I am sorry if I have been difficult of late, it is only that . . ." She sighed. "Well, I do like Martin and in time—"

"Now you are being sensible, my love," Drusilla approved.

"I should be sensible and grateful," Alethea said slowly. "I should have been much more grateful than I have been. Think of the vast difference between my lot at present, and four months ago. All this do I owe to Jean-Claude and to you." She paused and frowned. "If only—"

"If only what, my love?"

"If only I were not compelled to deceive poor Martin." Alethea took a nervous turn around the room and came back to face her aunt. "Sometimes when we are together, I find the truth on the edge of my tongue, begging me to release it. I have to bite my tongue to urge it back. I wish I might tell him—"

"Not yet," Drusilla warned. "Wait."

"Until I am safely married to Sir Martin? But then, will it not be even worse? His disposition is not all sweetness and light, Aunt Drusilla. If he were to learn that I cheated him—"

"I think he will not feel cheated, having you as his bride, my dearest."

"All the same, I would feel much more comfortable were he to know the truth."

"There are many facets to that truth that he might have some difficulty in understanding," Drusilla said slowly. "You must remember, my love, that you live in the same house with Jean-Claude, and as he is your uncle, no one would cavil—"

"Oh, yes," Alethea interrupted. "I know it is impossible to tell Martin or anyone else . . . but I could wish it were not. I hate to have this falsehood hanging over my head like the sword of Damocles."

"I am sure that there are many such swords in this society, my dear," Drusilla said easily. "You may believe my attitude too worldly and even surprising, knowing, as you do, my dislike of prevarication. However, it is my opinion that a vessel that has been tossed in as many stormy seas as yourself with no control over the wind and the rain deserves a safe harbor." She drew her niece into her arms and kissed her on the cheek. "No, my love, go forth and enjoy the evening—it is your evening, you know."

Alethea forced a smile. "I will do my very best, Aunt," she said, and hurried out of the room.

CHAPTER NINE

THE HOUSE FACING Berkeley Square was brilliantly lighted, a beacon in the night, indeed. Arriving with Sir Martin, Alethea was surprised at the number of post chaises, coaches, and curricles lined up on either side of the street, making passage almost impossible. At least, the lanterns on the coaches helped to light the road, else there would have been some difficulty in descending safely from Sir Martin's post chaise, given the indifferent glow from the streetlamps.

"Lord," Sir Martin muttered as he escorted Alethea up the walk to the front door of Lady Langmore's mansion. "I think she must have invited all of London." Then, as if aware that he had sounded carping, he added with an adoring smile at his betrothed, "But I do not mind—since I have the most beautiful girl in England with me."

"My dear," Alethea smiled up at him, "I fear you grow fulsome."

"You have no idea how much more fulsome I plan to be." He pressed a kiss on the top of her head. "I beg, however, that we will not need to remain long after the announcement."

"I will not complain if we leave," Alethea assured him.

"Will you always be so accommodating?" he asked lovingly.

She was spared the necessity of an answer, for they had reached the front door and it had been opened by the butler. They came into the hall.

"Lord love us," a plump young man some few feet behind Alethea and Sir Martin glared down at his companion. "Damned if I thought the Langmore'd have such a crush! Though I should have known." Despite his annoyance, he added with a smile, "Damned if I ever saw you in such looks, Sally." He pressed the tip of a gloved finger against her cheek. "An' I do believe it's real."

She did not pretend to misunderstand him. "Sure 'tis real. It's only old females like 'Arriette 'n Julie wot need to color up."

He laughed. "You're damned lucky they cannot neither o' em hear you, else there'd be blood running down both your cheeks . . . and other places, as well." He let his hand move over her plump buttocks.

"Well, they cannot," Sally retorted. She glanced at her gown, cherry red satin and cut so low that her full breasts seemed in imminent danger of popping forth from their nests. A necklace of small but perfect pearls encircled her neck. It was centered by a little ruby heart which she had thought very grand when the viscount had presented it to her, two months earlier. She no longer held the same opinion, and she meant to remind him that he had promised her a replacement when his next quarter's allowance came due. She visited a resentful thought upon his aged grandfather, the earl of Strathmore, who kept him on such short leading strings. Then, she forgot him as she brought her hand to her head to see if the red ostrich plumes she had fastened in her curls were still in place. They were. Eventually, she intended to have them replaced by a ruby and diamond tiara but, meanwhile, she had other matters on her mind.

As they entered, Miss Price caught sight of Julia Johnstone and Harriette Wilson with their escorts, the one a duke and the other a marquess. They seemed in great good humor, but when she greeted them, she was miffed because both young women gave her no more than a perfunctory nod. However, even that set-down could not trouble her this night. Despite her smiles, her interior angers lent a color to her cheeks and a brilliance to her eyes that no cosmetic could ever duplicate.

It was that color that Tommy had praised, and though

he could not have known it, it grew directly out of the information he had given to her as they drove toward Lady Langmore's house.

"There will be an engagement announced tonight . . . Perhaps a pair o' 'em, so I have heard."

"Really? And 'oo'll be gettin' married?" Sally had asked disinterestedly.

"Well, there's this Miss Alethea Saint Cyr, damned funny thing about her . . . Came out of nowhere, but seems she's been in this convent and she's the niece of the comte who's nosin' about Lady Langmore. Can you imagine, she'll be getting married too . . . and to that same count. At least he's a sight younger than her first husband. Dry old dog he was."

Sally hoped she had sounded as casual as her escort when she said, "And who might the count's niece be marrying?"

"He's a dry young dog." Tommy had laughed. "His name's Sir Martin Willoughby and he comes from a nest of Puritans, so I've heard. His uncle's high up in the church . . . bishop of something, I disremember what, and young Martin might as well be—for all he's never taken orders. He's a prig . . . a real prig . . . sort I never could abide."

Sally's smile broadened. She would find a way to put a spoke in Alethea's wheel and in several other wheels— before she was much older!

"Good Lord," Sir Martin muttered as he and Alethea were ushered into the drawing room where, to his bemused eyes, literally hundreds of people appeared to be congregated. However, when he was able to assess the number of guests about him, he decided that there were no more than some twenty-odd couples, and perhaps some twenty single men and women circulating freely, their voices blending to a babble that could easily have stemmed from the famous tower. He muttered that sentiment to Alethea, who nodded but, he feared, had not heard him.

He looked in vain for his hostess, but he did not see her. However, a second later, he did see the tall, slender form of Jean-Claude and pointed him out to Alethea. He was standing with the hostess, Martin realized. She looked very well, considering her advanced age. He could not, however, approve her gown, cut too low for one well past her first youth. Indeed, he was reasonably and regretfully sure that his uncle, the bishop, would not even approve Alethea's gown since it, too, was low enough to reveal the roundness of her bosom, a sight he jealously wished might be screened from other masculine eyes. He wondered who chose her clothing and made a mental note to ask his mother if she might recommend a mantua-maker who would see that Alethea was dressed less conspicuously, once they were wed.

"I did not expect so large an assembly," he said to Alethea, who smiled at him, but put her hands to her ears to signify that, as he had guessed, she could not hear him. That, however, was just as well, for in looking into her beautiful face, he quite forgot what he had wanted to say and wished only that they were already married and alone . . . He flushed at the images that had flashed through his mind. They were certainly not proper and, undoubtedly, they would have shocked the young female at his side. She was so utterly lovely, and also she breathed purity and goodness. In fact, though he was not generally very imaginative, he was sure that she would rival the very angels in heaven—in looks as well as character. It had often seemed to him that she was the very epitome of virtue. He frowned, remembering that his mother had expressed some doubts on that score, an opinion based on nothing save that she was partly French!

"For you know, Martin, dear, that that nation as a whole does not have a reputation for chastity. In fact, quite the opposite if one remembers the excesses of the Revolution . . . And then there was the court of Louis XV . . . that wretched creature, the Du Barry. In my opinion, beheading was too good for her; she should have been whipped at cart's tail like the common whore she was."

His frown grew blacker as, mentally, he refuted his mother's cavils, though he had not dared object in person. He had always been an obedient son, but never had he felt so out of sympathy with his mother as upon that day. Fortunately, she, too, had been won over by Alethea. His uncle, too, had liked her, and the bishop was particularly hard to please—being suspicious of what he called "modern females." However, both he and Lady Willoughby had been impressed by the comte and . . . He paused in his thinking as he heard Alethea give a little exclamation of surprise.

He looked at her and saw that she was standing very still, staring at something or, more likely, someone across the room. Ascertaining the direction in which she was looking, he saw only a large group of people and then, a flash of scarlet caught his eye and he noticed a young woman in a vivid red gown. She had two upstanding ostrich plumes of a similar hue in hair that was, he thought, a spurious shade of yellow. Indeed, to his shocked eyes, she was that abandoned creature about which the Bible had much to say. Into his mind flashed the words, "for the lips of a strange woman drop as a honeycomb and her mouth is smoother than oil, but her end is as bitter as wormwood, sharp as a two-edged sword."

How often he had those words intoned by the minister in the pulpit, but never had they seemed actually applicable until this moment. And why was Alethea even looking at her. She must not, she must not, his affronted senses told him. She must turn her eyes away from the scarlet woman "for her house is the way to hell."

He slipped an arm around her shoulders and, to his surprise, found her body incredibly rigid. He guessed that her shock must be equal to his own, seeing so abandoned a creature present in a noble house! Lady Langmore, damn her, had much to answer for!

"My dear," he said hastily, "it is passing warm in here. Shall we go into the hall . . ." He paused, because the girl in red was moving hastily in their direction, actually elbowing her way through the throng, and people were falling back, protesting but still letting her pass. There was a plump young man behind her, who seemed to be

trying to hold her back as she roughly pushed her way
through the crowd of protesting people. She was coming
in their direction, he realized. Her eyes were on Alethea
. . . and Alethea stood where she was, still as a statue,
staring at her. Seemingly, she was unable to move.

"Alethea," Sir Martin said urgently. "Come away,
please, come with me, now."

She did not seem to hear him, and then the red woman
was there, staring at Alethea, saying, "Well, 'ere you are,
then. I expect you're surprised to see me, eh?"

"Sally," Alethea mouthed.

"You . . . you'll never tell me that you know her." Sir
Martin stared at Alethea incredulously.

He received an impudent grin from the woman in red,
from the scarlet woman, from the strange woman with
the honeyed lips. "She knows me," the creature affirmed.

Was it his imagination? Had all conversation in the
room ceased? No, laughter and chatter came to him—
but from afar. He stared at Alethea. Her face was drained
of color. She said, "What do you want, Sally?"

Then, even as the Scarlet Woman, the Strange Woman,
opened her mouth to reply, Alethea's uncle, coming from
somewhere, stepped to Alethea's other side and put a
sustaining arm around his niece's waist. He said in a low
but firm voice, "What are you doing here, Sally?"

The girl laughed loudly. "I got as much right 'ere as
you, Jean-Claude, you 'n yer damned little whore. I got
an invitation."

"Sally!" her companion protested in a shocked tone.

It was then that Alethea seemed to come to life. She
said coldly and distinctly, "I am not and nor have I ever
been his whore."

"No?" The girl's ugly, mocking laughter seemed to fall
into a pit of silence, and Sir Martin was suddenly aware
that every eye in the vast room seemed to be fixed on
them. He was vaguely aware of Lady Langmore approaching them. Meanwhile, the woman named Sally
laughed again, even louder than before.

"No?" she repeated sarcastically. "An' will you tell me
yer 'is niece, Miss Unwin . . . *Unwin?* Hell, Unknown's

wot ye really are . . . Bastard's wot you are, 'n 'e be yer lover, right enough . . ."

Voices, rising and falling like the tides in an ocean, seemed to be coming from a long distance away, and in Alethea's mind was an image . . . jeering little girls, all pointing fingers at her and then, at the urging of one child, Sally Price, throwing clumps of mud and stones. Mud was splattered on her gown now . . . but she lifted her chin and stared back at Sally. "Liar," she said distinctly.

"Sally!" the plump young man with the red woman was saying. "Come away, for God's sake." He took her by the arm.

She did not look at him. She continued to glare at Alethea, saying loudly, "She can deny it all she wants, but she's 'is whore. Ask 'er where she spends 'er nights? Ask 'er!"

It was then that Jean-Claude slapped her hard across the mouth. "Salop," he snapped. "You ought to be whipped at cart's tail for your damned lies."

"Here . . . you! You'll answer to me for that, Comte." Tommy, his plump face flushed with anger, stepped forward.

"I will and gladly, Lord Furneaux," Jean-Claude said steadily.

"And you will answer to me," Sir Martin, finding his voice, spoke loudly. "This lady is my affianced bride."

"Yer bride, is it?" The woman in red's shrill laughter battered against his eardrums. "Why not? She might as well spread 'er legs for you as for the next."

"Good Christ, that is enough, Sally," Tommy growled.

"Name your seconds, Lord Furneaux," Jean-Claude rasped.

The room was silent then, silent enough for Alethea's voice to be heard as she said in clear ringing tones, "I beg you will not fight, gentlemen." She bestowed a brief, apologetic glance on Sir Martin. "I am sorry, Martin, but Sally here is right—she has given you a good part of the truth."

"Alethea, for God's sake . . ." Jean-Claude protested.

She did not look at him. She went on to say, "Jean-Claude de Bretigny is not my uncle. He is no relation to me. However, he is not my lover. He is simply my benefactor. As for myself, my name is Alethea—for the rest I do not know, since my father, whoever he was, did not believe it necessary to bestow a wedding ring upon my mother. As Sally Price has been moved to inform you, I am a bastard, and as such I hardly deserve your championship." Before any one of that shocked and silenced group could speak, she had picked up her skirts and, running through the room, she fled out the door.

"Alethea!" Sir Martin cried. Then, he was running, too, running after her and reaching the door of the house. He saw the butler staring bemusedly through the open portal into the street. He did not stop to question the man, but rushed out into the chill darkness and looked about him in a growing panic. Then, he found her—at the end of the patterned brick pathway leading to the house.

"Alethea . . . Alethea . . ." He came to her side. "Do you think I care what you are?" he cried. "I love you, and I know that you are good. It is your . . . it is the Comte de Bretigny who is culpable. And his reasons—"

She moved away from him, saying in a cool little voice, "It is not Jean-Claude, Martin. Everything I am, I owe to Jean-Claude."

He stared at her in anguish coupled with a growing anger. "Why do you defend him?" he demanded furiously. "He must have had a purpose in . . . in perpetrating this . . . this scheme, but nothing will make me believe that you are a part of it. You were forced into whatever it was, and by God, he will answer for it. He will answer with swords!"

"No, Martin," she cried. "Jean-Claude is not a swordsman. He is a scientist. You must not call him out. He does not deserve your anger. He has always been kind and good and . . . and I love him."

"You . . . love him?" he repeated.

"Yes, I love him with all my heart, with all my soul," she half-sobbed. "I am sorry. I thought I could marry

you, but I was wrong. You have been wronged, Martin
. . . but after all I am glad this happened."

"You are glad . . . glad?" he whispered.

"Yes . . . because loving Jean-Claude as I do, I never
should have entered—"

"You!" he interrupted furiously, striking her hard
across the face. "You whore . . . you whore of Babylon
. . . Leading me on, you and your damned lover. You
scarlet woman." He struck her again. Then, catching her
by the shoulders, he shook her hard. "Damn you to hell, I
would like to kill you—"

"Ere!" A tall shape came out of the darkness to
confront him. "Wot're you doin' to this poor little
girl . . ." The man, obviously one of the coachmen,
interposed his large form between Sir Martin and
Alethea. "I've 'alf a mind to—" As he spoke, Alethea
suddenly fled.

"Alethea!" Sir Martin, pushing past her would-be
protector, dashed after her as she fled into the darkness.

In a small chamber off the hall, Jean-Claude, impeded
from immediately following Alethea by an amazed,
shocked, and subsequently furious Lady Langmore, received a blow in the face from her ring-encrusted hand—
after the admitted truth of his deception.

"She is not your mistress!" she shrilled. "A fine lie, one
to add to all the others you have told me. Oh, oh, oh,
would that I were a man. I'd call you out myself." Her
eyes enormous in a face so pale that her rough stood out
in ugly patches, she added, "You have made a fool out of
me, Monsieur le Comte . . . Or is that, too, a lie?"

Jean-Claude said icily, "It is not a lie, Lady Langmore.
Nothing is a lie—save that Alethea is not my niece. I had
wanted to help her . . . She deserved my help, and that is
all."

"She deserved it, did she? And what did she do to
deserve this fine help, may I ask? What—save sleep with
you? And to reward her, you allowed her, your cast-off
whore, to be courted by poor Sir Martin and I . . . I . . .
all unknowingly would have aided and abetted this
nefarious scheme!"

"She is not my whore," Jean-Claude said steadily. "She has never been with any man, and Sir Martin would not have been the loser, Lady Langmore." He sighed, wishing she would cease her harangue and let him go. He was concerned about Alethea. Where had she gone . . . ? Was she with Sir Martin? He had to find her!

Lady Langmore glared at him. "And to think . . . to think that I would have married you," she cried hotly. "I would have actually taken you . . . a bogus count and a whoremonger to boot . . . to my bed."

He said coldly, "In order for a marriage to have taken place between us, I must needs have offered for you, Lady Langmore, which I do not recall doing."

She started back as if, indeed, he had struck her. "Get out," she screamed. "Get out of my sight. I never want to look on your face again. You . . . you disgust me."

He bowed. "I will bid you good evening, Lady Langmore."

Jean-Claude came out into a night that had grown appreciably colder. A few wind-borne snowflakes struck his cheek. There would be more, he guessed, and meanwhile, Alethea was out here in this biting cold and without even a cloak! He stared about him. Several coaches were moving out, their drivers cursing and growling as they maneuvered the cumbersome vehicles. More guests were blocking the roadway as they climbed into their conveyances. It was impossible to see anything or anyone in this crowd. Jean-Claude's concern increased. He moved forward, starting to cross the street, and then hastily jumped back as a coach came barreling toward him. In that same moment, a hand fell heavily on his shoulder.

"You . . . you French dog!" He was pulled around roughly and found himself facing an angry and anguished Sir Martin. "You will answer to me. Name your weapon, damn you to hell!" the young man cried.

"I am sorry, lad," Jean-Claude said wearily, "but I have no intention of fighting you."

"You damned coward!" Martin cried furiously.

"As you wish." Jean-Claude bowed and, turning on his

heel, started to stride away, hoping against hope that Alethea might have returned to the house. There was no use trying to ascertain her whereabouts in these dark streets.

He was caught by the shoulder and found himself looking into Sir Martin's face once again. "You filthy bastard, foisting your . . . your mistress on me," Sir Martin rasped as his fist connected with Jean-Claude's chin.

Caught unawares, he staggered back and, receiving yet another punishing blow to the face from Sir Martin, fell onto the snow-wet street, much to the delight of several coachmen and postboys, who had yet to be summoned to drive their employers home.

"A mill . . . a mill!" one of them yelled. Others took up the cry and a few of them started to form a circle about the two men as Jean-Claude got to his feet. He glared at Sir Martin. "Very well, you young fool, I will meet you if you so desire."

"I do desire, damn you to hell," Sir Martin retorted furiously. "Name your weapon and have done."

"Swords," Jean-Claude snapped. "Choose the place and send your seconds to me. Meanwhile, let me be gone. I must search for my ward."

As the men, disappointed in their hope for an immediate combat, drifted away, Sir Martin rasped, "Your *ward*? A likely story. Rather call her by her rightful name— whore, your whore. She as much as confessed it. She 'loves' you, she said . . . but you'll not find her. She eluded me and is gone."

"Then," Jean-Claude said in a voice sharp with concern, "I must look for her. She cannot be alone in these streets at this hour of the night."

Sir Martin glared at him in an ever-increasing fury. "Why not?" he demanded. "The streets are something your 'love' must know. Perhaps you yourself discovered her there, the scarlet woman, the strange woman with the honeyed lips, the—" He got no further.

Striking him down with a well-aimed blow to the chin, Jean-Claude said contemptuously, "I withdraw my promise to meet you . . . You are not worth my staining my sword with your blood." Turning away from him, he started walking in the direction of his house. As he had anticipated, Sir Martin did not follow him.

It took him close on a half-hour to reach his home. The snow was heavier, big flakes beating against his face, making it difficult for him to see, difficult to walk, also. He had slipped and fallen twice, and by the time he reached the house, his heart was pounding in his throat.

Where had she gone, the poor child? He had asked himself that over and over again—at the same time castigating himself for what he now realized had been a most foolhardy undertaking and doomed from the very outset! If he had been thinking clearly, he would have realized the dangers inherent in such a mad scheme. But he had wanted to help her, poor girl, poor beautiful child . . . so innocent and so cruelly treated by rich and poor alike because . . . because why? She was fatherless, a condition that cried out for pity and for protection, rather than the sneers and slights that had so often been her lot! Only Drusilla understood, and had she gone to Drusilla? But where else could she have gone? He reached his door, raised the knocker, then slammed it against its plate.

He had repeated that summons several times before the door was opened by one of the footmen, looking harried and confused. As he came into the hall, Jean-Claude was almost afraid to ask the question that had been troubling him all the way back. "Has Miss Saint Cyr returned?" he demanded anxiously.

"Aye, sir . . . but—"

"Where is she?" he demanded.

"She's not 'ere now. None o' them females is 'ere now—nor yer valet 'n Marie."

"They are not here." Jean-Claude stared at him blankly. "Where have they gone?"

"They took the travelin' coach, sir 'n bolted out o' ere, they did."

"When?"

"It must 'ave been an hour since, sir."

"Did they say where they were going?"

"No, sir, but they was in a very great takin', they was . . . 'specially 'er."

"Whom?" Jean-Claude demanded curtly and thought he knew the answer. His guess was corroborated as the man said, "Miss Saint Cyr, sir."

He cursed himself for being three-parts of a fool. Wrapped in thought as he had been, he had not even remembered taking the post chaise to Lady Langmore's rout. It must still be there. He would need to send Matt to fetch it—but Matt had driven it, had he not? He might yet be waiting on that street.

"Where's Matt?" he demanded.

"Dunno, sir. 'E left 'ere while the females was still preparin' to go. 'E were that angry . . . never saw 'im so angry, sir."

"Then, who drove them in the coach?" Jean-Claude demanded.

"'Twas James from the stables, sir. 'E's 'ad experience wi' coaches."

"I see . . ." Again he had not been thinking clearly. Naturally, Matt would have brought Miss Ludlow home. And where was he now?

Jean-Claude went to the door and, opening it, stared out into the snowy distance. The winds had increased and the snow also. It was too late to follow the women. He guessed that Drusilla would have been headed for home; he knew that she missed her house and had never been happy in London. But how far would she get in this storm? They would need to stop at an inn. Perhaps in the morning, he might be able to catch up with them. But there were matters to which he must needs attend here in London, the closing of the house. No! He would not close the house. He would return after he had seen Alethea. He sighed. He was bone tired and sore from his falls, else he would have gone now—storm or no storm-–he and Matt. And where was Matt?

Matt had reluctantly driven a flustered, tearful Miss Ludlow home. On the way, he had heard what had happened, and that had corroborated something he had

seen while waiting in the street and chatting with some of
the other coachmen.

A woman in red had burst forth from the great house,
followed by a fat little man who was actually shaking his
fists while she screamed at him, talking about rights and
Jean-Claude and Alethea. She had used words that Matt
would have liked to shove down her damned throat, the
throat of his sister Sally, looking like the whore he had
always guessed her to be.

He had moved away from the group to confront her,
but by that time, she and her furious little escort were
settled in another vehicle and the latter was bawling out a
direction Matthew knew. Unknown to anyone, he had
gone to seek Sally at the milliner's, and one of the girls
had archly told him about her "rise" to a snug little house
in Chelsea. She had also given him the directions, which
he had not yet used. He had been determined to use them
then—but Miss Ludlow had come out and he had had to
drive her home. Once he arrived at the house, he wasted
no time. He had made inquiries in the stable and was
given the route to the Village of Chelsea and, more
specifically, the street on which lay his sister's house.

He had arrived at her house to find the front door ajar
and to hear her screaming, "Very well, I'll be out o' 'ere
tomorrow 'n ye can go to the devil, damn you! Think I
cannot get myself somebody else, you got another think
comin'. I'm too good for the likes o' you, Tommy, 'n did I
ever tell you, you are too bloody fat to be a good lover.
Bein' in bed wi' you's no better 'n makin' love to a
cushion! Yes, I said I'd go 'n I will . . . There'll be plenty
want to take me in, you can be assured o' that. So go
on . . . get the 'ell out."

The fat man left, and such was his state of anger that
the door remained on the latch. Matt pushed it open and
came into an overdecorated room smelling heavily of
scent. She was there in her red gown, with two bedrag-
gled red plumes drooping about her face. She was
walking up and down in a fine fury and, as he stood
there, she picked up a vase and threw it against the wall.
Then, turning, she saw him and her mouth dropped
open.

"You," she finally said. "Wot're you doin' 'ere?"

He had not known what he was going to say or do. His anger was too great. Then, the words came. "I know wot you done, Sally," he told her harshly. "I know wot you done to one 'oo never 'armed you. You 'ated 'er all yer life . . . You spread lies about 'er 'n made 'er lose 'er position at the big 'ouse, but ye wasn't satisfied wi' that . . . ye 'ad to go further—"

"An' wot if I did?" She glared at him. "Wot's she to you? Or maybe you'd like to lay 'er, the way Jean-Claude 'as, ye would like that, I'm sure . . . the way ye stare at 'er in that dumb, moonstruck way."

"Damn you, 'e's never put an 'and on 'er 'n well ye know it, you little whore. You make me puke, 'n it's 'igh time ye 'ad ye comin' uppance." He had advanced on her then.

She had screamed and tried to get away from him, but she had tripped over her long skirt and fallen, and he was on her, and his anger—far too great to be contained—was unleashed. He brought his fist down on the side of her face and felt something crack beneath it. The sound further maddened him, and he began to strike her on both face and body, the hard blows falling indiscriminately on both, the while she screamed in anger and then in pain. By the time the beating had ceased, she was no longer screaming. She was lying curled up on the floor, her hands pressing against her battered body. Both of her eyes were blackened and swollen, her nose was flattened, and her front teeth gone—a horrid sight, indeed, a sight to make him shudder, to make anyone who saw her shudder. The wounds would heal—they were none of them mortal—but she would never look the same again, and he was not sorry. Sin should not wear a pretty face, and neither should cruelty.

CHAPTER TEN

JEAN-CLAUDE, LYING IN bed, had watched the dusk fade into dawn. The morning was cold and fortunately clear, a good day for driving, he decided. He hoped that Matt had returned. Where had he gone? Had news of his sister's denunciation reached him? If it had not . . . should he be told? But that was not important anymore. All that was important was getting out of the city and trying to find Alethea. He rose and dressed hastily. On coming downstairs, he met the butler and inquired after Matt.

"'E's out back in the stables, sir. Came in late last night, 'e did. Brought the post chaise back."

"Please send him to me. I will be in the library."

"Very good, sir."

Jean-Claude was looking over his household accounts in the library when there was a tentative knock on the door. "Come, Matt," he called.

However, when the door opened, it was not Matt but the butler, who entered looking grave. "Sir," he said hesitantly. "There be one Sir Miles Wortley to see you. It's urgent, 'e says."

"I do not know any Sir Miles Wortley," Jean-Claude said impatiently. "And I wish to leave for the country as soon as possible."

"If you please, sir, 'e says 'e's from Sir Martin Willoughby."

The events of the previous evening rolled back into his

mind, and Jean-Claude's first impulse was to consign Sir Martin to the devil! He needed to find Alethea and that before the day was much older. He wanted to comfort her, and that was all that mattered. Furthermore, had he not already put the whelp in his proper place? Yet, obviously he was not content to remain there, and perhaps he had best be taught a lesson, a final lesson which he would not soon forget. He said curtly, "Show Sir Miles into the drawing room, please."

The man was young, well-dressed and plainly ill at ease. Salutations were exchanged, then he spoke nervously of a grievous injury to Sir Martin's feelings and to his person, as well. He was much discomfited when Jean-Claude curtly interrupted him, asking abruptly, "When does he want the duel to take place and where? Let it be as soon as possible. I have business I must needs settle out of town."

His visitor breathed an audible sigh of relief and hastily named the following morning, a spot beyond the city, and suggested the name of a physician. He agreed with alacrity to Jean-Claude's choice of pistols over swords. He had decided upon the latter because a sword fight took longer. Matters being concluded, Sir Miles left hurriedly and, it seemed to Jean-Claude, apologetically.

Matt, returning on the heels of the departing visitor, was pressed into the role of second. At first he protested. "Ye ought to 'ave a gentleman attend ye, sir."

"Nonsense, Matt," Jean-Claude retorted briskly. "We'll keep this among ourselves. I have few friends here in the city and none I trust as much as you."

Matt flushed. "Shouldn't 'ave to fight at all. Damn my sister, but she'll 'ave cause to remember 'er part in this."

"Matt?" Jean-Claude gave him a long look. "Was that where you went last night?"

"Aye," was the grim response. "I did."

"What happened?"

"Gave 'er a bit o' 'er own back, I did. Ought to 'ave 'ad when she were little. May'ap, it be better now . . . She'll not be attackin' 'er betters again, she won't."

Jean-Claude nodded. He did not ask any more questions. Matt could be heavy-handed, and he was a veteran of several victorious encounters with men bigger and brawnier than himself. Jean-Claude imagined that he had used those punishing fists on his sister. There had never been any love lost between them, and Matt was still seething with rage over the attack on the tower that she had instigated.

Rising before dawn on the morning of the duel, Jean-Claude expected that young Sir Martin would be satisfied with a bullet flying harmlessly over his head. Angry as he was with the lad, he had calmed down to a point where he could well understand his attitude.

The young man had been bitterly disappointed and, obviously, he had been deeply in love with Alethea. Sally's cruel lies and, Jean-Claude reluctantly had to admit, her few truths, must have been so many arrows to his breast. And that Alethea had subsequently rejected him was also obvious. There was no doubt but that poor Sir Martin had been both injured and insulted by the events of what he was beginning to term that "fatal night." Consequently, it was only natural that he would want to salve his honor with a duel. However, he was quite sure that Sir Martin, too, meant to do the same. His religious training, something Alethea had mentioned more than once, would preclude any other course of action. Then, honor being satisfied, they could both leave.

Immediately upon quitting the dueling ground, he would hurry into his waiting post chaise and drive out of London. He had missed a whole day, but there was still a hope that he might catch up to Alethea on the road. He doubted if the three ladies would feel it necessary to drive as speedily as he intended to do.

The dueling ground—located in a clearing place surrounded by tall trees—lay some five miles out of London. The morning was cold and, much to Jean-Claude's relief, very clear. It was good driving weather—he could not have wished for better!

Sir Martin and Sir Miles were there when he and Matt arrived. His opponent had been surprised and also shocked, Jean-Claude thought, at the sight of Matt. He had, of course, expected a man of his own class, and his expression reflected disdain. Indeed, his whole attitude was such that Jean-Claude had second thoughts. Yet, to do other than that would interfere with his plans.

Sir Miles, whose place it was to drop the handkerchief that would announce to the opponents that they must fire, stood at a spot to one side, at an equidistance between them. He had an air of tenseness and even distress about him, Jean-Claude thought. He doubted if the young man had ever officiated at a duel. Probably, he was also thinking about the possible advent of the constabulary—unlikely, however, he thought, unless Sir Martin had summoned them to interfere in the nick of time and save him from a possible bullet. Given his actions on the night of the rout, he would not put it past him. In fact, it was surprising that he had summoned enough courage to satisfy his so-called honor yet a second time.

However, the physician, Mr. Stone, had tried to talk them both out of the duel and, given this final opportunity, Sir Martin had refused to take it. He preferred to go through with this mockery. They were in their places now, and Sir Miles was holding up the fatal handkerchief. At its fall, they would fire. They aimed. Matt moved back, and Sir Miles stood at attention, evidently steeling himself for his part in what the physician had not scrupled to call "this most unfortunate and unnecessary event." Then, suddenly, there was a loud explosion and Jean-Claude felt something strike him, sending him reeling back. Much to his annoyance, the pistol dropped from his hand. He was vaguely aware of something being wrong, and realized that there had been only one shot. He should have returned the fire. Why had he not?

"Damn you to hell, Martin," he heard Sir Miles cry. "You did not wait, damn you to hell."

"Did not wait . . . for what?" Jean-Claude asked vaguely, and on glancing down saw that his white shirt was turning red. Before anything else could register, he felt himself falling. He tried to save himself, but could not seem to summon the strength. In another second, he lay supine upon the chill ground.

Someone was at his side, looking regretfully down into

his face, and he was vaguely aware of angry cries. Then, on opening his eyes wider—and finding that movement to be an effort—he recognized the face of Sir Miles, a Sir Miles whose cheeks were bedewed with tears coursing out of his reddened eyes.

"Oh, sir," he half-sobbed. "I am so sorry."

"Come away," a curt voice ordered. "Let me examine him, please."

Jean-Claude looked up into the thin face of Mr. Stone, the physician. He whispered, "Did I . . . hurt . . . Sir Martin? Wanted to . . . to shoot over his—his head . . ."

"Sir Martin," the physician replied in tones of deep disgust, "is quite unharmed, sir."

"Ah," Jean-Claude murmured in relief. "Then my bullet went awry. I meant that it should and . . ." But pain, sudden and intense, smote him, and as something akin to realization flooded through his mind, he mercifully fainted.

The skies were gray, but patches of blue were to be seen between the rolling clouds. The weather was still uncertain, but at least it was no longer as stormy and wild as it had been. Jean-Claude, as he lay back against the squabs of his traveling coach, a blanket wrapped about his knees and his great coat over his shoulders, wished that he did not feel quite so weak.

Mr. Stone's words, crisp and to the point, as usual, were in his ears. "You would be better off, sir," the physician had said, "if you would heed me and remain abed another few days."

"I have been in bed." Jean-Claude had gazed on the man's thin, clever face with sheer dislike as if, indeed, his present infirmity were of the latter's causing. "I have been in bed," he had repeated, then added for additional emphasis, "for the better part of two months. I must get home, Mr. Stone. They've not heard from me, and I have not heard from them. Something is amiss, I am sure of it."

"Possibly," the physician allowed, "but you'd be the better for another week of recuperation. You nearly died, sir. The bullet was within an inch of ending your life."

"So you have often told me," Jean-Claude said wearily. "But I am not dead and I am myself again—or very nearly." He had avoided his doctor's censorious glance and had given only half an ear to his parting strictures.

Now, however, he was reluctantly aware of the roughness of the roads, had been all too aware of them for the last hour, angrily aware of them. Or was the anger directed at himself or, rather, at this persistent weakness? Never should he have accepted Sir Martin's challenge, he thought bitterly.

He grimaced, remembering his original liking for the young man. Obviously, he had spent too much time among his compounds and his experiments; he was no longer a very astute judge of character. He shuddered. Had it not been for fate's long finger, Alethea would have been married to this young rogue, who, at present, was exactly where he ought to be. No, he mentally amended, not quite. He ought to be in prison for attempted murder, but actually, he was at home, where he could hide his disgrace from the world of fashion—a world from which he was forever banished!

Everyone, thanks to a shocked Sir Miles Wortley, knew that Sir Martin Willoughby had pressed the duel upon the Comte de Bretigny with the express purpose of killing him or, to call his design by its rightful name, murdering him in cold blood. That had been evident, Sir Miles had averred, when Sir Martin had discharged his pistol before he had been able to drop the handkerchief.

That he had not succeeded in his fell design had been, according to Mr. Stone, a near-miracle. That it had been a miracle aided by himself, the physician had not mentioned. However, it was true. Despite his caustic manner and his cold, often sarcastic speech, Mr. Stone had, on occasion, remained with his patient all through the night and through half of the next day, as well, discounting his own weariness. He should, Jean-Claude was perfectly aware, have heeded Mr. Stone and taken those few extra days, but he had to know the fate of poor Alethea—Alethea, who, thanks to the intervention of God and his angels, had not become Sir Martin's bride!

"He is not worth so much as the nail on her little finger," he muttered and, as he conjured up her image, an ever-present fear rose like bile in his throat.

Where was she? His only hope was that she might be with her aunt in Drusilla's little cottage . . . But what if they had left the cottage . . . the village . . . for parts unknown? What if . . . He closed his eyes, seeking oblivion in sleep.

Much to Jean-Claude's disgust, the jouncing of the coach had made it imperative that, after all, he heed his physician's advice. He had been forced to remain at an inn on the outskirts of Malton some miles from Helmsley. He had remained there for the better part of a week. Then, when he had finally arrived at the tower, Matt had helped him inside and, because he was too weak to ascend the stairs, he had made up a bed for him on the first floor. He had fully intended to rise early in the morning of the next day and go forth to Drusilla's cottage—but, in the end, she came to him and, sitting by his bedside, she asked him angrily why he had not thought to summon her before. She also wanted to know why he had not thought to write to her concerning his condition. "I would have returned to London to nurse you," she had said crossly.

He bore her scolding patiently enough. Then, at a break in her diatribe, he said quickly, "What of Alethea, poor child. How is she?" Again, before she could respond, he added, "Where is she?"

"To answer the first of your questions, Jean-Claude, she is well enough. And she is in Scotland, visiting my second cousin."

"In Scotland," he breathed, half-raising himself. "Where in Scotland?"

"She is in Langholm. My cousin, whom I never think about, from one year to the next, is named Ruth MacIlwraith. She has a cottage in the hills and lives surrounded by a large, affectionate, and prolific family . . . There are children, grandchildren and great grandchildren. Alethea thought that she would like to tend children again and perhaps teach them. I wrote to Ruth.

She was delighted to have Alethea and said she would use her in both capacities. She has been there a little over a month."

He was disappointed to hear that she was not at home. He was also anxious over her state of mind. "How is she?" he asked.

"Well," Drusilla hesitated, "she was very unhappy at first—"

"Did she love young Martin, then?" he demanded and was visited by a vagrant memory, one he now impatiently dismissed as ridiculous.

"Not she!" Drusilla exclaimed. "The poor child was sore confused and, afterwards, of course, she was angry. I think she is over the worst of the situation now . . . Her letters have been most heartening."

"Will she be coming home soon?" Jean-Claude demanded eagerly. "I do want to see her."

"As to that, I do not know, Jean-Claude, love," Drusilla said thoughtfully. "This place has memories that she would as lief not consider. And, of course, there are some here still believe—"

"Damn them," Jean-Claude cried angrily. "Damn any of them who do not think her a veritable angel from heaven."

"Jean-Claude, my love, calm down," Drusilla urged hastily. "You must rest. I think I will be leaving you now."

"Come back," he begged, mentally cursing himself for his persistent weakness.

"We will," she assured him gently.

"We?" he demanded quickly.

"Miss Ludlow will want to see you, I know, as soon as she might. She did not want to come this morning for fear that two visitors would disturb you."

"Miss Ludlow is here?" he asked with considerable surprise.

"Oh, yes." Drusilla smiled. "She is living with me in the cottage. I find her a great comfort, and she is very helpful."

"Oh." He also smiled. "I am glad of that. I am sure she

did not wish to return to her brother." He sighed. "Oh, Drusilla, what a madness all this has been . . . And poor Alethea. I had thought to help her and instead . . ." He loosed another sigh. "It is all my fault, everything that has taken place!"

She put her hand to his head and gently brushed back his tangled hair. "Never think so, my dear Jean-Claude. You are not to blame. You wanted the best for her."

"And went about it in the worst possible way," he groaned.

"Jean-Claude," Drusilla said softly but firmly. "If it had been meant to be . . . It would have happened and nothing could have prevented it. Fate has something else in store for Alethea. You, a scientist, might not believe in fate, but I have learned to believe in it. And so, I think, must you."

"Man," he said bitterly, "is the master of his fate!"

She shook her head slightly. "I must differ with you. But we will not argue about it—until you are better."

On a day a little over two weeks after his return, he did feel better, much better. But though he remembered Drusilla's words, he was in no mood to argue with her. He had seen her and also little Miss Ludlow several times in the sixteen days of his final recovery. And now, coming to bid them a brief farewell, he kept a burgeoning excitement for which he had no name, well under control.

"I am," he said, "going to a meeting of the Royal Society of Edinburgh. Would it be possible . . . I mean, would Alethea mind were I to stop at Langholm and see her?"

"No, Jean-Claude," Drusilla said on a breath. "I think she would be very pleased were you to pay her a visit."

"I will take your word for it, then. You must give me her direction."

"Yes . . . I will give it to you," Drusilla said more composedly now. "But are you sure you are well enough to travel quite a distance—and over some very rough terrain?"

"I am quite well," he assured her. "And I would like to

see her. It would mean a great deal to me to know that she is happy . . . where she is now."

"I do understand," Drusilla said.

They were, he thought, talking at random and not saying very much and so, as soon as she had given him the direction, he took his leave, feeling . . . but he had no name for his feelings. He was only pleased because he was well enough to undertake the journey to Langholm . . . the journey that had at its end the promise of seeing Alethea again.

CHAPTER ELEVEN

JEAN-CLAUDE'S IMPRESSIONS OF Scotland were of crags, lakes, trees, and sheep, sheep everywhere, with small, black and white border collies rushing after them, chivying the young lambs. It had taken him three days to reach the border, and two more to ride up the road leading toward Langholm. He was weary and, out of necessity, he had come slowly—too slowly, because he had wanted to ride like the wind, driven by a variety of emotions, uppermost among them an eagerness to see how she was faring and to see if something hurled at him like a curse could be true—Alethea, whom he had wanted to help and had succeeded only in hindering and disgracing, she who had suffered so much already.

And what was he to say upon his arrival? There had been moments when he had wanted to turn back—black moments, when he had been overwhelmed by memories of the harm he had inadvertently done her with his wild scheme. All too often in his times of illness, he had dreamed of that night when Sally, clad in red and, in the distorting visions of those dreams, bloated with self-satisfaction, approaching Alethea, primed to topple the delicate and vulnerable structure in which he had encased her.

He had woken in tears—tears of weakness, of course, for his part in that wanton destruction. It had been his fault, his alone, and he knew a blinding shame because

186

Drusilla had, in the sixteen days of his recovery, never reproached him for it, even though she, too, had endured considerable pain and shame, herself. Many in the village who had once respected her avoided her. Sally, recuperating in a workhouse from her brother's beating, had swayed one of the women there—one who could read and write—to pen a letter to another friend who could read, and the gossip had spread, had grown larger and larger until the truth was no bigger than a grain of sand!

And what was he going to say to her . . .? He asked himself for the thousandth time as he rode up the steep streets of the village toward a cottage which, according to Drusilla, was on the outskirts of Langholm. She had described a whitewashed cottage, two stories high, with corbie gables that looked like steps running up to the peak of the roof.

There was a wind blowing now, bearing an amalgam of odors—a wind left over from March, though it was now mid-April, he reminded himself regretfully. He had wanted to make amends much sooner, but Drusilla had told him that she had written, and so Alethea knew why he had been delayed. He had half-hoped for a letter from her, too. Yet, what might she write to him, who had so badly bungled her life—with his "chemical solution" which had been no solution at all.

At the turn of the road and in a dip of land, Drusilla had said. There was a turn and to his relief, the road went only one way so he would not be confused and go in the wrong direction. He had traveled in too many wrong directions already! He rode on and saw the house, could not mistake it—there were the corbiesteps, crowsteps was another name for them. There was the whitewashed facade, a picket fence around the house and a wide yard out back which, of course, he could not see.

Alethea would be out walking with the children or she would be inside. It was ridiculous to wish that she might be waiting for him. She had no notion of the time he would arrive, and there were other reasons that would keep her from waiting.

As for himself, he could compare his emotions to those a much younger Jean-Claude had experienced as he rode in the direction of a much larger house—a castle, in fact. There had been poplar trees growing on that road and, he thought with a sudden surprise, it had been three weeks into March—and now it was April, still the spring, the early spring. And yet he felt as he had felt on that day long ago . . . Or did he?

Could he base so very much on the jealous words dropped by an angry young man? Could he, a man of thirty-six—no, closer to thirty-seven—be experiencing once more the emotions of eighteen? He tried to laugh and was not successful—laughter was far from him. Apprehension welled in his breast as he thought of all the years that had passed over his head and of the new gray strands in his hair since his illness, strands to keep that white lock company. He was a fool, more than a fool, to be in love with a girl of twenty, a girl in the very spring of her life, while he was nearing the autumn. And was he in love?

He had not consciously thought of love in these last weeks—he had thought mainly of wanting to see her again and beg her forgiveness. But now as he neared that house, these other almost terrifying sensations seemed about to overmaster him. He could not let that happen, he told himself. He could not approach the place where she—Alethea—was dwelling until he had regained his equilibrium. Indeed, he wondered if, after all, he were not a little mad. He looked beyond the cottage up the road to a stretch of wooded land. He needed to walk through it—to calm himself and to banish these thoughts which, like virulent gnats were attacking his mind. Was it possible that he was actually experiencing a return of the fevers that had so often visited him during the early days of his illness?

He could not tether his horse at the post rising by the gate, could not knock on the door of the cottage, could not see Alethea until he was calmer, until these turbulent feelings left him. He gently urged his horse forward . . . forward toward the stretch of greenery, a meadow, he noted as he came closer. And standing at the edge of the meadow was a girl in a white gown with a fluffy blue woolen shawl over her shoulders. Her hair, a ripe gold, was blowing slightly in the wind, and her back was toward him.

"Alethea . . ." The name sprang to his lips, but he did not utter it. She stood like a statue. The wind, growing stronger, tossed her skirts about her slender legs. "Young," was another word that came to his mind and hovered on his lips. She was very young, a young back and young straight legs and young golden hair—enough to convince him that his dreams were nothing but dreams and her spring was his autumn. She could look upon him as an uncle or even a father. He could expect no more. He forced a smile to his lips and opened his mouth to call, and in that same moment, his hands must have tighted too quickly on the reins, for his horse neighed sharply. Annoyed, he drew it to a quick halt.

She turned swiftly, her eyes widened. "Jean-Claude," she cried in a low, sweet voice, one he had never heard from her before. "Oh!" She ran toward him. "Aunt Drusilla wrote me that you would be coming, but I could not believe it." An overlay of anxiety shone in her eyes. "But should you be riding? I heard that you were badly wounded."

"I am recovered," he said. He added, "I expected to hear from you . . . once I had returned to the tower."

She flushed. "I wrote so often . . . so many letters, but they did not satisfy me."

"Three lines . . . three words would have satisfied me," he said.

"What could I have said in three words?" she asked. She caught at the bridle of his horse, as it seemed about to move away, and in that same moment, he dismounted.

"Oh, do be careful," she cried.

"I am being careful," he told her. "I took this journey in very easy stages."

"Aunt Drusilla wrote that you are going to a conference in Edinburgh. This is out of your way, is it not?"

"This is my way," he said simply, knowing suddenly

that he was right to speak to her as he was doing, knowing that she would understand him, knowing, too, that jealous young Sir Martin had told him the truth.

"Oh, Jean-Claude." She took the bridle of his horse and led the animal to the post, securing it. She came back and, putting her hands on his shoulders, she lifted her face for his kiss, which he pressed on her lips, holding her as tightly as his still-diminished strength would allow, his face wet with her tears and his own.

"We will not speak of anything that has passed," he said finally. "That is in the past. I did not come for a conference in Edinburgh. I came only because of you, Alethea. I love you. I want to marry you . . . but I was afraid to ask you to be my wife."

"You are not afraid anymore, are you?" She smiled mistily up at him.

"No . . . I do not think I have misjudged the situation."

She broke out into delighted laughter. "Oh, no, Jean-Claude, you have not misjudged the situation—especially if you are aware that I have loved you all my life."

"I was not aware of that," he said huskily. Before she could comment, he added, "I have learned that we are not far from Gretna Green. Should you mind being married there?"

"Oh, no, Jean-Claude," she murmured. "If you will wait . . . I will fetch my cloak and we can go immediately."

They came back to the tower by slow and easy stages. By mutual consent, they did not stop first at Drusilla's cottage. This night, their first after three weeks in Edinburgh, they wanted to spend alone. They reached the edifice at sunset and, against Alethea's protests, her husband insisted on carrying her over that threshold she had crossed so often on her own two feet.

"You are not strong enough yet, Jean-Claude."

He looked at her masterfully. "I feel as if I could move mountains."

She fixed him with a kindling eye. "You will have to do it chemically."

He laughed and kissed her, a light kiss that, as usual, turned into a passionate embrace. As they finally moved apart, he said, "I want to sleep in the tower this night. I sent word to have Matt place the bed there."

"In the tower . . . your stronghold, Jean-Claude?"

"Shall you mind, my love, considering . . . ?"

"Considering what?"

"A night when—"

She placed two fingers against his lips. "Shhh, I know what you are going to say."

"You always know, do you not?"

"Are we not one?" she asked.

"One," he agreed and kissed her yet again. "And," he said then, "in the tower I can see you by sunset and moonlight and dawn."

They climbed slowly up the three flights of steps and, again over his wife's protests, her husband lifted her, then set her down inside by the bed—now covered by a white linen spread.

It was not until she lay with him in that same bed that she saw the large, square object draped in a velvet cloth standing against the wall just beyond the foot of the bed. "What is that?" she asked.

"I will show you." He slid from the bed and, moving to the object, he lifted the cloth.

"Oh, Jean-Claude, the . . . the portrait," she murmured. "That is what happened to it!"

"I could not let him have it," he explained. He returned to the bed, saying passionately, "I think I knew then that I could not let him have you."

"Oh, Jean-Claude," she murmured happily. "Of course you could not." With the new lovely affection and intimacy that had replaced the awe she had once felt for him, she pulled him down beside her again and, pressing against him, she whispered, "That would have been no solution at all."

"Least of all . . . a chemical solution, my angel," he agreed as they drifted into ecstasy.

EPILOGUE

THE POPLAR TREES were heavy with new leaves, and the skies were a vivid blue dappled with wind-driven clouds as a great, cumbersome traveling coach went rattling up a dirt road in the province of Normandy, France. The vehicle was pulled by six gray horses, traveling with renewed speed toward their destination, which meant that it swayed from side to side with appropriate creaks and squeaks, sometimes to the alarm of its five passengers.

Still, despite the coach's jouncing and creaking, one of three children, an infant of some six months, remained fast asleep on his mother's lap, while a little boy of five chattered to his four-year-old sister as both stared wide-eyed out the windows at the unfamiliar landscape. Actually, it was not as unfamiliar as it might have been; they have seen quite a bit of the country in the last few days.

"Mama, why does not Papa ride inside with us?" the little girl demanded, a touch imperiously as might one who was used to having an indulgent father obey her every wish.

"Shhh." Annie, the abigail, pointed to the sleeping infant. "Be quiet, Thea. Your brother is finally asleep."

"No, Annie, she does not need to be quiet," the child's mother said gently. "Have you not noticed that Raoul will sleep through anything?" She smiled and turned to her daughter. "Papa wishes to ride to his old home on horseback, Thea. It is the way he was wont to come years ago . . . Do you not remember him telling you so?"

"When did Papa used to come here?" the little boy asked.

"A long time ago, Jean," his mother replied and gazed out of her window, feeling . . . But she was not quite sure what she was feeling. She had both wanted and not wanted to visit the château where Jean-Claude had been born and which he had left nearly a quarter of a century before.

In that time, Napoleon's star had risen and plummeted, and Louis XVIII had returned from exile in England to the French throne in a France which, judging from her observations, still remembered with great longing and regret the corporal who had become an emperor. Naturally, great changes had occurred in all of France and she, having seen the ruins of many a once-mighty château mournfully pointed out to her by her husband, feared to see his old home which, with its adjacent lands, had been recently restored to him. Was it a ruin? There was no one to provide him with that information. He was not in communication with the servants who had fled shortly after he had left for England, and those who had dwelt in surrounding châteaus had, for the most part, perished on the guillotine.

She did have hope that her Aunt Drusilla who, with little Miss Ludlow, had agreed to go ahead of them to Normandy and to the château, might have found it intact. If not, they would be staying at the Croix d'Or, an inn located nearby. And what if his old home was not a ruin and he wished to remain in France, despite the fact that their children were English-born and he prospering because of sundry chemical discoveries? When the journey had been planned, shortly after the king had made a point of restoring his lands, Jean-Claude had spoken about wanting his children to see from what tree their family had sprung.

Was that all? she wondered unhappily. During the three months since the message had arrived, Jean-Claude had seemed extremely preoccupied. For once, he who had shared his every thought with her had not divulged his preoccupations. He had merely proposed the journey. Actually, he had insisted upon it, making his plans without consulting her, presenting it to her as a fait accompli. If he had discussed it with her before making that decision, what would she have said?

She did have objections, none of which she had wanted to voice aloud when Jean-Claude said, "The comte and comtesse de Bretigny will be returning to their château . . ." He had kissed her, then, adding, "The princess will, at last, come to her castle."

He had been, of course, trying to give her confidence, trying to make her feel a part of that life he had put behind him. Still, there was no denying that while she now bore his illustrious name, she herself was in essence nameless. How many brides had crossed the threshold of his château in the hundreds of years that had passed since the first stone was laid?

Many had become the comtesse de Bretigny but they, she was sure, had all brought immense dowries to swell the coffers of the estate. Some of the most illustrious names in France had been added to his family tree, but Jean-Claude had taken unto his bosom a nameless bride! Was that why he had been so silent, so noncommittal throughout most of the journey? Was he entertaining long thoughts as to their situation, and was she not foolish to imagine that?

Every day, he gave her new proof of his love—every day he expressed his admiration for her and for his children. And how he had fretted over each birth—because of his concern over her "delicate constitution." She who, because of her healthy peasant ancestry—something that could not be discounted, even given her unknown grandfather and father—had released each child into the world with amazing ease.

"Mama, Mama, look . . . look at the little horses in the field. They are ponies!" Thea cried. "Oh, I wish I had my pony . . . then I could ride with Papa."

Alethea gave her a fond smile. "You will ride with him,

but only after we have arrived. You could not have ridden
with him before, child. You would have been very weary.
We must have covered close on twenty-five miles, this
day."

"I would not mind!" Thea cried. "Oh, I wish I could
have ridden with Papa."

"Me, too," said her brother. "I should have ridden
with him. I am older than you."

"Shhh, children," Alethea murmured. "You must be
quiet or you *will* wake your brother." She looked out the
window, striving to catch a glimpse of Jean-Claude and
was, as always, worried, wondering if he should have
remained so long in the saddle. Then she chided herself,
as he most certainly would have done had he been a
party to her thoughts. He had fully recovered from Sir
Martin's attack on him, that cowardly revenge that had
taken place fully six years ago and which ought to have
brought him a conviction for attempted murder. However, he had inadvertently paid in full for his sin.

Last year, the news had reached them that Sir Martin
had laid siege to the wife of a certain Lord Ellsworthy,
who was often away from his estates and in London.
Lady Ellsworthy had proved responsive to Sir Martin's
blandishments, and the husband, alerted to the situation,
had come home and challenged Sir Martin to a duel. As
was his wont, he had not waited for the signal, but this
time his bullet had gone astray. His opponent had had
better aim and Sir Martin, last of his line, had been
gathered to his ancestors.

The thought of his early demise troubled Alethea not
at all. She had a sudden image of him on that night he
had pursued her, screaming epithets at her. He had
looked as if he wanted to strangle her and, indeed, might
have so done had she not been able to elude him.

And why was she dwelling on that bad time—and the
worse time that followed when, at her own hysterical
insistence, she had forced Drusilla and Miss Ludlow to
leave London that very night! It was still impossible to
fathom her motives. She ought to have remained, ought
to have waited for Jean-Claude to return. Both women

had told her so—but she, overcome with shame and misery, had refused to listen and they, driven by her mad urgency, had obeyed. What had she really been thinking? Had she wanted to clear Jean-Claude's name, clear it by leaving him? Something of the sort might have fluttered through her mind and, on reaching home, she had been sure that her life was over.

She shuddered, recalling Jean-Claude's long silence. At first, she had interpreted it as anger at her flight and then, she had decided that, after all, he had made peace with Lady Langmore and married her. Then, when the truth about his injuries was revealed, she was in Scotland. She had longed to come home and nurse him—but had been adjured to remain where she was by her aunt and had seen the wisdom in that.

Oh, how happy she had been when her aunt had written that he was recovering and that he wanted to see her . . . And it had seemed to her that there had been more between the lines than had been written. Then, he had come to Scotland!

She had never forgotten the wild beating of her heart when she had seen him coming toward her, and had known instinctively why he was there . . . Now, her heart was beating wildly again at the thought of arriving at the castle he had described so often, the castle that lay not far from the De Mothancourt lands, where he had wooed and won the hand of Denise de Mothancourt. He had told her about poor little Denise . . . about his plan to return from England and wed her, the descendant of a family as old and as aristocratic as his own. Now he, a man of nearly forty-one, was returning to the Château de Bretigny with his baseborn wife and their three children.

An unwelcome memory smote her—the miniature of Denise. She had found it and admired it, only to have him snatch it away, apologizing afterwards, saying brusquely that it was part of the dead past. Yet she, recalling that moment, guessed that the girl might yet retain some hold on his heart. And would her poor little ghost not rise again in these familiar surroundings?

There was a sharp tap on the carriage window. Looking around, she saw Jean-Claude, dismounted now, his reins wound around his hand. In that same moment, she realized that the carriage had drawn to a stop. The two older children, grown somnolent while their mother lost herself in reminiscences, came to a noisy wakefulness. They pounded on the door, begging to be let out.

"Papa, Papa," Thea screamed. "Are we here, then?"

A postboy opened the door, and the baby also set up a shrill plaint.

Jean-Claude, laughing happily, lifted out his daughter and his son and helped the abigail from the coach. Then, relieving his wife of the wailing Raoul, he placed him in Annie's arms and, assisting Alethea down, he put his arm around her waist and led her beyond the coach, pointing up the road that stretched ahead of them. "There, my love, is our château," he murmured. "And look, it stands as it has always stood for nearly six centuries, give or take a few additions over the years."

"Oh, Jean-Claude, I am so happy for you!" she cried as, unmindful of the servants, she received his rapturous kiss. It was only after they had moved apart that she really saw the tall, wrought-iron gates and beyond them, at the end of a long, tree-lined carriageway, the huge edifice of stone and brick with tall, circular, pointed towers and a multiplicity of windows and chimneys. Impulsively, she turned back and caught her son in her arms, lifting him up.

"See, see, Jean," she murmured over a pounding in her heart and in her throat as well. "There is the ancestral home of Papa . . . and it will be your home, too, my love."

"Papa . . . Papa . . . I want to see it, too," Thea demanded.

"Eh bien, ma petite. Voila!" He lifted his daughter to his shoulder.

Thea, Alethea thought, looked amazingly like her father. Her eyes, though vividly blue rather than gray, were the same shape as those of Jean-Claude. Her features were similar, too, softened only by femininity. The boys, he had often remarked happily, resembled her

more. Did that really make him happy, or was he yet
haunted by his lost Denise?

He had broken into French, something which he did
less and less at home. It was wrong, she knew, to feel so
intimidated by this structure of brick and stone that
represented the heritage of Jean-Claude, Jean-Claude the
chemist, who was winning more and more recognition
and respect in England! Jean-Claude her husband, who
was suddenly the comte de Bretigny again, come home at
last with a bride who did not go by the name of Denise de
Mothancourt!

Had her Aunt Drusilla been able to read her thoughts,
she would have been very angry. Her aunt had pride—
and Alethea had always had that same pride. But on
occasion, her past arose to haunt her. Alethea Unknown,
whose father was a cipher and whose mother might have
been a whore. Sally had said that . . . Sally had spread
the tale through London, and Lady Langmore had kept
that particular pot a-boiling until she had, some three
years ago, broken her neck at a water jump during a fox
hunt on her country estate.

Jean-Claude, sizzling over Lady Langmore's sneering
allusions to himself and his bride, repeated to him by
more than one colleague, had called it "heaven's judg-
ment," one that he insisted had also been meted out to
Alethea's other foe—Sally.

Alethea shuddered again, thinking of Sally. She now
lived at home with her widowed father, keeping house for
him. She had become a thin, cowed creature with all her
ripe beauty gone, her features battered out of shape by
Matt's heavy fists. *He* was married, very happily, to
Katie, who had prospered the year she had spent as a
milkmaid. She had come home much improved in looks
from eating regularly. It was better to think of her than of
poor Sally. Matt, however, had never regretted his actions. "Pa should've done it long ago . . . Above 'erself,
she were, 'n needed the meanness beat out o' 'er."

And was not she, Alethea, above herself, too? Or was
she being ridiculous, entertaining these sentiments? It
was ridiculous to be intimidated by a house!

"Venez avec moi, mon ange." Jean-Claude was at her
side. Over his shoulder, he called back to Annie, telling
her to keep the children with her for the nonce. Taking
his wife by the arm, he looked down at her adoringly and
then, with the perspicacity he had always demonstrated
when with her, he said, "But what is troubling you, my
love?"

"Nothing," she lied valiantly. "I am so anxious to see
the house . . . But why cannot the children come with
us?"

"Because," he slipped his arm around her waist, "they
will be seeing it very soon—but now, it is for us." Asking
the postboy to hold his horse, he lifted Alethea to the
saddle and swung up behind her, urging his steed to a
gallop.

In a few moments, they were at the gates which were,
to Alethea's amazement, opened by two men in the green
livery of Jean-Claude's house. Obviously French, they
grinned broadly and bowed often. However, before she
could do more than notice them, she and Jean-Claude
were riding up the long road to the immense château. In
a few more minutes, he dismounted and, securing his
horse to a post on the carriageway, he said merely,
"Come."

Putting his arm around her, he brought her up a
flagstoned path and up a circular flight of stairs to the
great building, flanked by a small wall running its length.
Reaching a massive wooden door, heavily carved with
wreathes of leaves and flowers, he lifted a brass knocker
in the shape of a wreath and brought it down heavily
against its plate.

Alethea, noting that the door and its knocker had been
recently polished, said with relief and pleasure, "My
aunt must be in residence. I hope the servants she has
hired will be to your liking."

"I know they will be," he said.

Against her will, Alethea felt a little at a loss. She had
come to expect an empty house with weeds growing over
the driveway. Instead, there was new gravel spread upon
it, and it must have been at his request that her aunt had

overseen these improvements. Did that not mean he intended to remain here? And did she really want to live in this imposing palace?

Her chaotic thoughts were interrupted as the door swung open and, standing in the aperture, was her Aunt Drusilla. Words bubbled to her lips and, suddenly, she could not voice any of them. Speechlessly, she embraced her aunt and then, in the shadowy hallway, she saw Miss Ludlow and would have entered, had not Jean-Claude scooped her up in his arms and brought her inside.

"It is the custom in France, as well, to carry the bride over the threshold," he murmured, as he set her down. Then, he was suddenly surrounded by a group of servants, old and French, all talking at once and some weeping, the while her aunt was explaining to her that the servants had come flocking back to the château once they learned that the count was coming home.

Before she had time to question her further, Drusilla was impatiently asking Jean-Claude about the children and he, while leading his wife out of the hall and toward a long staircase, was advising her to collect them and bring them in. He added that he had much to show Alethea, and surely she must understand.

Drusilla laughed and said that she did.

The floor, Alethea noted, was inlaid, and the graceful winding staircase was covered with a soft, sunken runner of oriental design. The balustrade was carved with strange, exotic flowers and vines, and when they reached the upper hall, she found an immense chandelier, a-drip with crystal drops, catching the sunlight from a long window.

"Your aunt . . . has worked wonders," he said with a catch in his voice. "I told her what it had been like . . . and now it is much the same."

"And so beautiful," Alethea breathed.

"Yes, beautiful." He nodded, but his eyes were now on her face. Then, he led her toward a double door with polished brass knobs. Opening one side, he revealed a vast chamber with a shining floor half-hidden under a faded Aubusson carpet in shades of old rose and gold.

The graceful furniture came, Alethea knew, from the period of Louis XV, and if some of the satin backing on the chairs was frayed and if one of the caryatids holding up a magnificent marble mantelshelf was partially shattered, the other remained in excellent shape. Above them hung the oil painting of an elderly man in powdered peruke and the court dress worn at the time of Louis XIV. The portrait showed signs of having been ill-treated, but if some of the paint were peeling, it was not entirely defaced, and she could detect a certain resemblance to Jean-Claude or, rather, she amended mentally, it was the other way around.

"Was he your grandfather?" she asked.

"My great grandfather," he said rather huskily. He added quickly, "Look at the ceiling . . . they could not touch the ceiling."

She gazed upward and her eyes widened as she looked at a vast painting of satyrs, nymphs, mythical beasts, all gazing at Orpheus playing his lute. That he and his audience were clad in the court dress prevalent at the time of Louis XIV, while the musicians surrounding him strummed chitarroni and lifted flutes to their lips as satyrs leered from painted glades, did not detract from the charm and beauty of the work.

"This is the first drawing room," Jean-Claude explained. "Dearest Drusilla has worked wonders here already, as I knew she must. She has whispered that she has not been able to devote as much time to the other rooms—but they will soon be its equal, I know." He visited a long look on Alethea's face. "I hope that you approve this house, my love."

She said faintly, "Yes, of . . . of course, I do. It is beautiful . . . and very grand and . . ." She faltered into silence, not knowing quite what she must say.

He said what she had hoped he might not say. "You will see that, in time, this house will be restored to its former glory. You . . . would you mind spending some part of the year here, *mon ange?*"

She heard doubt and hesitation in his tone, but she had read hope in his eyes. The time she had feared was coming to pass. She said hesitantly, "Do you wish to . . . to live here in France and not in England anymore, Jean-Claude?"

"No, my love. I want our children to know both worlds," he assured her strongly. "Still, it is time and past that you took your rightful place as my countess. I wish you to be presented to the king . . . That has long been my dream, but does it frighten you?"

Alethea met his questioning gaze and sought for an answer that would conceal the truth, the truth that she felt inadequate to the house, to the magnificence about her and, above all, to the role in which he obviously wished to thrust her. Denise de Mothancourt would have entertained no qualms, she knew, but Denise was dead, and she was second best.

"No, no, no, you are not!" he burst out. "I will not listen to such madness."

"M—madness!" Alethea repeated incredulously. "I . . . I do not understand you. I said nothing. It is you who must have gone mad, Jean-Claude."

"Ah, I knew you would tell me so . . ." He laughed and then sobered quickly. "No, my dearest love, I am not mad. Do you imagine that I do not know what you are thinking, my Alethea? That in six years of having been your lover and most fortunate husband, that I do not know and, occasionally, regret the workings of your mind?" He stepped to her side and put his arm around her. "You are not my second love—but my first, my dearest.

"When I knew Denise, I was young . . . just eighteen. It was true that we were brought up together, but in those days, I had no real conception of love. My one passion was chemistry. Denise knew that and was jealous of it. She did not scruple to tell me so.

"Later, when she died as she did, I convinced myself that I was her sorrowing lover, mainly because any other love must needs have interfered with my chemistry, and while I busied myself—happily—with my cauldrons and my concoctions, a little girl of my acquaintance suddenly grew up and a man of mature years, named Jean-Claude, put chemistry behind him and grieved because he feared this child, so suddenly and so beautifully a woman, would never care for him.

"He did not dream that this blooming young girl could ever love a man of his age. Then she surprised him—a surprise conveyed to him by one Sir Martin Willoughby in an excess of jealous rage. And even then, he was not sure he believed it . . . But she, the girl he had come to love with all his heart, the girl he had more than loved—had, indeed, worshiped—corroborated Sir Martin's words.

"Alethea, my Alethea, you have always reigned over my heart, and it is time that you became also the queen of my castle. For our children's sake, too, we must be dwellers in two worlds. My heritage is an old one—our children must know it and be proud of it, and you must take your place in the world. You are not only the bride of a chemist, you are the bride of a comte. You cannot disagree."

"But I do," she said firmly. "I agree that our children must know and appreciate their heritage, I agree that we must spend some of our days here in France. But Jean-Claude, my only love, I am neither the bride of a chemist nor a count. I am simply your wife, and my place is wherever you desire it to be—because I am also a part of you."

He kissed her fondly and then passionately. "But, of course, my love. And now, shall we go and welcome our children into our home?"

"Oh, yes, Jean-Claude," she said softly and happily. Then, taking the arm of the man whose love and adoration she would never doubt again, she moved with him into the great hall and, at his side, descended the stairs of their new home.